MINIMAX

OTHER BOOKS BY ANNA LIVIA

Incidents Involving Mirth
Incidents Involving Warmth
Bulldozer Rising
Accommodation Offered
Relatively Norma

Minimax

a novel by

Anna Livia

The Eighth Mountain Press
Portland, Oregon • 1991

LIBRARY OF CONGRESS CATALOGING-IN-PUBLICATION DATA

Livia, Anna. 1955 -
    Minimax : a novel / by Anna Livia. — 1st ed.
      p.   cm.
    ISBN 0-933377-12-6 (cloth : alk. paper) : $22.95. — ISBN
    0-933377-11-8 (trade paperback : alk. paper) : $9.95
    PR6062.I895M56 1991
    823'.914—dc20   90-42350

Cover design by Marcia Barrentine
Cover art by Claudia Cave
Book design by Ruth Gundle

Manufactured in the United States of America
This book is printed on acid-free paper.
First Edition 1991

10 9 8 7 6 5 4 3 2 1

Published by The Eighth Mountain Press
624 Southeast Twenty-ninth Avenue
Portland, Oregon 97214
(503) 233-3936

For Dympna Jones, my mother

TABLE OF CONTENTS

IN THE BATH

M innie was in the bath where she had been chased by Baby Vicky's washing machine. Baby Vicky lived upstairs and was a very clean girl. Mostly it was just dust and dishes but on bad days it could grow to five machine loads of washing followed by three hours spin drying which made the floorboards shake, as well as the awful noise, and however high Minnie turned the volume, she could not play her opera tapes loud enough to block out the vibrations. In any case, she felt that opera should not be used in this way. Not that anything can stop opera being opera, but Minnie had sensibilities about these matters. In brief, Minnie fled, and the only place in her small flat in which the shuddering and moaning of Baby Vicky's spin drier could not be felt was the bathroom which, being four steps below the level of the rest of the flat, did not share the same floorboards.

Baby Vicky is a very minor character both in our heroine's life and, sadly, in the lives of her own nearest and dearest. Soon a man will marry her and she will live as happily ever after as she did before. She is, however, to be thanked for getting Minnie into the bathroom where our story begins. Minnie does not ask Baby Vicky to ration her washing machine just in case cleanliness is Baby Vicky's opera. Baby Vicky is a chiropodist and, what with the elephant customers trooping up and down and trumpeting on the stairs, and the shudder-moan of the washing machine, Minnie thinks she might as well be living beneath a brothel. But that is because this is the way Minnie's mind works and has nothing to do with the highly respectable Baby Vicky or her elephants.

Finding herself in the bathroom, Minnie decided to have a bath. For the nine years before she had moved into this flat, Minnie had lived in a series of bed-sits with shared bathrooms in which it had not been possible, or courteous, to do anything but bath. But in this last, private bathroom she had discovered and, she sometimes felt, perfected those joys enhanced by hot, wet, naked solitude. She liked taking her clothes off, freeing her breasts and stepping into water she could linger in. Only here had she at last dared to play her operas at volume instead of turning down the soprano as she drew breath to unburden her passionate sorrow. Minnie had not wished to disturb her fellow tenants; there is something intransigently unoperatic about a household full of women washing themselves and their smalls in the hope that modern men still prefer old-fashioned girls.

Here where no sad razor caught the fuzz of another woman's legs, and no scarlet lipstick waited at the ready for the pout, the cupid's bow, or the quick dab, where the hope of a man lingered round no new cherry plum nail varnish, Minnie bathed the bath of the woman's woman. In place of the simple towel and bar of simple soap, province of athletes and asexuals, bath preparations had become highly complex. First Minnie collected her cassette player and her favourite opera which at this point was *Die Zauberflöte*, known in English as *The Magic Flute*. Minnie liked to sing "Pa pa pa; pa, pa, pa" in tune with the love-smitten birdcatcher. For years she had been declared entirely unmusical and almost certainly tone deaf, until the day she read the words *Voi che sapete*, Cherubino's aria in *Le Nozze di Figaro,* in the frontispiece of a novel, savoured that secret message, *you who know*, and wondered how the tune went. She wondered so much that she went out and bought for £2.50, from W.H. Smith, *The Marriage of Figaro*, famous scenes and arias and listened. It was like discovering lesbianism after having resigned oneself to celibacy. Now Minnie would cry when certain arias were sung, like *Che farò senza Euridice?* (what *would* she do without Euridice?) and *Ardon gl'incensi* (the bathroom filled with the scent of burning incense). She could not attempt to sing like those women and so she satisfied herself with "Pa pa pa; pa, pa, pa," knowing all that it stood for. Next Minnie made a fresh pot of Darjeeling tea and took a gooseberry fool out of the fridge. Then came a procession of bath salts, bath oil, bath vinegar, bath seeds, bath pearls, bath oysters and many-tentacled bath octopi which dropped ceremoniously into the bath water, there to await Minnie's pleasure.

During these preparations Minnie heard the sound, miraculous above the drier and the chiropodist's elephants, of the post slipping through the letter box and hitting the welcome mat. She picked up five letters and took them to read in the bath, where she remained for the next three hours listening to the *Flute,* drinking tea and refilling the bath with hot water. She opened the letters: one from Beryl, her mother; one from Laura, her stepsister; one from Ingrid, her little sister, all living in Perth, Western Australia, where Minnie had left them ten years before. The fourth letter was from Ranier in San Francisco upon whom Minnie had an absorbing but pleasantly unrequited crush. The fifth Minnie very nearly dropped into the bath as soon as she saw the return address and if she had, and the water had rendered illegible the contents, then this story would have ended very differently. The fifth letter was overprinted "Natalie Barney" and bore a New York postmark. The reason why the name "Natalie Barney" almost caused the drowning of the word was simple, and was this: the name of the woman who wrote the book whose frontispiece, *Voi che sapete,* had brought the way, the light, the joy of opera to Minnie after a thirty-year musical mutism, was none other than Natalie Barney. Minnie had written a letter to this woman six months previously, a letter clearly marked "fan mail." But that had been six months ago, and the time for even the most cursory "profound thanks for the trouble you took to write" was long since past.

For those of you with an unbridled curiosity for the contents of other people's post, I will divulge that each of the five letters is reprinted in entirety within a very few pages. Minnie read, and reread, each letter several times. Then she reached three decisions: she would fly to Australia, she would fly to San Francisco, she would fly to New York. In that order. The Minnie who, ten years ago, had been unable to make or receive phone calls from anywhere other than the bedroom cupboard (we understand our American sisters call this "the closet") had made one flying leap into the sophistications of the twentieth century. She could telephone anywhere in the world from the bath. Incoming calls she simply did not allow by the (very) simple method of never, on any pretext, giving anyone her phone number. When she read her mother's letter offering a free trip to Perth, Minnie dialled a travel agent and asked about flights.

"I'll shop around. May take a little while, I'll call you back."

"No," said Minnie in a tone that had never heard of argument. "I'll ring you at twelve."

Two acts, three gooseberry fools, and a one hundred percent turnover in bath water later, Minnie rang again.

"If you go in September there are no substantial discounts available. I can do you an Air India for just under a thousand, that's the cheapest. You know, you'd only pay an extra forty if you bought a round-the-world trip."

It was at this moment that Minnie's lightning brain decided it might as well pay the extra forty itself and stop over in San Francisco and New York. Minnie had always wanted to go to the States and now, by the simple expedient of flying to Australia, she would fulfil a lifetime's ambition. It should be added, lest anyone is about to misunderstand anything, that Minnie loved her mother passionately and her sisters were her number one, absolute favourite females. The only reason Minnie had not herself bought a flight in the intervening years and reheated her joy in their presence was that the grimy, grinding, awful circumstances of her London life had not permitted it. You may, or may not, get to hear about them. We, me and the author, assume you are reading this because you expect to be entertained, amused, uplifted and as we can see nothing, really nothing, remotely uplifting about poverty and misery, we may decide to leave that bit out entirely, or content ourselves with bitter hints. Fill in details of your own misery; you'll know what we are (not) talking about.

"One round the world ticket with stopovers in Perth, Western Australia, San Francisco, California and New York, New York. I'll pay now with my Visa card."

Poverty and misery had not prevented the well-known high street bank from thrusting upon Minnie a credit card which, had she used it, she could never have hoped to pay off. This was the Thatcher consumer boom when everyone was mortgaging themselves to Conservative policy. Next Minnie phoned British Telecom to send a telemessage to her mother. Beryl did, of course, have a telephone but since she had the same blanket policy toward incoming calls that Minnie had—indeed Minnie had merely copied her mother in this as in so many of life's problems—it would have been quite pointless for Minnie to try and ring her.

"ARRIVING TUESDAY FOURTH SEPTEMBER STOP WIRE ME A THOUSAND STOP LOVE"

Next Minnie rang Ranier's ansaphone.

"I fly into San Francisco on fifth October. Be lovely if you could meet me. Afraid Genevieve is no longer appropriate. My flight number's PA101, ten thirty in the morning. Your time. And thank Nea for the offer of her spare room. It'll be great to see you again."

After this Minnie hummed a few bars of "Some Day My Prince Will Come" before she realised what she was doing, and stopped.

It was impossible for Minnie to inform Natalie Barney of her intended presence since, examined more closely, the return address on the envelope amounted to no more than "New York" and a ZIP code. Why did she bother with the ZIP code? To make you think she'd given you the address. Apparently Natalie Barney was as chary of the postal system as Minnie and Beryl were of telecommunication. Minnie scribbled a brief, enigmatic note which she would type up later and send via the publisher. Enigma was certainly a good ploy; anyone who muffled her own address was bound to be a devoted obscurantist, Minnie calculated, having a fondness for obscurity herself.

The likelihood of her note, however carefully obscured, reaching Natalie Barney in time for her to make any use of such information as she managed to glean was remote, seeing how long a perfectly ordinary fan letter from the general public had taken: six months. But Minnie knew, even at that early stage, that she would meet Natalie if not in Australia, then in San Francisco, if not in San Francisco then in New York. Furthermore, she knew that this was the real purpose of the trip, however familially it was dressed. The only way of avoiding Natalie was to stay in London, and bump into her on the Portobello Road, like the man who seeks to escape Death whom he is destined to meet in the marketplace and who walks away into the hills only to find that Death has stopped to rest there and is sitting on the next rock.

And the letters which caused this flurry of activity? We promised to let you read them and make of them what you wilt.

Darling Minnie,

Thank you so much for your letter. You sound as though you live entirely on air, and cheese sandwiches. Your sister Laura was asking only the other day: But what kind of place does Minnie live in? What sort of job has she got? Is she earning pots of money like they say Poms all are now they've got

*Maggie Thatcher? You know, Laura-type questions. And I
realised that I simply haven't a clue. I suppose you must have
been living somewhere, working somewhere, eating something.
Am I, after all these years of blissful tranquillity and self-ab-
sorption, to start worrying about you? You would say…No, of
course you wouldn't. None of us would. Except Laura and,
since we adopted her, she has absolutely no intention of ever
being poor again in her life. Perhaps that's why. I expect that's
why. Well, darling, I won't pry, but I do hope you have enough
woolly jumpers and they say a human being really can live,
quite well, on a diet of cheese sandwiches as long as she eats
tomatoes as well. Could you manage a tomato?*

*We all loved your description of supper with Genevieve,
nice for you to have someone to laugh with. I suppose she must
have fed you. Do tell her about the tomatoes.*

Minnie paused in her reading to squirm. What she supple-
mented her cheese sandwiches with was gooseberry fools and
plenty of them. An excellent source of vitamins. But the thought
of Genevieve feeding her, having anything in common with
Genevieve any more, let alone laughter, caused a bitter grimace.
There was much Minnie had not told her mother. There were, she
supposed, things her mother had kept from her in the same spirit.

*Laura and her John are getting on very well again. She
won't speak to him, and has refused to sleep with him, but
they're getting on very well. She is competing with her sister
Moira for the Housewife of the Year Award. I'm afraid Moira
is still on what is jocularly known as "the game," though how it
can be a game when there is no way of Moira winning, I do not
know. Her great passion in life is her steam iron. Do not scoff
at the commercials, Minnie. Those women who raise a perfectly*

pressed cuff and exclaim, "I love my new super-adjustable alu-
minium ironing board with heat-resistant cover," are telling the
absolute truth.

Moira meet Baby Vicky, thought Minnie, inventing a cosy future
for the two of them where they could give up feet and fucking and
open a laundry. Vicky would wash and Moira would iron and the
time between the washing drying and the iron steaming would be
filled by the two of them diving onto the double bed and crum-
pling the clean, crisp sheets so that the whole cycle could begin
again. But it does not do for a sexual outlaw to meddle in the affairs of others, however convinced she may be that she knows
what's best for them. That is the province of your mother and your
best friend. But think how useful it would be, and do let's be
utilitarian about this, how useful it would be to have really objective advice from one who knows you intimately and has no axe of
her own to grind on your skull, advice from she who knows every
creak of your floorboards, every bottom sheet soaked in Biotex to
get rid of embarrassing understains, the extra whisk of the vacuum
cleaner before that important date, the hasty emptying of six waste
paper baskets, contents unknown but she could make a good
guess. Your mother may say: "Well, it's your life, dear, and all I ever
wanted for you children was that you should be happy, but if you
ask my opinion, I'll give you it, for what it's worth. I always
thought John was a sweet chap and if you ever did think of settling
down you've found good husband material there."

And you know she means that John is a lawyer/doctor/accoun-
tant/insurance broker and lawyers/doctors/accountants/insurance
brokers are per se and a priori good husband material. In fact, the
only reason men train as lawyers is to make some woman a good
husband and the reason why there is a thirty percent increase in
the number of students applying to law faculties, against a thirty
percent downturn in the number applying to engineering faculties,

has nothing to do with the re-emergence of London as a major financial capital (capital generates discord, it is understood, and discord generates lawyers, and vice versa, of course) but is due entirely to the desire of an increasing number of men to become husbands. Your girlfriend (your girl friend, I mean, not wishing to presume) may say:

"John's got lovely eyes."

And you know she means he is ugly/jowly/paunchy/spindly/short-assed because lawyers/doctors/accountants/insurance brokers are per se and a priori ugly/jowly/paunchy/spindly/short-assed and since eyes are always lovely (who do you know who is famed for really ugly eyes? look how well Tiny Tim did with his), she mentions eyes in complete confidence of your continued friendship.

But the outlaw in the basement, she can tell you frankly and without prejudice that while you always creak/launder/vacuum/empty before your date with John, the new young man, the useless wastrel minstrel who came the other night required none of these fastidious preliminaries to foreplay, and you laughed more with him than she has ever heard you laugh in her long career as your neighbour. And what is life without laughter? And what is a good husband without a smiling wife? If you're lucky the useless wastrel minstrel will turn out to be Bob Geldof and you will live happily ever after and call your baby Fifi Trixibelle after the outlaw in the basement. Of course, if you're unlucky he will turn out to be Boy George.

Sniping at the mores of the sexual majority from the cover of bath water and a sheet of opera is all very well, but Minnie lived on the planet too. She drew family trees in the bath foam to remind her of the nucleus of her nuclear family. A complicated three-dimensional soapsud showing the mothers and sisters, stepsisters and stepsisters' sisters, stepfathers, stepgrandmothers and aluminium stowaway stepladders. This last was needed to get from step to step; it showed that while Laura and Moira were sisters, and

Laura and Ingrid were sisters, Ingrid and Moira were not related. And where did Minnie fit, twelve thousand miles away and queer to boot? Where did she fit? There would come a time when she must emerge from the bath, leave behind the foamy warmth and walk abroad, preferably clothed, and Agony Aunt as relational qualifier, or indeed career definition, is open to misinterpretation. Besides, after years of capping, cropping and pole-axing, the local councils are hardly going to decree that every block must have its basement outlaw for the preservation of harmony higher up the superstructure. Be sensible.

From the familial triangles Minnie switched to a series of soft curves. She joined herself with Genevieve, then watched that union slowly melt as the foam popped and crackled. She joined Ranier to Nea at the other end of the bath, a topological San Francisco. That union dissolved in its turn. With increasing satisfaction Minnie drew curves between herself and Ranier, herself and Nea, and, momentously, herself and Natalie Barney. But nothing lasted. The very softness of the foam, which made the tracks so easy to imprint, made it impossible for any to remain visible for long. Where is rock? Where is stone? Where are the ugly/jowly/paunchy/spindly/short-assed queer lawyers/doctors/accountants/insurance brokers? Perhaps there is one working in your office.

One day when Laura had brought the kids over for a "change of battleground" as she calls it, she and I were sitting in the family room with a cup of tea. Ingrid, who's been staying here now her baby's nearly due, waddled in and started explaining to us two hardened mothers the best way to give birth. There came a terrible row from the lounge where the kids were playing the piano, and Son stumbled toward Laura, shaking with infant fury. Son is a sturdy blond slug but at that moment he looked fit to destroy the world: big sister Zebbee wouldn't let him help play the piano. "Zebbee says she hates me," he sobbed.

*Laura sent Zebbee to reconsider in the spare room, "Girls who
hate their brothers cannot stay in nice company."*

Minnie, having no discrimination and precious little left in the
way of politics, lapped up the cosy domestic drama. Why was there
no one at work to send people to bed to reconsider when they
began to hate one another? Where were the mothers sitting on
sofas drinking tea who could so peacefully solve the problems of
the world? Minnie was not unlike those hard-nosed businessmen
who spend much of their time in the air, jetting between business
meetings with a computer on their laps, who suffer from aeroplane
phobia but are ashamed to admit it. They somehow manage to
have themselves seated next to a young mother with a small baby
so that when she soothes it they can close their eyes and pretend
she is talking to them. Minnie had, however, a vestige of her former
self who had managed to survive the onslaught of conservative
politics and internal disillusion: her alter ego, Milly. Milly could be
relied upon to insert a strident note into the cosiest kitchen.

"Oh those babies," Milly droned in Minnie's ear, getting foam up
her nose. "Those thirty-something babies. A significant proportion
of a whole generation of women succeed in not producing young,
so significant that they actually manage to affect the population
growth. Abortion restrictions are lifted and by the end of the
eighties there is a serious shortage of labour in the teenage and
early twenties age group. So forty-year-old women can get jobs, go
to college; the places have not already been taken by the young.
Faced with this glorious success, what do women do? They turn
thirty and have babies so that by the time the kids are old enough
to leave school, there will be no jobs for the mothers and they will
have to console themselves as of old with good works and nervous
breakdowns."

For unrequited love was not alone among Minnie's problems.
She had, also, unrequited political ideals. Or perhaps it would be

safer to say that she had an alter ego who would not let her take a
calm back seat and enjoy a long withheld taste of prosperity or, if
not full-fledged prosperity, comfort at least. For it is a fact that a
woman who is comfortable cannot rebel and a woman who is a
rebel cannot be comfortable.

*Do come over and visit us all again. I am even in a posi-
tion to say "My shout, mate." Or, if you've been away too long
to understand that, then, "This round's on me." Now that my
John's got his physics Ph.D. and is servicing the local lasers, he's
bored but surprisingly well paid. My nice boss—who we met on
a boat, must tell you sometime—made a mint out of the stock
market crash. Like listening to a pilot talk a plane down from a
radio tower to hear him making deals. When the journalists
hound him for explanations of his "meteoric wealth," he says
modestly, "Merely a question of knowing the future." So now
he's filthy rich and living in expensive Dalkeith with his yacht
and good luck to him, I say. The secret of his success, I would
also say only no one asks me, must be connected with his habit
of staying awake all night and sleeping during the day. I suppose he listens to the financial reports on the other side of the
dateline. He has a strictly liquid diet, but so many do, and in
every other way he is exactly like all the other young blond financiers one has ever met. I could dine out on Vivien stories
(that's my boss's name, Vivien), he has the most amazing luck,
but as he's been preternaturally good to us all, and since I've
not the remotest desire for company, I eat a fresh morning lettuce and a sandwich in the park instead.*

*So do come, I'd love to see you. As would the rest of the
rigmarole: Ingrid, Laura, Zebbee, John, John, John, and Son.*

All my love,
Ma

Minnie paused to wonder a moment about this "preternaturally good" young blond financier. Could her mother possibly be matchmaking? Surely not. Surely nothing. Her mother would like her to be married. Perversity was fine, until the right man came along. Minnie might have considered the proposition had her mother's boss been a preternaturally *old* blond financier. She wouldn't much mind cooking and cleaning for six months till he died and left her everything. Then she remembered the other reason men marry. She wasn't sure whether to be pleased or troubled that she'd found it so easy to forget.

The next letter was a note, folded inside Beryl's.

Hallo Minnie,

Mum said she was writing so I told her I'd give her a letter for you. She really means it about the money and paying your fare so don't worry your hedgehog head about that. We haven't heard from you for ages: are you still a hedgehog? Or have you grown your hair back? All the pictures in the papers of lesbians they have their hair very short but Ingrid, who takes a professional interest, says lesbians don't go to the barber as much these days. She says you used to see them in there in rows in their shirts and ties but now they go to the ladies' salons and have their nails done and their cuticles removed. Have you got cuticles? or have you had them removed? I am a bit out of touch with all that.

The house is just how I want it. We have five bedrooms, lounge room, family room, laundry, bar and a reticulated lawn so I just turn on a tap at the wall and this underground hose squirts water at all the plants. Then I put down my coffee, lean over, turn the tap off again, and the watering's done. Only wish I could reticulate the kids. We're all doing well and my sister Moira's rolling in it what with the American military and the Russian navy. Moira says the girls prefer to do the Russians

*because they don't have so much AIDS. Mum probably already
said that Ingrid is pregnant. Her John gets drunk and beats
people up, but he's never beaten Ingrid. He has two bulldog
mixes which bite, but only when they're chained.*

Lots of love,
Laura
Z z z S (this is Zebbee's signature)

Don't you hate it when a woman annexes her husband or her
children and puts their names on the bottom of a letter clearly
written only by herself? Especially if you've never met the husband
or children concerned.

The third envelope contained a postcard from Ingrid.

Hallo darling,
*I am very pregnant and very happy and I am going to have
a baby. We are going to call her Lolita. I already know she's a
girl because when Loviebuttons swings the crystal it goes anti-
clockwise over my belly. Mum and her John are doing good. He
tells her how fax machines work and she tells him how they
don't.*

See ya soon,
Ingrid

Arguments rose in Milly's mind against Ingrid naming her baby
Lolita. It was time wasted which would have been better spent ac-
customing herself to life's little sorrows, being grateful it wasn't
Minnie's baby and inventing appealing and suitable nicknames.

Ranier's letter was almost as short as Ingrid's.

Dear Minnie,

   Sure you can come stay while you're in San Francisco. Nea
(my ex) has spare room and you and Genevieve are welcome
to it. Let us know when, and we'll arrange for someone to pick
you up. I work nights but have a lot of friends. My Faust com-
plex bristles as I write that. As soon as you say you're really
happy, they come and take your soul away.

Lesbianly,
Ranier Golding

Genevieve had been Minnie's lover for ten years. A one-night
stand who stayed for breakfast. Until one day, nine days ago, she
did not. Minnie had toasted two pieces of bread, spread each with
butter and thick-cut Seville marmalade and only one piece got
eaten. This is the kind of misery to which we promised to allude,
on which we promised not to dwell. Have you, dear reader, ever
had an unhappy love affair, irrespective of whether s/he was good
for you, whether all your friends agreed in chorus that you were
better off without her/him? Well, so had Minnie. She examined
Ranier's letter with the microscope of the unrequited. Ranier would
banish her to the spare room of an ex-lover, would she? And
welcome Genevieve without a second thought. Clearly, she did not
fancy Minnie, was not even at this moment devising a cosy nest
where they could be alone together. This Minnie already knew but,
as she was fond of repeating, "Show me the woman who is good at
taking rejection and I'll show you the terminally autistic."

Natalie Barney's communication consisted of five words.

Come. I must meet you.

Minnie surged out of the bath, waterlogging three airmail enve-
lopes, tripping over the lead to the cassette recorder and overturn-
ing the wastepaper basket with the remains of the gooseberry fool.
She pulled her suitcase from under the bed and began to pack. It
was not until she was considering which knickers to bring: the
holey, the loose or the sordid, that she realised she still had no
clothes on.

IN THE BULRUSHES

→ 2 ←

*C*lothes were a problem. Minnie was a dinosaur. A small dinosaur. The last of the dodos, then. What does a dodo wear? Which shops sell shirts for dodos? Social change was no longer a media star, except in Eastern Europe where it performed the fascist goose-step, and the divided Left were cutting each other up into little pieces. This was at least in line with current marketing strategy, dividing the human body into smaller and smaller units so a product could be provided to "deal with" each unit. Nose-guards for spectacle wearers, specially curved brushes for the back of your teeth, finger protection for frequent pencil users. So far the hackers seem to be slashing away without thought for financial gain, motivated by jealousy, envy, greed, lust—the old favourites—but it would occur to someone soon that money is to be made from selling one's fellows. And why not? Everyone was busy making money and buying property, "the only sensible move," and making babies to put in the property, and embarrassed by anyone still poor and still possessed of that unslaked urge to overthrow the system. The urge was Minnie's only possession, and so she hung onto it, long past expediency, long past sense. What does one do when one discovers that the movement into which one hurled oneself, body and soul and finance, consists fifteen years later of little more than nostalgia and career moves? Is it the same idea when shared by fifty thousand or by two? Who, Minnie wondered, was the other one? Maybe they would know where the dodo clothes shop was.

Minnie decided to give up living and go shopping instead. For reasons to do with the misery to which we promised only to allude, she had discovered recently that her wardrobe was sadly lacking. Having lost the job to which she had devoted herself for eight years, Minnie had been for an interview at a recruitment agency. "When can you come in," the woman on the phone had asked, "so we can take a look at you?" Looking was, apparently, all she had in mind. As soon as Minnie sat down the woman had leaned over and declared, "You look quite lovely as you are, but you'll never get a job dressed like that. Don't you have something else?" Minnie did not. "You know you are getting a bit long in the tooth, dear. How old are you? Thirty-three!" Too old and too disreputable to get a job, Minnie had gazed at herself in the mirror of the nearest Wimpy Bar and wondered what she was doing wrong. She was sure she had washed and ironed whatever it was she was wearing because she always did, and her socks must be alright because she'd thrown the really dreadful ones away.

Minnie carried that mirror vision of herself down the high street and picked away at it with a mind more used to undermining the state and assessing her chances with beautiful women. Neatly ironed navy-blue chinos, a green flasher mack and a grey briefcase. What was wrong with that? Her hair was long with grey wings like Susan Sontag only Minnie's were natural whereas Genevieve's lover's ex-lover knew the fag who'd put Susan's streaks in for her. Could it be that word-processor/secretaries were not meant to look like Susan Sontag? Minnie wore no makeup, could not even re-member what all the bits were called. There was lipstick and eye shadow, but they were easy. Wasn't there also a thing you put under your eyelashes and another for your cheeks and a third which went over the cheek stuff and something else again which went behind your knees? The recruitment woman had said that firms expect their staff to dress to suit the ambience. Minnie, trying desperately to grasp this new concept, had said brightly that at least one got the choice between matching the wallpaper or the soft furnishings. The woman had snapped that Minnie had evidently never heard of power dressing. Minnie had not.

Determinedly unabashed, Minnie strode forth to conquer another new world. She headed for Marks and Spencer which was where she had been buying knickers these last ten years. Each time she rounded the corner of the gooseberry fool shelf a line of frothy white lace waved at her from the lingerie department. Minnie had gone straight from school uniform to jeans and chinos, but like Margaret Thatcher, she still bought her underwear from Marks and Spencer. Maybe the firms the recruitment woman had in mind would not have employed Mrs. Thatcher either.

There were racks of cream-coloured blouses and pale blue angora jumpers. There were all-cotton culottes and beige pleated skirts. What do women wear? Minnie looked anxiously at mothers and daughters buying white raincoats with detachable lining. If she stared too hard somebody would wonder what she was doing there. Probably the security guard. Minnie snatched up a navy-blue wool jacket and skirt and hurried toward the fitting rooms for a moment's privacy. What about those men who went away to Casablanca and came back as women? Somebody must have taught them how women dress. But how would Minnie explain, when she arrived in Casablanca, that she didn't need the operation, just the instruction? No doubt there were magazines. Yes, surely there were, with knitting patterns and recipes and photographs of fashion models and a bit underneath that told you what it was, how much it cost and how to accessorize. Minnie frowned. There were, she remembered, so many magazines. She thought perhaps the ones with the knitting patterns were not the ones with the clothes hints.

"Did you want to try that on, madam?"

"I suppose I must have wanted to."

"It looks a little large. If you don't mind my saying so."

"They come in sizes?"

"Of course. You won't find a 'one-size' suit. What size are you?"

"I don't really know."

At jumble sales, Minnie's familiar clothes haunt, you just hauled out whatever caught your eye from the tables of castoffs and handed them to one of the helpers. She counted up what you'd got and you usually paid two quid for the lot. If something didn't fit you when you got it home, you gave it away to the next jumble sale. The only item you couldn't buy there was knickers. Well, could you?

"Hmm. What size bra do you wear?"

Minnie didn't wear a bra. Not that she'd burnt hers, exactly, but she had been grateful to the women's liberation movement for allowing her not to replace the old ones when the straps ripped or the little hooks came off. She had found bras extremely uncomfortable and they never fitted. Whatever cup she bought, she always had bits of breast peering over the top. Sexier without.

"Umm," she said, anxiously.

The fittings-room assistant decided Minnie was a foreigner, despite her accent. Many foreigners speak perfect English just to fool you. Marks and Spencer has a well-deserved reputation for its help and courtesy to blind and wheelchair-bound customers; the assistant had listened to a staff lecture on the subject only last week. Patience had been the keynote and patience is probably the best attitude to adopt when dealing with foreigners.

"How big are your breasts?" the assistant asked with her best attempt at a no-nonsense, business-as-usual stance. If one went to the trouble of describing the colour and tinge of a mango to a blind person, it was only logical to spell out the basic information needed to assess a woman's size to a foreigner who, no doubt, used a different system.

Minnie considered the question. She could think of only one instance where the exact contours of her breasts were relevant.

"It takes both of my lover's hands to cover one," she replied truthfully.

The assistant turned not a hair. This was England.

"Is he a large man," she enquired, "or a small man?"

"A woman," said Minnie, "of the middle height."

"In that case," the assistant said, her tone brisk and efficient, "you'll be a size thirty-six."

"Fine," said Minnie, looking relieved. "And if my lover had been a man?"

"In that case," replied the assistant, "he would only have used one hand."

"What a pity," Minnie exclaimed.

The assistant frowned. The subject was closed.

Minnie continued along Kensington High Street. She dropped into Next and Dorothy Somebody but could not bring herself to try anything else on. The blue wool skirt suit had looked smart, like the manageress of a Marks and Spencer fittings room. And then there'd be the tights and the matching cardigan and the shoes and a change of blouse and a handbag. Oh my god. The handbag. The recruitment woman had been very convincing about the need for Minnie to take herself in hand if she ever hoped to re-enter the booming British economy; the finality of her interviewer's tone washed around Minnie's mind like saltwater in the bilge, slowly eroding the old oak timbers. Even the length of Minnie's service seemed to count against her. "How long were you in your last job? Eight years? Eight? But, my dear, that is a very long time." The interviewer had sounded shocked. Well, Minnie thought, as she bumped into a dog-walker juggling six leads, it's in the agencies' interests for everyone to stay in each job the shortest possible length of time. If we all worked in the same places for years on end, the agencies would be out of a job. This sudden realisation brought with it a rise of cynicism, sufficient to sit Minnie down and order her an orange juice.

With deep relief and even gratitude, Minnie spotted a woman on the other side of the coffee bar whose clothes, even at that distance and with people in between, she wholeheartedly coveted. As the woman walked past her toward the door, Minnie admired the soft, sweeping folds of the silk: pale pink shantung, like Beryl's mother used to wear.

"I say," Minnie said, leaping to her feet, "I've been admiring your suit. Wherever did you get it? It's just what I want." The woman smiled a practiced smile and gave the name of a dressmaker in Milan.

"How much does she charge?" Minnie asked.

The woman winced no more perceptibly than had the fittings-room attendant and mentioned a figure a little in excess of two thousand pounds. Minnie was not abashed. "It appears I have taste," she thought to herself, "even if I don't have money."

The job that Minnie had lost after eight years of devoted service and to which, one assumes, she was able to go jumble-suited and fashion-comatose? This is skirting close to the misery we promised not to elaborate, but many people do like to know about employment. It helps them assess the character's class position, and then they know where their sympathies should lie. Minnie worked for a small inner-city collective which set up computer databases for other small inner-city collectives. You might ask how such a job can last eight years since the number of small inner-city collectives requiring databases must be limited and, once set up, a database does not need servicing. But no. Only persuade a group to buy themselves a computer and they are yours for life. Ask the Jesuits. Ask IBM.

The reason Minnie was forced to quit this worthwhile and hardly lucrative employment? The reason for her flight to Australia, toward an impossibly unlikely love affair with an author she had never met? The reason why Beryl should suddenly remember this first daughter, half a world away and offer a return ticket, and in the peak period too? Minnie wrote to Beryl, not of the material circumstances of her life—no mother's cockles would be warmed by tales of low wages and much soup—but of the extraordinary and depraved idealists who inhabited her world, stories she could not tell in London where everyone knew everyone on the extraordinary depraved idealist circuit. But the depravity of the idealists was like the ears of King Midas: impossible to speak of, impossible to keep quiet. As Midas's servant told the bulrushes, so Minnie had told her mother. The bulrushes whispered the secret among themselves till it grew to a roar with the wind and the whole kingdom heard of Midas's shame.

What depravity? Which idealists? Could it be anyone I know? It's now playing in a neighborhood near you. Funds granted and mysteriously disappearing; facilities agreed and never built; intimidation of witnesses; destruction of evidence; the usual minutiæ of life in a metropolis with the addition of pomp and speeches. Minnie had been so downcast by the latest depravity that she had almost entirely ceased going to the launderette. Instead she had stocked up on new Ariel Rapide for those difficult days when you feel like washing things by hand. Otherwise she was sure to have bumped into someone who would with high glee have insisted on telling her the stop-press news. It was that kind of launderette. The bulrushes whipped the depravity into a seven-day scandal which, turned away from Minnie's flat by the closed front door, had changed direction and landed full-frontal in Minnie's workplace. It could almost have been planned as public repudiation of any gains the Left might have made in the last few years: all the benefits the poll tax had bestowed upon the opposition. There were court appearances, car chases, people thrown down stairs, broken jaws and, following hungry in their wake, like buzzards to a sky funeral, journalists from those papers which thrive on decomposition. "Bad enough what this government is doing," said Milly, "the National Health, the ILEA, the GLC, all those council house sales and all those interest rate increases throwing all those kids onto the streets. How can you bear it when you see them begging, 'hungry and homeless,' humiliated, not even looking you in the face? London's a Third World country for them."

The day Minnie resigned she bought a length of hosepipe with an attachment so it would fit onto her car exhaust. She planned to drive to Trent Country Park late one moonless night and empty a full tank of petrol into her lungs by way of the internal combustion engine. She stocked up on codeine, sleepers and aspirin; bought a medicinal bottle of gin to go with the antibiotics she had been warned not to mix with alcohol. She began to lock up her kitchen knives. Sitting on tube platforms she would grasp the bench firmly with both hands; no one wanted an incident which would delay all movement on the Circle Line for at least half an hour. Minnie was nothing if not intense and intensely involved in this movement now pouring its gorgeous strength into slitting its own throat. Liberty was a glorious thing to fight for, but where was it nowadays? Crouching unrecognisable as the choice between Brand X which eats dirt and Brand Nu which does away with unwanted odour.

Minnie was, moreover, and above all, a lesbian. And lesbians get hysterical about the least little thing. Have you ever watched a bunch of dykes trying to work out the bill in a crowded restaurant? The debonair city gent will have unfolded a few twenties—they always deal in cash, not for them that vulgar American plastic—before you have time to seek your bowler. Even the blue-rinsed ladies of the Women's Institute have their own arcane method of keeping score; like idiot savants with calendar skills, they can tell to a meal who's turn it will be to pay the bill on a certain afternoon in November of the year 2000. Lesbians are a race apart. Lesbians take positive delight in doing the same simple arithmetic five times for the pure pleasure of getting it wrong.

What saved Minnie from the range of suicides for which she had prepared was an unexpected and felicitous effect of the latest scandal. Whenever anyone began to tell her the juicy latest, Minnie's mind would fill with Maria Callas in *Lucia di Lammremoor* singing "Ah ah ah ah ah" and bouncing around on the high notes, effectively blocking out anything vile idealist Y was said to have done to sweet innocent idealist X. Since Minnie regarded opera as the personal gift of Natalie Barney without whose frontispiece, *Voi che sapete*, Minnie might have gone through life bereft of sopranos, she had written the fan letter which had, six months later, produced the reply, "Come. I must meet you."

There were other things. Before Genevieve had gone, grotesque fantasies would form in Minnie's mind immediately prior to orgasm. If Minnie forced out the fantasy, she didn't come. Since the fantasy only appeared at the exact point when all Minnie wanted in the whole world was to come, she allowed it ten second headroom. Time enough for the orgasms to be effected. Time enough for Minnie to walk around with a perpetual chorus of "I am a monster," "I'm turning into an animal," "I'm turning into a man." It was a relief when Genevieve did not come back.

In brief, Minnie had been pursued by a serpent across rough and rocky country. Fainting with exhaustion, rage and fear that this bitterness, this bile, would blight her life, she was wide open to the invitation from the three enchanted ladies who had appeared before her in the guise of letters from Beryl, Laura and Ingrid and were exhorting her to calm down, get fed and be loved. Minnie was, she discovered, hungry. A hunger gooseberry fool had been unable to satisfy. Sex and politics had turned from blueprints for a better world into nightmare backstreets of the old. Work had become a trap whose bars were Minnie's own competence, hardened into indispensability. For some years she had felt like Tony Last in

Evelyn Waugh's A *Handful of Dust* ("Evelyn Waugh," thunders Milly, "have you no class consciousness?"; "Oh yes," Minnie replies, "just enough left to read Evelyn Waugh."), obliged to read aloud from the complete works of Charles Dickens every evening in the South American jungle, going to sleep hoping to make it to the next canoe out of there, waking to find he has been drugged again, and the canoe has departed again, ignorant of his existence.

When Minnie heard the sound of an aeroplane, like a magic flute, in the air above her bathroom she jumped for it. To her credit, her slim sense of self-preservation, and Beryl's excellent upbringing, Minnie decided on rest first, lust later. She was aware this was more upbringing than innate good sense. Indeed at the worst, at the bottom of the slimy dark pit where there is not even water to tread but thick, endless mud, the one thing which, prior to opera, prevented Minnie from sucking the hose, wielding the knife, swallowing the pills, plunging under the train, was the simple phrase, "I cannot kill myself because my mother loves me." Beryl loved her daughter and Minnie lover her mother.

IN THE BOSOM OF HER FAMILY

➤ 3 ≪

*L*ove is not, unfortunately, everything. Mother and daughter might have continued to love each other, each in her own way, at a distance of twelve thousand miles through a sentimental, Vaseline lens. They did not need to test their certainty by once again occupying the same living quarters. Close up, all the little creases and rages would be visible, all the old irritants would set to work again. Minnie felt that her reasons for coming were not entirely noble, not entirely mother-centred. She found her mother's world as difficult to appreciate as the fashion racks in the department store. What is it that distinguishes a really lovely pair of culottes from an unspeakably dowdy pair? In London she was always meeting Baby Vicky on the front doorstep and Baby Vicky was always off to a wedding. Courtesy would prompt Minnie to say how nice Baby Vicky looked and to express a hope that the wedding would be a good one. But what makes a good wedding? Minnie had no idea. The woman who lived in the basement was always going off to rock concerts and although Minnie had never been to one, she could at least imagine that if the rain kept off, and the speakers worked, and the bands turned up, and the drug busts were minimal and you met someone nice, then you would come home saying it had been marvellous, or "dishy" or "crucial" or whatever it was one said to express pleasure after a rock concert. But weddings? Minnie imagined that a concert, at its best, promoted a sense of spiritual togetherness amongst the green-haired, leather-clad, nose-ringed throng. But the theological basis for a wedding is the spiritual difference between men and women such that they must be tied in some visible way with the dire warning that "whom God hath brought together let no man set asunder," or however it went. Oh well, perhaps it was the hats.

In the bosom of her family Minnie lay down and slept. When she awoke, she was thirty-three and it was dinner time.

"Go on then," said Beryl's voice just outside her room. "Go and bounce on your Aunty."

Whereupon a blond slug and a grown-up four-year-old catapulted through the door. Then overcome by their own daring, they stood staring open-mouthed at the reclining figure.

"Oh," bleated Minnie, who hadn't quite got used to "daughter," so found "aunty" rather a strain. "You can't come in yet, I haven't wrapped your presents."

Zebbee seized Son obediently by the hand and marched him to the door. Minnie stumbled to the chest of drawers and looked for something to wear. Her travelling clothes had disappeared into her mother's washing machine. Gone were the days of sticking her legs into whatever surfaced first in the jeans drawer; the words of the recruitment woman rang in her ears no fainter for having been uttered a week ago. If one could not get a job, one could not participate in the economic world but was thrown back on sentiment, so personal, so terrifyingly changeable, such a factor in Minnie's present discomfort.

Minnie had returned to England ten years ago clad in pink and black with forays into a very clashing pink and green. Hard times had since drained every spark of colour from her clothes and waved a navy blue wand over her closet. There had been no time for colour and navy was cheap and serviceable, the two least enticing sartorial attributes.

When Minnie emerged at last, she very nearly stumbled over two small children sitting, eyes closed, hands out, in front of the door.

"What on earth?" she exclaimed. One has to watch closely to get to know and distinguish small children, appreciate the curious thought processes that go on in their extraordinary heads.

"You told them to wait for their presents," Laura explained. "They're waiting."

"Good grief. But I didn't expect them to do it. At the mention of 'presents' my friends' kids would simply and methodically have ransacked my suitcase."

"These two are Laura's," said Beryl, "and they do what she says. Kids' Lib never reached Western Australia."

Minnie supervised the unwrapping of multicoloured balloons, a quantity of little acorns which would, with patience, build a model of the Taj Mahal, and a green inflatable water snake with a red forked tongue. The doorbell rang.

"Oh Lord," exclaimed Beryl from the kitchen, "the parrot's got the macadamias. Would one of you answer the door?"

Even as she asked, a very slow-moving Ingrid limped into the living room.

"Sorry about that. Lost my key and then I found it again. Hi, darling." This last was to Minnie as Ingrid flopped down onto a big old sofa. Minnie gazed at her baby sister in disbelief. It was possible for Laura to have grown two practical, purposeful children; Laura had been thirty-five years old all her life. But Ingrid? Ingrid was still just a little thing, learning to walk, falling over and having to be picked up. Yet all the indications were that she was about to have a baby herself. Minnie beamed with honest joy—some things had remained simple—and hugged Ingrid carefully around the bulge.

"Have you been buying lots of lovely, frothy baby clothes?"

Minnie cooed. The false note hung, jarring, in the air.

Ingrid smiled peacefully.

"Babies don't need much."

"Where will you live?"

"On my land," said Ingrid. She pulled out a set of photographs featuring five acres of prime Australian bush. A little rise, a little valley, a lot of trees, some nice rocks. No water and no house and no road and no electricity and no gas and no telephone and no plumbing and no shopping centre. Minnie decided to start small.

"But, water, Ingrid. You'll need water to clean the baby and wash its nappies and sterilise its bottle and give it a refreshing drink."

"We're getting a rain barrel," smiled Ingrid peacefully.

"You need rain," said Minnie.

Ingrid gazed peacefully toward the window where dark clouds could already be seen gathering obediently in the previously clear sky. The parrot was huddling disconsolately on its roost. The forecast had not said rain that morning so the parrot had left the most succulent almonds on the tree for teatime, and now they would be washed out.

"Barrels need a large catchment area," Minnie insisted. "They don't just fill from the sky; they collect water that runs through the gutters from the roof of a house, for example." She tried not to put too much emphasis on the word "house," not wanting to rub in the fact that Ingrid did not have one.

"We've got a house," said Ingrid, bringing out another picture. This one showed a battered tin shed attached to someone else's bungalow.

"Isn't it in the wrong place?" suggested Minnie. "Wouldn't it need to be on your land, to feed the rain into the rain barrel?"

She was, momentarily, interrupted by a loud thunderclap. It really was too hard on a parrot, the parrot was thinking, to be forbidden the family macadamias and deprived of the best almonds, all in the same day.

"Loviebuttons is going to knock it down," Ingrid was explaining peacefully, "and Mum's John is going to carry it out to my land."

To avoid any confusion caused by the shared first name of their various menfolk, the women of the family referred to their own husbands, sons and boyfriends as "Loviebuttons," and to everyone else's as "your John," or "her John," as applicable.

Minnie pictured Beryl's husband with his scholastic pallor and wondered how he planned to carry a ton of metal, brick and wood the fifty or so miles from Perth to Gunderdin where Ingrid's land was situated. Questions like: How did the land become yours, Ingrid? would certainly have been greeted "By mutual consent, Minnie" or "Just seemed better that way," so Minnie refrained from asking. It was not, however, in Minnie's makeup to ignore questions of money. Sisterly courtesy might postpone her giving voice to them but they roiled about the canyons of her mind nonetheless clamorously for that.

"Loviebuttons is borrowing his mate's low-loader," Beryl threw in, peering round the corner from the stove, trying to count how many were coming to dinner. Ingrid, smiling peacefully, brought out a picture of a low-loader.

"How do those twenty-foot jarrah roof beams get onto the low-loader, Ingrid?" Minnie asked, expecting a technical explanation involving winches, cranes and gantries.

Peacefully, Ingrid brought out a picture of Loviebuttons. Minnie glanced. A young man and a tree standing in close proximity but at a peculiar angle. The tree appeared not to be touching the ground.

"Where is the bottom of the tree?" she puzzled.

"In Loviebutton's hand," said Ingrid, peacefully.

"Open secret what Ingrid sees in her John," laughed Beryl from the entrails of the rabbit. Minnie was baffled. And the parrot, who had hopped onto the windowsill for a closer look, could not see what the fuss was about. Loviebuttons had no feathers, he was a dingy beige colour; the parrot swooped off in an access of scorn. Why, that green inflatable water snake with the red forked tongue was a lot more fetching.

"Ingrid's John is so strong he can lift trees?" said Minnie slowly, feeling her way.

Beryl, Laura and Ingrid nodded encouragement.

"Oh." A dim bulb glimmered in Minnie's head. "That's meant to be sexy, right?"

The three women nodded again. Minnie glanced back at the picture.

"And the angle at which he's carrying that trunk, it could be mistaken for an erection?" Erection, was that the right word? Men's anatomy and its hydraulics were rather forgettable, she found.

Beryl guffawed, Laura giggled and Ingrid smiled, peacefully. Minnie was taken aback. She was unused to straight women being straightforward about the joy of straight sex. Those she knew in London steered their way through conversation as though they had resolved that particular tension in the early seventies and had felt no throbbing since. Whatever Milly might have to say about ninety percent of women not achieving orgasm during penetration, Ingrid would go right on smiling peacefully and holding out her photograph of Loviebuttons. Her family's choice in Johns was now clear to Minnie: Beryl's was clever; Laura's was nice; and Ingrid's was a sex kitten. Minnie felt a great sense of achievement in decoding heterosexual hieroglyphs.

"Mum," Minnie said next day over tea and toast, having refused the yoghurt, melon, avocado, corned beef and baked beans of which Beryl assured her there was plenty. Beryl's bottom drawer was filled with baked beans. She had read somewhere, in something Minnie had sent no doubt, of a humble homebody whose one act of rebellion had been to fill a cupboard with tins of beans. "Mrs. X's incompetence as a housewife, spending all the grocery money on beans, is her way of maintaining sanity under oppression," the author had decided. Beryl had thought to herself, Baked beans, how sensible, and was tempted to take the name "Housewife X." She had read somewhere else, probably Lady Troubridge's *The Book of Etiquette,* that it is customary for the mother to give the daughter breakfast. So she did her best. She did her best.

"Mum," Minnie repeated, "was Ingrid having me on about the baby?"

"Well," said Beryl vaguely, "she is nine months' pregnant, dear. Something has to happen. And of all the possibilities, a baby would probably be the nicest."

"No, I mean that she hasn't done anything about it?"

"She must have done *some*thing," said Beryl.

"About...about...its *things.*"

"Nappies?" suggested Beryl. "Doesn't one like to mention them by name these days? What do they do in London about such *things*?"

"In America they dry the baby's bottom with the hair drier," mused Minnie. "Supposed to be more sanitary."

"Hard to imagine a baby's bottom as a temple to hygiene, but far be it for me..."

"But Mum," said Minnie firmly, "Ingrid told me she's taking her baby out to her land where she doesn't have any water, let alone a house. And when I asked after its pretty, frothy frocks, she just laughed. Other mothers..."

"Other mothers?" repeated Beryl. "Tell me all about it."

In the bustle of having Minnie to stay, Beryl had forgotten to buy parrot food. The parrot had endured two days of candied almonds and salted peanuts, but now it was putting its claw down. It wanted cuttlefish and dried wobbegong and it wanted them bought from Cents, the paupers' store. While Beryl and her John were hard up they could not bear to shop at Cents, made Beryl feel like white trash just walking in the door. But now they were both earning real money, the parrot reckoned they could afford it. The produce was dirt cheap and Cents left the fins and head on their wobbegongs while more up-market establishments cut and filleted. There was nothing the parrot liked more than the head of a wobbegong. It was like, well, like *Salome and the Head of John the Baptist* which Beryl was so fond of reading to Zebbee. The parrot had not been filled with unmitigated delight on hearing of the birth of first one, then two, now three human infants. It associated them with plucked tail feathers and ignominious pursuit but there were advantages, it discovered. Like being read to. No one ever thought to read to a parrot but they were rather thrilled to find one perched on the armchair above the child.

In this fashion the parrot had heard the contents of Minnie's entire correspondence with her mother, many of the sisters' letters, including the most recent batch. It had added its own words of encouragement. "Pa pa pa," it had sung, "pa pa pa," the song of Papageno which it naturally considered its own, meaning, "We are both strange birds seeking the one creature who can love us as we wish to be loved." But Minnie had not replied. She spurned comparison with a parrot, even such a red and green feathered beauty. Well, the parrot would bide its time. It eyed the green water snake; that red forked tongue was so sexy, why it could circle one's entire head and lick one's ear. The parrot longed to sprinkle the snake's tongue with hazelnut, then peck it off. While an inflatable water snake might not be a parrot's soulmate, it would put a little gaiety into a dull afternoon. Though the parrot had the strangest feeling that afternoons with Minnie around were going to get quite interesting.

"I know," said Beryl with a sudden spark. "Let's go to Cents. It's just across the reserve, don't even need to get the car out. We can have a lovely time browsing round the shelves."

"Oh yes, let's," glowed Minnie enthusiastically, inspired by the same inexplicable impulse as Beryl. "What fun. I've been longing to push a shopping trolley round a supermarket. Let's hope there's a long queue at the checkout so we can take our time leaving the store."

Once the fish and the nuts were safely in the trolley, the parrot cast about for other items they might buy. If they came home from a shopping trip with so little to show for it, they might, after the flame of naked parrot hunger had dissipated, come to wonder what had possessed them. It was not that the parrot feared discovery, but raging lust can be embarrassing when seen from outside, through the eyes of another species, and the parrot did not want those two casting about for an explanation which might lead them to the garage where it fully intended to be having it away with the friendly water snake.

Minnie could not help noticing that her mother flipped two dozen disposable nappies and three pairs of plastic pants on top of the pile of tinned tomatoes and baked beans already sitting in the trolley. Responding to the same inexplicable stimulus, Minnie found herself cuddling a large, floppy, washable yellow doll with which she crowned the pyramid. All those of you who wonder what causes a woman to have a baby, and what causes her female friends to come round clucking and cooing and to chat, endlessly, of the comparable softness of nappies, may learn the secret now: a woman gets her maternal instinct from the parrot.

"Stocking up on nappies?" said a familiar voice.

"Thought they might come in handy one of these days," said Beryl vaguely.

"Gonna put them in the bottom drawer with the baked beans, are ya?" said Laura.

"Two dozen nappies never hurt anyone," said Beryl.

"Think Ingrid really hasn't got anything for the baby?" asked Minnie.

"Yeah," said Laura. "She has. But they left them in store down in Bridgetown till they could find a place to live up here."

"What profit a woman two wardrobes full of clothes in Bridgetown if she has her baby in Perth?" asked Beryl.

"Knowing Ingrid," said Laura, "she's got it all worked out and just isn't letting on."

"And do you?" asked Minnie.

"Know Ingrid?" said Laura. "Well, I used ta. We used ta rave on to each other about every little thing. You know how sisters are."

Minnie grinned sadly and shook her head.

"But since her new John came on the scene, it's been harder to talk to Ingrid. He gets drunk and picks fights. Keeps on at my John to fight and prove he's not a coward."

Sensing that Minnie was about to say something derogatory about Ingrid's John, Laura took the defence. "He's as soft as silk to women and children, Ingrid's John. It's only blokes he likes to beat."

"You can understand that, Minnie," said Beryl.

"Come on," said Zebbee, who had collected everything they needed for the barbie. Her daddy was out deep-sea fishing that afternoon, part of a boat trip Laura had bought as a birthday present. She had found the address of the boat company amongst a list of suggestions in *Woman's Way* under the heading "Happy Teenagers: Here's How." Tomorrow there would be fish to cook, so tomorrow evening they would have a barbecue. Laura surveyed the contents of Zebbee's trolley, checking her daughter had bought Loviebuttons's favourite mayonnaise with the added sugar.

"We're having a barbie," said Laura. "Wanna come, Minnie? I've invited Simone and her girlfriend, Lex."

"Simone?" said Beryl. "From Ingrid's hairdressing salon? You mean she's…"

"She says she's…," said Laura, "and Lex says, 'None of your effing business.'"

The green inflatable water snake was not the cheap date the parrot had supposed. It was, as it turned out, partial to head of wobbegong but it expected more than a little macadamia relish before it would put out. Low-level flattery and heavy preening were not enough; the snake wanted the champagne works. The parrot would have to find somewhere else to send Beryl and Minnie; the afternoon was going to be a long haul.

Beryl was putting the beans away when the post arrived.

"Minnie darling," she called, "would your politics be seriously compromised by having tea with a practising prostitute, or are all women still your sisters?"

Minnie was at that moment in her bedroom, gazing at the letter from Natalie Barney: "Come. I must meet you." Domesticity was all very well, and the food was excellent, but now that she had rested and supped she had begun to feel there was more to life. There was, she remembered, sex. Where had that old memory surfaced from? Family ties and the soft fondness of sisters were a blessing indeed but she wondered how long she could restrain herself before throwing her clothes into a suitcase, leaping on the first plane to New York, and presenting herself stark naked on Natalie's doorstep. In all likelihood, however, Natalie would have a doorman, not a doorstep, and not even Minnie felt brave enough to present herself stark naked on Natalie's doorman. The other little obstacle was that Minnie still did not know where Natalie's doorman was situated.

* * *

"Is this a purely theoretical question, Mum?" asked Minnie, "or are you translating a tricky passage from your Russian primer? *Glasnost* is having unexpected results."

"Laura's sister, Moira, has invited us to tea. She says that officially she's working this afternoon, but unless a Russian ship pulls up in a hurry, she won't get a call."

General goodwill climbed into Beryl's immaculate white Kingswood to visit Moira. Beryl worried about Laura's sister. Had worried more when it looked as though Laura might give in and invite her to stay in one of the five bedrooms belonging to the re-ticulated lawn. Moira had developed none of the thick skin and lashing cynicism of the prostitutes of contemporary fiction. Well, it took Beryl's mind off Ingrid's baby and Minnie's secret sorrow. On the other hand, the whole familial role kept Beryl away from her nice Russian irregulars.

Laura reckoned if they accepted Minnie, they should accept Moira. Different people did sex differently, that was all. How come she and Ingrid turned out the two normal sisters? But then there was how she felt when she saw Moira, her little sister Moi, dressed up in red silk camiknickers for some bloke to, well, do what they did. Mostly Laura tried to put it out of her mind and have a good time with Moira like the old days. Which hadn't been very good, but she was going to put that out of her mind too. She had Zebbee and Son now.

Minnie felt better than she had done for years. Meals appeared that she had neither cooked nor paid for. No one told her about E additives, caffeine, white sugar = white death, aluminium = Alzheimer's, or too much salt hardening the arteries and better use sodium-free. No one seemed to want to throw anyone down the stairs for tolerating, or not tolerating, sadomasochism. Most places there weren't even any stairs. She was meant to have an attitude about Moira being a prostitute, a well-researched, articulate, po-litical argument, but she was too weary, life was too hard for rhetoric. Or rather, she felt too well, euphorically well, to think much beyond "Poor Moira. She must hate it." Soon, Minnie supposed, she would have to allow her brain to work again but at the moment it was still too dazzled by the warmth, the sun, the bright colours and the constant stream of obvious affection. They had stopped off at Sweet Sugar High to buy gooseberry fool for Minnie, himmeltorte for Laura and a nice feuilles de chêne lettuce for Beryl. If Minnie could not have sex, she would stuff herself with gooseberry fool.

Milly was raging that having tea with a prostitute was tantamount to living off immoral earnings, even if you did bring the cakes yourself and why, she might ask, was Minnie condoning the most basic level of female oppression when she should be doing everything she could to get Moira off the game and into honourable employment. She might well ask. Minnie might well reply that there was precious little that was honourable about the jobs Moira could get. Then they might well have an argument. But Minnie was drooling over the prospect of sweet, sticky, creamy fool and paid not the slightest attention to Milly.

Moira lived in respectable Victoria Park. Her neighbours told each other she did night work, a euphemism which must have been invented for the benefit of the children, who were entirely uninterested, since the men had all, on occasion, used her services, and the women gossiped freely. When meeting her on the street, or bumping into her at the local shops, they would ask after her family, mention the weather, and observe that the garbos were bloody late with the bin collection again. This was not new world tolerance but small-town necessity: the fewer the people, the more you have to make allowances. She and Laura were competing for Housewife of the Year Award. What Moira's profession might have detracted, her house more than made up for; it was cool and calm, giving the impression of shade and waterfalls. Apart from the ironing, she lifted not a finger to order her home but hired a daily for the cleaning, a weekly for the rough, a laundress for the wash and starch, a monthly for the windows and a new service she had found in *Woman's Way* to shampoo the carpets.

As Beryl pulled up in the Kingswood, Moira lounged on the front verandah, lifting weights with her feet. An ice trolley stood in the kitchen, laden with ice cream cake and raspberry pavlova, ready to be wheeled into the garden under a tree, should English teas and picnics prove to coincide.

"How about a game of Scrabble?" Moira suggested after she'd settled Beryl on a rug with a large cup of tea, shown Minnie round the house, explained the new industrial-strength vacuum cleaner to Zebbee and passed on the latest news of the steam iron to Laura.

"Cake first," said Laura. "My two might be more interested in the ball bearings in your Hoover, but it's exactly half an hour since we bought the himmeltorte and I can't keep my mind on anything else."

Minnie and Beryl gorged on gooseberry fool and lettuce respectively; Laura plunged into the himmeltorte and Moira ransacked the pavlova, for each had brought to the table the thing she liked best to eat.

"If the kids don't finish it I'll take the ice cream cake to work for the girls," said Moira. "It's my turn to bring goodies."

They spread out the Scrabble board. Minnie put down a "quoin," Laura a "pique," and Beryl an "oxymel," double-word score.

"Aren't we smart," said Minnie.

"No," said Laura. "We've been playing Scrabble a long time, is all. Bet no one knows what these words mean, they just picked them up from the last game."

"Probably never meant anything," said Moira. "The first person who made them up was a good liar and a bad loser."

"Can you imagine being proud to be a good loser?" Beryl was musing, and Minnie was replying, "Show me a really good loser, I'll show you a really certifiable autistic," when a loud shrill noise rang out in the vicinity of the raspberry pavlova and Moira's wrist.

"Why've you set your wrist alarm for 4:32, Moira?" asked Minnie. "I'm curious."

Laura giggled.

"That's my beep," said Moira. "Gotta go to work." She turned to Minnie. "Will you take over my letters and make the words in my place?"

"Yes," Minnie promised solemnly.

Moira stood up and brushed grass off her skirt. She went into the house to collect her coat and handbag. Then she kissed everyone goodbye. As she waved through the car window, backing carefully into the road, it was hard not to think of where she was going, what she was being summoned to do. She looked so much like a young housewife off to animate a Tupperware party. The others carried the tea things back into the house where Zebbee was loading the dishwasher. Beryl looked round the clean, well-equipped kitchen in which the owner never cooked.

The Scrabble game was destined to freeze permanently at "quoin," "pique," "oxymel." Despite her solemn promise, it was not possible for Minnie to make Moira's words for her.

IN BETWIXT AND BETWEEN

⇒ 4 ⇐

Minnie felt a return of the old rage: if Moira was still selling her body in the nineties, had women made no gains at all in the last twenty years? They were wearing miniskirts in the sixties, they were wearing miniskirts now, and the only difference that Minnie could see was that before, the skirts had been orange and mauve velvet, whereas today they were black leather.

Hobble skirts would, she supposed, describe a straight line between one's personal appearance and one's subject position. Though it is rather difficult to walk a straight line since one has two legs, one on either side of one's body. You might as well be walking a tightrope, anxious all the time lest you fall off. A long balancing act between moral probity and personal taste. The dictates of personal taste are often dignified with the universality of an ideological blueprint. The clever learn cunning, alter their vocabulary, say "It is good" where they used to say "I like it,"; say "It is offensive" where they used to say "It does not suit me." Often a new idea passes only into the vocabulary, not into the hearts and minds. People learn to talk right, their radical new lexicon at the mercy of the next grudge that comes along. Then they can offload old words for new and nothing need change but the manner of its expression. You have friends, no doubt, who, finding that "Get the fuck out of here" made them appear churlish, have altered their phrasing to "I need space for myself at the present time." Laura, at least, knew she was playing a game of Scrabble and that words like "quoin, pique, oxymel" were good for scoring points but had no outside existence.

Minnie borrowed Beryl's car and drove the two streets to the barbecue. She was touched, and a little overwhelmed, that Laura had invited women to meet her. Family and dyke life usually took place on separate planets. She had supposed her stay in Perth would be a kind of stopover from real life while her batteries re-charged. And here they were doing it in Perth too, in Laura's backyard, eating fish Laura's husband had caught. Being a lesbian was becoming a very common or garden affair, it seemed.

"Brought the car?" Laura greeted her in the driveway. "It's only five-minutes' walk. You're turning into a real Aussie."

"It's this shirt," Minnie grinned. "Didn't want to crumple it and Mum's iron's died."

"My sister Moira has a new steam iron with aluminium ironing board and heat-resistant…"

They laughed.

"I told my John's mum about Ingrid, what you said, about her planning to take the baby out to her land and leaving all the baby clothes down at Bridgetown. John's mum had a word with his sis-ters and his sisters-in-law. They've had enough babies for two football teams and a pack of cheerleaders. They're going to bring the castoffs for Ingrid."

"G'day, Minnie," said Laura's John coming in from the garden. "Good to see ya again. Barbie's goin' well. Could do with a stubby, but. Thirsty work. You girls want somethin'?"

"Aw, make us coffee will ya, darl?"

John trundled cheerfully out again. Minnie and Laura sat down for a minute.

"Where are the kids?"

"Out there with John. He's really good with them."

"Sounds like you've got the perfect setup."

"I'm bored," said Laura with a dangerous flatness in her voice. "I heard this song on the radio, 'Is that all there is?' I keep humming it to myself. Even... well, you know. Even...in bed."

"You could always..."

"No," said Laura sharply. "I could not. I want the house, the garden, the kids, even the dear old husband. Sometimes I get fond of the boredom. It makes me feel... safe."

"Stops you feeling like Moira."

"I'm nothing like Moira," Laura snapped.

"Oh I want my lawyer/doctor/accountant/insurance broker too."

"The ugly/paunchy/jowly/short-assed one?"

"You have them here too?"

"You wrote to mum about them."

"It's funny you calling her mum. Someone asked her once how many daughters she had and she said two, the pregnant brunette and the blonde. She meant you and Ingrid. It made me feel quite strange."

"I'm sorry."

"We keep apologising to each other."

"Yeah," Laura smiled. "Do you really want to marry respectability?"

"Not marry..."

"Well no, but a respectable...girlfriend? Is it a 'girlfriend' you say?"

"Me, I say lover."

"That's sexy."

"Would be. If I had one."

"Oh. Don't you?"

"She left me."

"And there's no one else?"

"Oh yes. Lots. At least two. There's this author, lives in New York. I wrote her a fan letter and she wrote back."

"What she say?"

"'Come. I must meet you.'"

"How romantic. But I'm a happily married mother of two. Oh I do miss the gossip. People think that as soon as you have babies all you want to talk about is nappies. What's there to say about nappies?"

"I see they're making them in two styles now, blue for the boy and pink for the girl. I mean what's the difference?"

"Now, Minnie. Try and remember."

Minnie laughed. "I have a song going through my mind too. 'You're obsolete, my baby, my poor old fashioned baby.'"

"Should have seen it. It was this long but. Carpet shark. Tricky bastards they are. So this bloke only lets it go. I couldn't believe it. Pay forty dollars to go out in one of them deep sea boats, present from Laura mine was, and he never caught a bloody thing. Started getting seasick. Face went all green. They've got waves out there, I will say that. We all looked the other way so as not to embarrass the bloke. This other guy though, mate of mine…"

Laura's John was bright with remembered excitement, his speech peppered with "wobbegongs," "grey nurse," "red-lipped morwong" and "western blue devil." He had started the barbie coals burning, laid out the steak and sausage—with his fish in pride of place—set the chairs up and sent Zebbee in for more plates. Minnie was drinking orange juice and wondering whether a "dugite" was a fish or a hook, the last story had them so entangled it was hard to tell.

"Your mum's boss took me out once. Mr. Vivien. 'R.V.' he likes to be called. Good bloke. Nice yacht. I do spray painting; cars normally, but he said it'd be just the same on a boat, so I did a design for him."

"What did he want?" asked Minnie politely. She had run out of "Mmm's" and "goodness me's."

"That was pretty weird. He showed me this old coin, real antique, with this woman's face on one side and "If you're squeamish, don't poke the beach rubble" on the other. Said I was to do a blowup of the face and spray it on the prow. I made a tracing and drew the blowup freehand."

"Freehand?" Minnie whistled through her teeth. "You must be good."

"Yeah well," said John modestly, "it's my trade. Should be good or they wouldn't pay me. Usually it's sun flares and comets' tails on the fins of racing cars. Anyways, I'd done the preparation and I was sketching the outline on the yacht but it wouldn't take."

"Wouldn't take what?"

"Wouldn't take nothing. Thought maybe there was something wrong with my paints. R.V. shelled out for new stuff. Nothing doing. Each time I'd paint on the outline, it'd stay there a few minutes, then it'd disappear. I called my boss, and he come over with some of the blokes from the garage. He'd never seen nothing like it. You know how gloss disappears into the woodwork if you haven't varnished or undercoated? It was like that, but this was metal paint. I said to R.V., 'R.V.,' I said, 'Your yacht has taken a dislike to that lady's face.' So he says to me, 'Well, paint me a picture of the yacht then, and put that on the prow.'"

"What's the yacht called?"

"Girl's name. His wife I reckon. Natalie Barney."

The whole world picked itself up and performed two cartwheels before righting itself again, leaving Minnie sitting dizzy and stupefied on Laura's reticulated lawn. Why did no one throw a bucket of cold water over her? "Jealousy is self-inflicted torture," it says so in *The Joy of Lesbian Sex.* John continued as though he had told the story a hundred times before.

"He's not stupid but. That R.V. It was coming up to the Atlantic Cup, though you'd say Perth is the wrong side of the world for the Atlantic. Pretty soon the whole of Fremantle was swarming with American yachtsmen. When they see Mister Vivien's yacht, with the yacht painted on the prow, they all ask him who done it. He tells them it was me, right. So they got on the phone: can I do them a picture of their yacht on the prow of their yacht? The men want that. The women want a picture of their daughter on a T-shirt. Same difference. I was made. I tell you, I was made. Couldn't keep up with the orders, had to get everyone in the family to help out: your mum bought the T-shirts, her John did the paints, Laura kept the books and Ingrid answered the phone. Came at the right time but. We needed the money, house had just jumped its price and we wouldn't have had nowhere to live..." Before John could launch into another fascinating but lengthy story, Zebbee trotted up.

"Mummy says your lot have arrived, Minnie."

"So what do you do?" Minnie asked, after the introductions had been made.

"I bake cakes at Sweet Sugar High," said Simone, adding, "your family eats most of them."

Everyone laughed. It wasn't very funny but it was very nice to laugh.

"And you?" Minnie turned to Lex.

"Used to be a bus driver, then I did panel beating in John's garage and now I'm a screw. And if you wanna know if I'm a good screw, you betta ask Simone cos no one else is in any position to find out."

"Don't you feel sorry for the women you have to lock up?" asked Minnie.

"Not really," said Lex. "It's a men's prison."

"Your hair's grown since I last saw you, Minnie," said Simone. "You look like Ingrid."

In the dusk Minnie blushed. Ingrid was beautiful. Wherever they went there was always someone, male or female, who would stare at Ingrid to the brink of rudeness, shake themselves, and beg to take her picture. That was, so Beryl had said, how the family first encountered Mr. Vivien. He had photographed Ingrid on a wine cruise through the Swan vineyards and asked were there any more at home like her. Sounded a bit iffy, as they say, but Mr. Vivien was a perfect gentleman and whisked Beryl out of her boring lawyers' office and into his employ almost before the boat docked at Barrack Street Jetty. Ingrid walked through life in a pleasant trance where all she need do was set her head on one side and smile and that which she wanted would be done. As stubborn as she was beautiful. If some misguided person suggested she do something she did not care for, she would set her pretty head on her shoulders, brace her majestic but usually languid frame, and not smile until the unacceptable had been withdrawn. Minnie was nothing like her. Indeed the two sisters had once spent a good hour examining themselves and each other, before a mirror in a campground bathroom: bones, limbs, colour and texture of those parts of the body in which details vary, facial features, hair: all quite different in the one and the other. "Different fathers," they had concluded, shaking their very different heads, "different fathers." A woman who had been showering throughout the examination crept out of her cubicle and scurried away, gazing covertly at them as she passed.

"I used to wear it in a one," replied Minnie.

"One what?" asked John.

"One inch all over," said Minnie. "We all went to this barber shop in Gurkha Parade. All the dykes. Sat there in a row waiting to be done alongside old men come in for a shave, schoolboys with hair over the collars dragged in by dad, workmen getting spruced up for a date. Surrounded by these ads for shaving cream and Durex."

"Do-what?" asked John.

"Sheaths, condoms, rubber johnnies," Laura told him.

"So the barber says, 'Do you want the usual?'" offers Lex. "Starts lathering your chin and whetting his strop."

John gazed at Lex and Minnie in fascination, glanced at Simone who sat demurely by the barbecue, a somnolent Zebbee on her knee, and across at Laura, who was cacking herself laughing. He felt pleased, and a little protective, that they should be having this conversation in his garden. Laura would explain it all later.

"So the barber says to me, 'Got a special offer here, right up your street. Five condoms for the price of one.'"

Lex roared appreciatively. Zebbee woke up and glared. Simone shook her head in mock despair. Laura shot a glance at John to see if he had understood. He was smiling affably but a little puzzled.

"Got five fingers, see," Minnie explained, wiggling them in the air to demonstrate. "One condom for each finger. To stop my lover getting pregnant."

"I thought it was an AIDS joke," said Simone. "They're telling lesbians to wear mouthguards and rubber gloves these days."

"They've been telling us to keep our hands to ourselves and shut our mouths for the last few centuries," said Minnie. "What's new?"

"And not just lesbians," put in Laura, to Minnie's surprise.

Minnie's musing was cut short by an explosion in her left ear. Milly had made a sincere effort to hold her tongue. It was good for Minnie to relax and enjoy herself, but it had gone too far. Milly could contain herself no longer.

"How *dare* you?" she demanded. "How *could* you? Look at you, with your long hair, telling butch jokes from the fifties."

"They're not from the fifties," Minnie objected, "they're from twelve months ago, last time I cut my hair. If we went and sat in that barber shop on Gurkha Parade, we would see the same thing happening today."

Minnie wanted to find out more about Natalie, and the yacht, but Milly, voice of Lesbian Nation, would not let up.

"You failed miserably as a butch, Minimax," Milly lashed out.

"Yes," Minnie agreed. "It hurt my pride, but as it did no other damage I decided to cut my losses and grow my hair. It's sexier, it's prettier…"

"No real woman admits to being pretty," Milly objected.

"That's right," said Laura. Minnie was never sure when her conversations with Milly were overheard. "Every woman in the world thinks there's something wrong with her."

"Bobbly nose," sighed Simone.

"Wispy hair," sighed Laura.

"Political obsolescence," sighed Minnie.

"You see some real beauts in changing rooms sometimes," said Simone, "and you look at them and you think, 'Now she is absolutely gorgeous.'"

"Scandinavians," said Laura. "Creamy golden skin, perfect breasts, long legs…"

"Scandinavians in changing rooms shouldn't be allowed," said Simone. "You just don't know where to look."

"And they're probably wishing for the skin of an English rose, flashing Latin eyes…and for everyone to go away and leave them alone," said Minnie.

"I like…" John ventured.

The four women turned toward him. The kids were now curled asleep in deck chairs, their little feet warmed by the smouldering barbie. John thought about bodies for a moment. He probably should have done this before he opened his mouth, but no one seemed to mind waiting a while. Minnie was gazing at Son asleep and thinking that perhaps the real point of having babies is watching them put their toes in their mouth. John's mind was having a hard time divorcing the body from the person inside. Women seemed much better at the long cool objective glance. He gave up.

"I like how Laura looks best."

Laura squirmed. It was true. She was what he wanted. And he'd got her. What was wrong with her? Why wasn't she delighted that after seven years of married life she was still her husband's ideal woman? She got to her feet with a jerk. She was meant to smile lovingly at him, present a vision of marital harmony. That was what he wanted, she could feel him wanting as she looked down at his naked thighs in their short shorts. He was a good-looking bugger and great with the kids. "Great with the kids." First they're

"good husband material" and then they're "great with the kids."
She wasn't. She was irritable and temperamental, loving the little
darlings to distraction one minute and the next telling them to go
play with the traffic.

"Anyone else want another drink?" Laura disappeared into the
house.

"You shouldn't tell queer jokes in front of straight people,
Minnie," Milly persisted with her usual determination.

"Why not? We're not a secret society. Most families have at least
one of us in their cupboards, dancing with the skeleton."

When she rejoined the conversation, she learned that Lex had
lost all inhibition and got onto gynecologist jokes.

"This dyke goes to her doctor and the doctor says, 'You have the
cleanest, neatest vagina I ever saw.' 'Gee thanks,' says the dyke. 'I
have a woman come in three times a week.'"

"This dyke goes to see her doctor and the doctor asks what con-
traception she uses. The dyke says she doesn't use any. So the doctor says is she sexually active. So the dyke says oh yes, she's extremely sexually active. So the doctor says well doesn't she mind if
she gets pregnant. So the dyke says she'd be absolutely thrilled,
and so would the Catholic Church. So finally the doctor asks if
she's a lesbian and the dyke agrees with the diagnosis. So the doctor asks, 'Well what instrument do you use?' so the dyke says,
'What do you think? A grand piano.'"

Minnie laughs wholeheartedly. Milly looks sour.

"Can't you see? That joke is on us. It says we aren't real women."

"Good grief," said Minnie. "Most of us can't afford the clothes."

"Think *we* can?" asked Laura from the kitchen. But her voice did
not carry.

Encouraged by her success, Lex continued with her favourite
Bangladeshi jokes.

"God's got it all wrong, you know. He's meant to destroy people
not property. These Bangladeshis breed like rabbits, so he sends a
flood to get rid of them. And each time there's millions of pounds

worth of damage, the Aid Agencies have to start from scratch with the wells and the hospitals, but the bloody Banglas just cling to the trees and when the flood goes away they all come down, fertile and destitute as ever."

"See!" crowed Milly triumphantly. "You started this. If you hadn't put her up to it, Lex would never have got onto this pernicious racist rubbish." It was Milly's personal and very private opinion that the Aid Agencies should be intentionally promoting homosexuality instead of handing out untested birth control pills with nasty side effects.

"Isn't it curious," Minnie retorted, "that pernicious racism makes you so triumphant."

Was it not possible to fly away, leave nasty hypocritical England in its self-congratulatory cloud, make up your mind to enjoy yourself and face no more battles?

"Have you met Natalie Barney? Can you swear on oath that she and this Vivien are just good friends?" The questions were on the tip of Minnie's tongue, and they would have changed the subject like a lodestone rock, but she could not bring herself to ask. Where would she be without even a romantic fantasy? And what if John said, "Sure, Natalie and Vivien are lovers, everyone knows that."?

It was late when Minnie drove home, but Beryl and John were still up. They were having the sort of understated quarrel that characterises the long-married.

"But I always have my Russian on a Tuesday, dear."

"But I asked you, I specifically asked you if I should buy tickets to the physics evening. And you said yes. So I did. Did you think I was planning to go on my own?"

This was exactly what Beryl had thought, if the question had registered at all. She had almost certainly been absorbed in a Tolstoy translation at the time.

"I didn't realise it would be a Wednesday, dear."

"It's not a Wednesday, is it. There wouldn't be any problem if it was a Wednesday. The physics evening is on Tuesday."

"But I always have my Russian on a Tuesday, dear."

Minnie came in bursting to ask her mother about Natalie and R. Vivien, but this might involve her in some awkward explanations of her own. She had so far told her mother nothing of importance of the life she had been living in London, though she knew her mother was waiting. One cannot so easily at thirty-three sob on one's mother's shoulder, "Genevieve was a bad woman but I still miss her, and if all the good guys have turned into worms or sanctimonious jackals what place is there for me in the world? So naturally I escape into romance and write letters to America."

She could not say, "There is no effective opposition in Britain, there is the Labour Party but it has ceased opposing, even unilateral disarmament is not what it was. There is no politics, only the Whiners versus the Diners, red-necked, blue-blooded. And have you ever wept bitter tears because the Labour Party is not what it was? Of course not, you don't want to look ridiculous."

"Minnie, darling," said Beryl, "would you like to go to John's physics evening?"

"Love to," said Minnie. A good time to find out about Natalie without giving anything away. What with the requirements for small talk and pause-filling, the most extraordinary remark could be passed off as nerves. Minnie experimented in her mind: "Mum, Natalie Barney was my role model and now Vivien has her name spray-painted on that yacht, I mean what is this?" "What dear? What's that about the yacht? I expect he named it for his mother. They get very sentimental, self-made millionaires. Do pass John the butter, you know he likes it on his radishes."

"There you are, dear," said Beryl to her husband. "You can take Minnie to the physics evening."

Then she collected her last cup of tea for the night, the Russian classic she was reading—but then Russians only write classics—and went off to her nice bed.

"You'll like them," John was saying. "They're nice."

Minnie was whistling, for no apparent reason, "Sweet Mystery of Life at Last I've Found You." It happened to be one of the parrot's favourites.

"I'm sure I will," said Minnie, a little dazed as always when her mother's vagueness was discovered to hide purpose.

"Funny thing about whistling," mused John. "I wonder why people do it. Can't sound anything like the same as when played by a full orchestra. I suppose they hear the rest of it in their heads and the bit of tune they force out through pursed lips is an outward and visible sign of an inward and invisible grace."

"Mmm," said Minnie, surprised in the act of listening to him. "I sing 'Pa pa pa' in the bath, you know, the bird-catcher from *Die Zauberflöte*, and it stands for all the notes I can't reach."

It suddenly occurred to her to wonder whether this John was the same one Beryl had had last time she came over, ten years ago. That one had driven taxis, Minnie seemed to remember, but perhaps he'd had an Oxbridge chemistry ægrotat all along and been able to convert. Beryl had drifted off with her hot-water bottle already. It was the usual sultry West Australian night, but Beryl *liked* hot-water bottles. It might, Minnie felt, be a little tactless to ask John. If he was the same man, he would be hurt that she did not recognise him. If he was someone else, he might not like to be re-minded that there had been another before him. You cannot tell with men where their sensitivities will lie.

At the first note of Minnie's rendition of "Pa pa pa," the parrot raised its sleepy head from beneath its wing and squinted through the window. The snatch was over almost as soon as it started.

"Another goddamn beak-teaser," muttered the parrot. It was in a foul mood. It had lavished all afternoon and a full packet of crushed hazelnuts on that slimy piece of overinflated PVC and got nothing but a peck on the cheek for its pains. All hot air and no action, that water snake. And this female Pommy pooftah thought she could fool around with the three magical notes of *The Magic*

Flute as though she was humming some meaningless crap from "The Sounds of the Sixties" about San Francisco and wearing flowers about one's person. Didn't Minnie know what tremendous forces she summoned with those three notes? Well, the power was unleashed now; that'd teach her.

Beryl's John meant to stay up and ask Minnie how the evening at Laura's had gone. Underneath his physics notes where he had been calculating the measurements of the hitherto unidentified thingy in his laser, he had written "Barbecue Minnie." He was now rather anxious to ask the question so he could cross out the reminder. He feared that if he left it too long he would forget what the message meant and be forced back upon a more literal meaning, and that might not be right at all. But Minnie began to hum, out of nowhere, a little ditty about gentle people and odd sensations. John found the mixture of drone and discord in Minnie's singing voice so painful to his, rather musical, ears that he felt it might be best if he simply went straight to bed and let Beryl deal with the social niceties.

"And what do you do?" asked Minnie.

This year the physics evening consisted of dinner first, educational divertissement second. Last year, fearing that members might come for the dinner but disappear into the woodwork before the educational divertissement, the food had been put second, waved over hungry physicist noses like a crunchy orange carrot. But, unfortunately, hungry physicist stomachs had rumbled throughout the presentation and this year the order had been reversed.

"I'm not a physicist," offered a nice-looking woman whose husband was wearing the same clothes as Minnie. "I'm a baby doctor.

'Neo-natal,' technically. My husband is a professor, I'm afraid, but the rest of the time he's a volunteer fireman."

"Not enriching uranium, then?"

"Oh no. He's in microwaves. We live out near Mundaring Weir and it's been so dry this year the fire risk is very high. John widens windbreaks and is on call in emergencies. They ring him at work sometimes and the department secretary has to explain he's giving a lecture on subatomic particles. The distressed householder tells her to fetch him out; the particles can wait, the hills are on fire."

"You have a nice sense of priorities in Western Australia."

"Some rain would help."

"Oh yes," said Minnie unselfishly. "My little sister wants rain to fill up her barrel. For the baby."

"To swim in?"

"For everything. They haven't any water at all at the moment."

"Hmm," said the nice-looking woman in a considering sort of way. "How old did you say the baby was?"

"It's not born yet. She's nine months' pregnant."

"No water?"

"No water, no electricity, no gas, no house, no road, no letter box, no indoor plumbing and no shopping centre. Lot of nice rocks, trees and a valley."

"Hmm," said the woman again. "You know in Western Australia the state is fifty percent responsible for the welfare of its children? If your sister so much as mentions a little qualm about the water supply to one of the other mothers while she's lying-in, they won't let her leave the hospital till they're satisfied the baby will have what it needs."

"Oh," said Minnie bleakly. It sounded rather as though her jolly habit of speaking anxiety aloud was about to cause her sister serious trouble with the welfare people.

Before there could be any question as to which hospital Ingrid was booked into and which authority she came under, there was a shuffling of chairs and a preparing to stand up.

"You can come this way now," said a young man who was desperate lest one of the scientists should ask questions on matters he knew nothing about. In the ordinary way he was happy to discourse for hours on any topic, knowledge or no. In fact, the less he knew, the less there was to inhibit him. But not with scientists present. That was too much to ask.

He showed the awesome assembled into the Omni Theatre whose ceiling and walls formed a projection screen shaped like the inside of a globe, which stretched back over the viewers' heads. He told them about the new seventy-millimetre film which projected larger-than-life scenes close up and made you feel you were, for example, right in the body of the plane as it flew over the sea. With the canny insertion of a few indisputable facts like "seventy millimetres" and a sample spool for the physicists to pass around, the young man began to regain his aplomb and more customary role as the "Great Projectionist Behind the Screen." There were, he explained, microphones every two feet to give the feeling of the plane rushing toward you over the runway. The screen itself, he explained, was composed of latex stretched over alloy supports. The alloys in question could only be referred to by number, apparently, reminding Minnie of an adolescent with acne who can bear to spell the word but not say it. Then he explained about optics, referred to as a series of percentages, and Minnie found herself drifting off. In order to see the numbered alloy supports behind the screen, the lighting had been changed so that the screen itself was now invisible and a black darkness surrounded them. Minnie, absorbed in the confusion of thoughts which had piled up uncatalogued in her mind—Ingrid's baby, Moira's profession, Lex's jokes, and the mysterious Natalie Barney—found herself walking like a somnambulist toward the darkness, forgetting, because she could no longer see it, that the screen was in the way. The lecture was over, intellectual pretensions satisfied. The film projector was turned on. The assembled physicists and fire fighters could sit back and imagine themselves in the cockpit of that marvellous World War Two fighter plane taking off right in front of them.

Minnie walked into something unexpectedly soft which blocked her passage into darkness. It appeared to be the cockpit of a World War Two bomber. She was bumped along a runway, then lifted up into the air without even a glucose sweetie to stop her ears popping. She was speeding over the waves and into the sky; the joystick was in her hand and felt quite familiar, maybe because she'd been clinging to it so hard to stop herself feeling seasick. Her mother's description of R. Vivien came into her mind and she wondered if that was who was guiding the plane like a millionaire talking his brokers into playing bear in an erstwhile bull market and trying not to upset them with expressions like "a hundred and forty million." Minnie wasn't feeling the least upset, and if it was R. Vivien guiding her into the plane, and the plane into the air, despite both their natural propensity for gravity, then it was a job well done. Any friend of Natalie Barney's was a friend of hers. Their affair was probably a thing of the long past, leaving her mother's boss with a weak spot for dykes in distress.

"If you believe that," hissed Milly from inside a parachute, "you'll believe a hundred impossible things before breakfast. Wherever this old crate is going, you can bet your women's lib life membership that you're not on your way to Natalie Barney's New York apartment."

With this, Milly bailed out.

"I am not an old crate," said a voice from the black box. "If I was good enough for John Niven, I can fly one plucky little woman across the Acheron. Sorry, Pacific."

The plane appeared to be flying itself. Minnie gave up asking, How? Why? Is there some transcendental purpose which will explain my presence off the Earth? She gazed out at what looked like icebergs and frozen villages but which were merely clouds.

The physicists in the Omni Theatre watched spellbound as the bomber took off. Like John Niven they too would raze Feberbruch to a heap of ashes, and the English Rose would cry tearfully into her radio transmitter, "You're so brave, John, what a brave man you are." But instead of the seat in the cockpit being empty, so that the physicists might better imagine themselves seated there, it appeared to be filled by a young woman who was not even wearing goggles, flying jacket and a gas mask, as each knew he would have done. As one man they turned to the Great Projectionist Behind the Screen. He sat with a look of thunder, reangled some of the most expensive slithers of glass this side of the Murray-Darlings and appealed to the stowaway to give herself up. The message moved toward Minnie foot by foot as it passed from one microphone to the next, like a train roaring into a station. Minnie continued to sit, goggleless and unconcerned, her hand on the joystick, her eye on those far off icebergs which changed shape so alluringly.

"Bail out, bail out, bail out," boomed the Great Projectionist. You can tell when a message is official because it is always relayed three times, and like tannoy announcements in railway stations, it is always impossible to tell what the official message is. Custom has it that one waits, politely perplexed till it is over, then one turns to the equally unenlightened who informs one, "Next train don't stop at Ongar," or "Soviet-American forces have let off a nuclear warhead and we're to proceed in an orderly fashion to the nearest shelters on the Piccadilly Line," according to temperament. After a while a consensus is formed amongst the uninformed and the most popular version prevails. Either everyone on the platform sits out the next train, or they collect their bits and head for the exit. If one is lucky one comes across a headless chicken and can consult its entrails.

Minnie was singularly unmoved that the fantasies of thirty physicists were meeting total frustration. She was musing to herself how nice it was to be able to sit back and have someone else take control.

"I'm going to have to kill it," announced the projectionist and with a beating heart he hit the switch.

The plane plummeted out of sight followed by a length of black film with odd scratches, a series of numbers and a blur. The projectionist would not know till he reeled back the entire film whether any of it had suffered serious damage. The girl was not his province, probably the young sister from *High Fliers,* jealous that her brother gets to stand on the plane wings and she doesn't. When he remembered the wings stunt, the projectionist was profoundly relieved he had killed the film when he had. That untutored idiot, that mere slip of a Sheila, would have fallen off and the fantasies of the physicists would have been dashed on the rocks at the bottom of the Grand Canyon.

When Minnie heard the call, from somewhere in her inner ear, to open the door of the plane, attach her left foot to the struts by a handily placed white silk aviator scarf, shift her weight to this foot, detach each hand in turn from the door handle and stand in fifth position on the plane wing, sliding her right foot up her left calf for a smooth arabesque, arms above her head performing that time-honoured sequence from *Swan Lake*, "I, here, am Queen of the Swans," she was not the least surprised. If the voice had requested her to dance the opening sequence from *La Bayadère* she would have offered no demur, but taken up position confident that the rest of the *corps de ballet* would somehow materialise around her.

"Have to drop you off, old girl," said the same confident contralto, and Minnie felt no more anxiety than if the driver who had offered her a lift had muttered, "Nowhere to park, dear, have to let you off at the lights."

"Untie the scarf," the contralto continued. "And when I say 'jump,' jump."

Minnie jumped.

She found herself walking up the driveway of a house in a warm Western country which was not Australia and did not remotely resemble New York. Before her was a car whose bumper stickers exclaimed, "LOVE YOUR MOTHER," "FAT JEWISH LESBIAN," and, oh glory, "EAT RICE, HAVE FAITH IN WOMEN." Minnie knew she had come to the right place, whatever that was, and wherever she was. Behind the car was an enormous heap of wood, too disorganised to be called a woodpile; in front of the house was a wooden porch and a bed of geraniums. Minnie knocked on the door. It was only when she set down her suitcase that she realised she had been carrying one.

The door was opened by a woman with thick dark curly hair and, though she was not Irish, green eyes. She was wearing a magician's cloak and a black felt hat with a veil.

"Oh hi," she said. "You got here. Well, that's it out there. Think you can handle it? Just stack 'em, okay, so I can pick them up without hurting my back and the ones on the bottom stay dry. And bring some onto the front porch for the fire. I'm Nea, I expect you guessed, short for Naomi."

"I'm Minnie."

"Thought you had a different name. Carol or something. Oh well, got a lot of names myself: Nea, Naomi, Flipper, High Priestess Orisha of the Crossroads. I'm going to sleep for a few minutes. You'll be alright?"

"Fine."

"Good trip?"

"Pleasantly uneventful."

"Hey, what did you bring that thing for? Moving in? Why didn't you just leave it at Ranier's?" Nea pointed at the suitcase, which Minnie had been carrying round the wood heap.

Minnie had herself been wondering what was in it. She opened the catch and peered inside.

"It's my clothes. They're still a little damp. I should hang them out."

Nea showed Minnie the clothesline.

"These really yours?"

"Why would I carry someone else's wet clothes in my suitcase?"

"Can't say I admire your taste. These are all blue and grey. Let me lend you something less like a rainy day at the morgue."

Minnie considered this. Tempting to dismiss the last ten years in London as a "rainy day at the morgue." Sadly Minnie shook her head at the tight piece of pink fluff which Nea held out.

"You must be joking. Pink and orange. My friends would laugh at me."

"What? Why? Don't tell me you're supposed ta be butch or something?"

Silence. From somewhere in the woodpile Milly laughed unkindly.

"Oh girl! Oh boy!" Nea whooped. "Just put it on. No one's gonna even see you in the woodpile."

Minnie tried on the fluffy pink and orange jumper. It drew a firm, fluffy line round her breasts.

"Whoo! Girl! Now I see why you don't wear clothes like that. Where you from anyway?"

"I don't know."

Whereupon Nea fell asleep. It was only after Minnie had moved the entire enormous stack of wood onto the front porch that she realised she had no sense of time and therefore no idea how long she had been doing this for nor how long Nea had been asleep. She supposed that if that was Nea, Ranier's ex, then this must be San Francisco, in which case it was behaving just exactly as the rest of the world expected it to.

"Good show," John was saying. "Pity about the burnt film at the beginning. Didn't make much difference, though."

"No," Minnie agreed, "I'd never flown a World War Two bomber before, but they make it easy for you, don't they?"

John laughed and nodded. "It's very realistic. Makes you feel like you're right there in the cockpit."

"Where did you go on your flight?"

"Oh, just buzzed around over the ocean, swooped up and down a couple of times. You go somewhere special?"

"Yeah. I got all the way to San Francisco. I think," said Minnie. But why? she wondered. It felt like I was being rescued from something. But what? she wondered. Of all the social events I've attended since coming to Perth, tonight's was easily the least demanding. All I escaped was a woman in a green silk tie telling me how she and her first husband flew the Grand Canyon back in 1947. And I would have quite liked to hear about that. Why not whisk me away before Moira's beep went off, or before Lex started telling those awful jokes?

"Minnie was very good-humoured," John told Beryl.

"I'm sure," said Beryl. "She's a good girl and I'm so antisocial. I really only like Russians."

"I thought we should have a party," said John.

"A what?" asked Beryl.

"Invite too many people, buy too much booze, cook too much food…"

"Why?" Beryl demanded. "Why on earth should we do that?"

"Well," said John, "I think Minnie would like to meet more people. We could ask everyone: all the family, of course, and the physics department, and those friends of Laura's."

"Simone and Lex?"

"Simone and Lex," John agreed. "Good idea. And your nice boss, Mr. Vivien. It's time we invited him back."

"R.V.!" exclaimed Beryl. "Now I wonder what Minnie would make of him. I'm almost tempted to let you go ahead just to find out." She paused. "Look," she said finally, "have a party, darling. Invite anyone you like. But let it be perfectly understood in advance that I will not cook, or clean, or entertain, or even speak to anyone I have no wish to speak to. I shall have a long bath while you prepare whatever you see fit to prepare. And when the party

starts I shall pour myself a stiff double brandy and flirt outra-
geously with whomsoever I should happen to feel like flirting."

John looked gloomy.

"Cheer up, love. It's an excellent plan, now I come to think of it.
And sure to be good for Minnie. I feel she has a secret sorrow, a
mother feels these things."

IN THE BACK

⇒ 5 ⇐

*B*eryl's John began preparing food seven days before the party. It seemed to him an auspicious length of time for Creation. He got out his calculator, a good wad of graph paper, his compass and protractor, a ruler, a calendar, the week's weather forecast, list of goods planes flying into Perth with itemisation of foodstuffs carried, and a ten-volume work entitled *The History of the World, Part Ten: Food.* He decided on Mongolian because, according to the book, it only takes ninety seconds to cook. Prawns less.

"And seven nights to chop," thought Beryl. It was not tact which caused her to keep the thought to herself but the perfect understanding that she who advises, supervises, and supervising cookery means foreseeing every disaster without being able to forestall a single one.

John's calculations, his lists and timetables, his charts and diagrams soon spread from the garage, which was his workroom, through the bedroom and from thence outward until there was not a room in the house which remained unmoved by Creation. Arcane but carefully scripted messages from John to John punctuated most social encounters as they were picked up, read aloud and pondered.

"Put sixty figs in a wide, two litre jar to marinate for six days in an excellent port wine and seal hermetically."

"Thoroughly wash a live lobster weighing not less than five pounds."

"Place scampi, Dublin Bay prawns, langoustine, and giant shrimps on a mound of rice washed in fourteen waters," read Beryl over breakfast and a quick lettuce. "Changed his mind about Mongolian."

"Mummy," said Minnie curiously, "what's this?" At the bottom of the parrot's aviary she had found what appeared to be notes for an overhead projector. Beryl examined the object.

"Oh my," she said in a voice of wonder. "Minnie, do look. It's a plan of my oven with the temperature and cooking time required for seven separate dishes mapped out each in a different colour on a series of transparent overlays. How...?" she began to say, as in "How ever did it get into the parrot's cage?" when the parrot in question stuck its head on one side and, in a parody of Ingrid, began to sway, shifting its weight and lifting each foot in turn off the branch, singing, "Dance, Cockie, dance Cockie, dance," as it had been taught to do when confronted with the interrogative.

"Blimey," commented Minnie. "Mum, when you ask John to make you a cup of tea, what happens? Does he place a thermometer in the water, do a quick calculation subtracting the resulting figure from boiling point, then set the oven timer for the number of seconds left to boil?"

"No of course not, dear," said Beryl. "He pulls out a tea bag and puts it in a cup like anyone else. Now, would you like to meet me for lunch in Dalkeith this afternoon? R.V. popped over to London to buy a newspaper but the garden's lovely and you should see the lettuce beds: frisée, batavia, lollos rosso and biondo, radicchio, quattro stagioni, feuilles de chêne..."

"Oh Mum," said Minnie. "You've got an interest."

"Don't patronise your mother, dear, it can only backfire."

"Why doesn't Vivien order the paper from a local news agent?" Minnie asked. "Or get a subscription?"

"That's a good idea," said Beryl, "but I think he wants to try out some new laser printers my John's been working on. Got tired of fading letters and endless typos and you can't change the print if you don't own the press."

At noon sharp Minnie pulled up at the gates of the Vivien luxury home in expensive Dalkeith. Beryl's John was practising his soufflés, working out the formula for guaranteed buoyancy and writing scientific instructions for the use of Beryl's Magimix; he didn't like to lend Minnie his Datsun Handyvan in case he needed a better magnifier for the sugar granules and had to rush over to his lab. Minnie parked the double-decker campervan in front of Vivien's bronze gates with the bas-relief ravens and pressed the bell.

"Name and nature?" twanged an electronic harp.

"Minnie," said Minnie. "Millicent Beryl-Débar. I've come to eat lettuce with my mother." You never knew when these devices were wired to a truth detector like the one Beryl's John had been rigging in the garage, before he got interested in the Readers' Digest *History of the World, Part Ten: Food*. Beryl might say, "Meet me for lunch," but what she had in mind was lettuce. The heavy bronze gates swung gracefully open, their electronic hinges playing a melodious few bars of "Ride on, Ride on in Majesty."

"Better than squeaking and grating eerily," thought Minnie, "like in a vampire movie, but just as disconcerting."

It will have been the bas-relief ravens put vampires in Minnie's head. Such a woman for notions. Disconcerted might not be the first emotion Hammer Horror sought to instil in its breathless audience but this was not a Hammer Horror. It was the great gate of the luxury home of Mr. R. Vivien, West Australian millionaire and yachtsperson. Minnie drove the campervan through the gate and round the drive without so much as a *frisson* of *"Lasciat'ogni speranza, voi ch'entrate."* ("Abandon hope all ye who enter here," *grazie a Lei, egregio Signor Dante.* Or may we call you John?)

Beryl glimpsed the top of the campervan over her typewriter and came down to show Minnie through the house and into the back. She could as well have taken her round the garden, but the hose was on and it did not occur to her to turn it off; besides, Minnie would have missed the period features.

Minnie gazed in silent wonder at the black marble staircase, the enormous lapis lazuli vase which graced the bottom of the balustrade, its malachite sister at the top. They walked through a long gallery in which the world's most gorgeous sopranos appeared to be catalogued and waiting their next curtain call.

So lifelike was the statue of Maria Callas that Minnie expected her to break into *La Bohème* at any moment, chasing the notes into the high ether like silver bats in a silver belfry. The windows looked out, not on the mock Tudor monstrosity of the millionaire next door, but on the slate roofs of nineteenth-century Paris. A trick of the light, landscape architecture at its finest. Minnie reached for Maria Callas's tiny marble hand. It was, of course, frozen. Beryl ushered her on. Beryl did not approve of opera. It was like horse-riding: sure to warp a girl for life should she be exposed to it in her tender years. The hot, sweaty, finely muscled body of the horse did something to the thighs of a young girl akin to the effect of a soprano on unwary ears. Beryl could not say exactly what that effect was, but she knew it prevented girls marrying and producing grandbabies and was therefore to be avoided. Safer to surround them with Sounds of the Sixties and send them roller skating.

The gallery led into a high-ceilinged, many-windowed octagon where pictures of beautiful women hung on every wall. Their eyes followed Minnie's path with unambiguous longing. "Djuna Barnes, Artemisia Gentilleschi, Queen Christina of Sweden, Romaine

Brooks, Una Lady Troubridge, Greta Garbo, Psappha, Countess Elizabeth Báthory…" Minnie read the labels aloud, expecting to come upon Natalie Barney who, although Minnie had never seen her, was sure to be beautiful, given her sexy books and her reputation as a lover. The strange anomaly among the women of the Octagon did not strike Minnie till she was sitting in bright sunlight in the garden with her mother, munching lettuce and watching the boats on the Swan. She continued through the house, ears unassailed by the screams of Transylvanian peasant girls.

Beryl showed her into a conservatory stuffed with sickly smelling plants: white violets, arum lilies and black orchids. In a corner by the Lethean lotuses were tubs of bonsai orange trees outside a thick oak door which opened to reveal an oriental hanging of gold brocade. Minnie pulled back the curtain and glimpsed a room painted black with heavy shutters keeping out the daylight. On the floor was spread a magnificently woven carpet, its bottomless black picked out here and there with dancing lights of sapphire, ruby and emerald. So fine was the design it seemed to Minnie that the lights moved slowly across the carpet, as though someone had encrusted the shell of a tortoise with precious jewels and set it to measure its slow, smooth pace from one side of the room to another. When the lights stopped dancing, Minnie fancied the tortoise had died. Then the heady scent of incense mixed with the hothouse flowers and burned in the enclosed air with the finely tapered candles which, Minnie realised, afforded the room what little light it held.

"Good grief how *gothick*," she muttered. "Any moment now a woman is going to swim out into the bay and fuck a shark."

"Oh, R.V. usually keeps that room locked," said Beryl vaguely. "He says he brought it with him intact from the nineteenth century and he doesn't want our modern air messing with it."

"It certainly is a period piece."

Minnie and Beryl left the house through the almost overpowering smell of hot thyme in the herb garden. They passed a pretty little sundial marked out by paving stones and grass where one told the time according to which stone one's shadow hit.

"R.V. worries about shadows," Beryl explained. "He thinks one day we may all wake up and find they have deserted us."

Minnie forbore to comment.

"R.V. likes me to have lunch in the garden when the tourist cruisers come past," said Beryl.

Minnie looked puzzled. It had not escaped her attention that this was the third time her mother had mentioned Vivien's name in as many minutes.

"Look," said Beryl, "There's one." She pointed out across the Swan to a rather unexceptional pleasure boat. "You'll see what I mean in about five and a half minutes. Just time to run and get the tape recorder."

The cruiser rounded the bay and pulled in toward Dalkeith as Beryl finished setting up the recorder. Minnie heard the muffled noise of the boat's loudspeaker. "What...?" she began.

"Shut up and listen."

The boat pulled closer and Minnie could see the white shirt-sleeves of the tour guide.

"And now, to port, that's your left for any landlubbers aboard, we are passing expensive Dalkeith where the West Australian millionaires have their homes. Such famous names as Pond, Murphy, Court-at-Home, Vivien..."

"Wave," said Beryl. "Don't argue, Minnie, wave when mother tells you."

Minnie and Beryl stood up on the parapet and waved at the delighted tourists who waved back delightedly and clapped.

"R.V.'s still rather a new millionaire, you see," said Beryl. "When they call 'Vivien' over the water it makes him feel immortal. He believes that if we wave, the guide will move him to the top of the list. I think he needs to add a few more noughts to his name first."

Minnie did a mild double-take: was this R.V.'s fantasy or Beryl's own? There was something Minnie did not like. There was something funny about the luxury home and there was something funny about its owner's hold on her family. Enthralled, she thought to herself, they are in the thrall of R. Vivien.

"Jealous," sang Milly from the herb garden, which was curiously lacking in garlic. "There is no connection among these quite disparate acts, except the one you are making in your head. People frequently spin a huge symbolic net out of events it suits them to tie up. There is, in fact, but one indisputable link tying R. Vivien to a loved one of yours. It is a link you would like to dispute but, since you can't, you leap to the opposite extreme and seek to bury it in a complicated mass of connections. Clearly, Vivien is, has been, or wants to be, a lover of Natalie Barney's."

"All I can say," growled Minnie, "is this Vivien has had a big effect on my family."

"Oh certainly," said Beryl. "My John was driving taxis until R.V bought the patent for his new laser printers and got him into the University of Western Australia Physics Department. And I had that beastly job where they made me take dictation all the time."

"Whereas your chief function here is to eat lettuce sandwiches in the garden and wave at pleasure cruisers," Minnie interrupted.

"Oh, no," Beryl corrected her. "My chief function is to have an upper-class English accent, like yours darling, and answer to the name Agnes Beryl-Débar."

"Huh," said Minnie scornfully, "I thought you'd dropped the double barrel."

"It was merely resting," said Beryl. "One never really loses it. However low one falls, one doesn't sell the samovar, darling."

"That's exactly what I mean," said Minnie, scratchy as a chicken. "Last time I was over, everyone except Ingrid was a staunch socialist. You were starting a new life in Marble Bar and Australia was in the grip of a pan-feminist energy hit. Now you're all accumulating consumer durables with built-in obsolescence and fawning over a parvenu millionaire. Moira's not the only one selling."

"Shouldn't you have looked a little closer at the free ticket you were offered, which, I might add, is taking you, bar the last forty pounds, all the way to America, your heart's desire? 'Wire me a thousand,' she says, cool as can be. Where the hell do you think the money came from?"

"Vivien," Minnie sighed. "All roads lead to R. Vivien."

She sat upon a bench in an esplanade of cedars, a flight of stone steps leading down to the bay, the boathouse and the moorings. There was a polychrome enamel plaque upon the back of the bench on which Minnie expected to see the name "Vivien," seeking immortality by providing a seat. It said, "*Avenue des Anglais,* Nice 1954." Minnie was as surprised as if she had found a hand towel in Vivien's bathroom labelled "Hotel California." Was the bench stolen after a romantic tryst?

Breaking the silence, Beryl spoke. "Do you have something on your mind? You don't confide in me very much, darling. I know it's difficult when we live so far apart. I was worried about you in London. You would write on those nasty little blue aerogramme forms on which you have room to describe the weather but precious little else. I knew if you were happy you'd have chosen paper which allowed you to be your usual long-winded self."

Minnie was so pleased by this insight that she neglected to bridle at the description of herself as "long-winded."

"I'm sorry, Mum. London was so awful I thought it would only upset you since you couldn't do a thing about it. I'm grateful to be here. It gives you weird ideas, living in a place like that for any length of time." Sitting surrounded by cedars on the west coast of Australia, upon a bench which came, God knew how, from the south of France, Minnie felt some pretty weird ideas rising right there and then.

"I don't expect my daughters to be grateful," said Beryl mildly. "I want you to enjoy yourself."

"Oh I am," said Minnie. "I am. But it's a bit of a worry about Ingrid, isn't it." In her concern to distract her thoughts from the supernatural, Minnie picked on Ingrid as an emblem of domesticity. So normal, so ordinary for mother and daughter to discuss the sister's advanced pregnancy. Something in the air should have warned her that this afternoon no topic would remain long on the comfortingly straight and narrow.

"Ingrid always lands on her feet," said Beryl, joining Minnie by the low wall. "I don't know where she gets her genes from. She's so different from the rest of us."

"Different fathers," laughed Minnie. "What I'd like to know is where the hell she got the money to buy that land of hers." What mischievous imp caused Minnie to ask that question in such a setting?

"The compensation," said Beryl inexorably, as though opening the lock gate so that the whole explanation must come rushing through.

"What compensation?" asked Minnie.

"For her foot."

"What foot?"

"Her right foot," said Beryl. "Darling, you can't possibly have forgotten."

"I haven't forgotten," said Minnie. "I never knew. Mum, what happened to Ingrid's foot?"

There seemed to be ravens, huge black ravens, circling overhead. Minnie turned, it was only the new Vivien flag flapping in the wind.

"It was cut off," said Beryl.

"No!" shouted Minnie. "Don't say things like that."

"It's true, dear," said Beryl.

"Oh how horrible. How horrible. Why didn't you tell me?"

Minnie started to cry. Ingrid had such pretty feet, such soft little baby feet, innocent and high-arched. Minnie imagined that tender flesh ripped apart and sewn up, the stitches resembling the botched job on Frankenstein's neck.

"I wrote to you, darling," said Beryl, "I told you all about it."

"You didn't," shouted Minnie. "I never knew." The tears were streaming down her face. Had Genevieve been intercepting her letters even then?

"You can't have got my letters," said Beryl. "We thought you had, though, because next thing we knew you'd sent Ingrid that lovely blue shawl."

Minnie shook her head. "I saw it on the Portobello Road and liked the colour. It wasn't even new."

"It was sweet of you," said Beryl. "Ingrid loves it. She's putting it by for the baby, for little Lolita. The only garment that poor child has so far."

"Apart from the two dozen nappies and plastic pants you inexplicably bought from Cents," said Minnie, the shock easing a little. "But, I didn't notice," she continued, "Ingrid's foot, I mean. Does she limp? She walks slowly, but I thought that was the baby."

"Not really very well up on the effects of pregnancy, are you Minnie?" Beryl smiled gently. "It was about a year ago. There was an accident at the salon, Johnny Francois's. Ingrid was washing the floor when one of the new driers fell on her foot. Apparently there was a metal blade sticking out the side. They should have folded it back inside the cover but the driers had only just been installed. Well, it sliced right through between the sole of her foot and the bones. Had it encountered bone, it would have bounced off, but there was only flesh and it cut through that."

"Oh my God," groaned Minnie, "my poor baby sister."

"We thought we'd have to sell the house to pay the medical bills at one point," said Beryl, moving from the horrific to the practical as smoothly as one does after a calamity has become family history.

"And I never even knew," said Minnie miserably. "It's awful to think that could happen to my own sister and I wouldn't even know."

"You know now," said Beryl, "and it's alright, really. Ingrid limps, but she can walk. She's walking better and better. It was a clean slice and they sewed the sole back on again right away. She can't stand for very long but then neither can I with my varicose veins and neither one of us was ever going in for tap dancing. She hated hairdressing and the compensation bought that lovely five-acre plot."

Minnie breathed deeply. She had had no part in this drama from beginning to end. Did she resent missing the crisis?

"She was on crutches when she met Mr. Vivien on the river cruise. It was him organised the compensation."

Again, the overpowering sensation that behind every twist and turn lurked Vivien. Minnie attempted lightheartedness.

"Will she really call the blessed infant 'Lolita'?"

"I wouldn't worry about that," said Beryl. "Zebbee will take one look at the new interloper, listen to it crying, and dub it 'Rory.' Word seems to have got round that Ingrid is destitute and about to give birth in a stable, if not a manger. They'll be forming an orderly queue to lay gifts at her feet any day now."

"Gold, Frankenstein and myrrh?"

"Oh, no," said Beryl, not noticing the slip, "Only men bring that sort of useless rubbish to a newborn baby. The women will bring all-cotton layettes, little woolly jumpers, romper suits and solar-powered steriliser kits." Beryl eyed her daughter. Minnie was pale and still looked a little shocked. Best change the subject, draw her out about herself.

"Like some more lettuce?" she suggested. There was a lot of iron in a green leafy vegetable. "If you want to make a start on the gooseberry fool, don't worry about me. R.V. doesn't like people to eat raw steak in his grounds, the blood upsets him, but apart from that, no worries."

Minnie found a lot of comfort in the wet, creamy sugar dripping onto her tongue.

"All these hints about beastly London, which God forbid I should find myself back in, I imagine you are not really talking about geography, Minnie?" Was this the best place to ask for details? Certainly, it was not.

"Oh you know, Mum. Twelve women die crossing the road, they

reckon they're committing suicide because that's the kind of thing women do. Twelve men die crossing the road, they declare it an accident black spot and put in a traffic light overnight."

But Beryl did not know.

The new Vivien flag was flapping energetically in the breeze and, as Minnie looked out over the bay, something came floating toward her through the air, something grey and yellow, with a silver lining. An escape craft at last? But it was the clouds, the clouds which pass up there, the marvellous clouds which were going to fill Ingrid's rain barrel. Even the weather had lost its innocence.

The cypresses whispered above Minnie's head, like waves on a beach. They appeared still until she fixed her gaze on one branch, one cluster of leaves and then it moved as though it was her look which animated it. In that pretty garden, with the sound of cypresses in her ears, sun and shadow playing catch across her bare legs, the smell of herbs floating across from the garden in such a rich bouquet that she might stand forever picking out the individual scents of thyme, sweet basil, mint, and fennel, Minnie felt more lonely and alone than ever on an unlit back street of the city. What could she have done at such a distance anyway, if Genevieve had given her Beryl's letters and she had known of Ingrid's accident from the start? That Genevieve should steal her letters was more painful, more humiliating with its endless spiral, "Why?" Why did she? Why had Minnie? Why hadn't Minnie?

Then she remembered the row of portraits in the Octagon Gallery: Queen Christina, Psappha, Romaine Brooks, all beautiful, all women: might she have confided in one of them? At last the anomaly in the lineup hit her.

"Notice anything about those portraits?" she asked Milly.

"Whole gallery full of beautiful women," shrugged her alter ego.

"Milly," said Minnie impatiently, "everyone knows what Sappho and Queen Christina were famous for, but the Countess Elizabeth Báthory? Are we supposed to accept her as one of us? Last heard of she was bathing in the blood of virgins to keep her five-hundred-year-old skin looking young and fresh."

"She liked bathing with women," Milly shrugged again.

"She had an iron maiden in each of her five castles in whose arms unwitting servant girls were impaled."

"She liked hugging her lovers nice and tight."

"She would bite her servants' faces and consume their flesh."

"She liked to nip a sweet rosy cheek."

"She was brought to trial after a young girl went into the castle to fetch water and her husband-to-be complained to the Lords when she failed to return after three days."

"Men are always complaining when women fail to return to them."

"She was responsible for the torture and murder of seven hundred women."

"She had a bad press."

"Don't you think you ought to be a little fussy where you look for your role models?" Minnie demanded. "Sadomasochism has been with us for a long time and so have its apologists. What would you think of a guy who said Vlad the Impaler was his hero?"

Now everything clamoured to Minnie at once. The black room with its tight shutters keeping back the daylight; the curious absence of garlic in the herb garden; Vivien's dislike of bloody steaks; the fear that the shadows would disappear; the unhealthy hold over her family; Ingrid's inexplicable, and retrospective, accident. Minnie knew without looking that were she to search that black room, she would come across this Vivien, not stepping out to buy a newspaper but lying in a coffin till nightfall.

"Mum," said Minnie.

"Yes," said Beryl.

"Mum, I don't know how to put this. When they do role-playing to simulate difficult real-life situations, they never include this one, so I'll probably do it all wrong. It won't make me feel any different about you, I just need to know. I mean, whatever you answer you'll still be my mother and I'll still confide in you as much..."

"Or as little…"

"As before."

Minnie took a deep breath, opened her mouth, and asked, "Mum, are you a vampire?"

Silence. Beryl sat with a variety of emotions, waiting for the question.

"Mum," Minnie repeated with increasing horror. "Are you a vampire? Has Vivien turned you all into vampires?"

Still Beryl waited for the question. To cover what she assumed must be her daughter's embarrassment, she gazed out across the Swan and noted that there were a lot of jellyfish washed up on the beach and it would not be safe to take Zebbee and Son swimming in the river for a couple of days.

When her mother still did not reply, or even respond, though Minnie had asked the question several times, she turned away to fix her eye upon some comfortingly solid object in an attempt to still the reeling within. There was the flag flapping from the turret with the Vivien arms: a black raven on a violet ground. Minnie steadied her dizzy gaze by a contemplation of the straight lines of the turret. They led her to the top of the tower, where the flagstaff stood, and on, by inexorable progress, to the flag at the top. What Minnie saw there stilled all her jitters to total paralysis. The flag was not flapping. It hung at an unlikely angle into space and moved as little as frozen washing upon a frozen washing line. Minnie looked at the river. No boats moved, the seagulls seemed painted in air. Beryl's face was set in an expression of waiting. She had not heard the question.

"Vampire, vampire, vampire," shrieked Minnie. It had no effect. No effect, no echo; it was not even carried on the wind.

IN THE BAY AREA

*T*hey had thought maybe a lovely midweek picnic up at Yanchep but Ingrid's clouds seemed to have settled in for the duration: little Lolita needed rain? Leave it to the heavens. They had thought maybe a stroll round Underwater World but the touchpool was being disinfected and the sharks were "stressed." All in all, a trip to the local library seemed the safest bet. Then Ingrid, staying at Laura's till Lolita's appearance, thought she might have labour pains, but didn't, but wanted to keep indoors anyway.

Minnie was at a singularly loose end. She wondered whether washing and ironing would help, since they did such a lot for Moira and Baby Vicky. She drove to Victoria Park in the campervan to borrow Moira's iron. Moira was out at an Estée Lauder demonstration in the Downtown Carillon, but a shirtless young man, whom Minnie understood to be the boyfriend, given his lazy familiarity with the interior arrangement of Moira's house, told her to go right on in and help herself.

Back home she sorted her clothes into whites and coloureds (navy blue and black.)Then she threw everything into the machine together; what was the use of putting on airs? While the washing spun she thought about having a bath, the two activities being now indissolubly linked. But then five letters would arrive, and she wasn't sure she could cope. A shower, then? They were over so quickly there was no time for anything untoward like post delivery. Minnie was stark naked, covered in soapsuds, absorbed in steamy shower fantasies, more soap, more hot water, when she heard a noise. Or five.

The post person's motor bike was braking.

The telephone was ringing.

Beryl's John was bellowing.

The parrot was calling.

The washing machine was shuddering.

Minnie flung on her dressing gown, flattening the soapsuds. First she answered the phone: Nea in San Francisco. Could Minnie please remove the pile of wood she left on the porch? It was blocking the door and Nea would like to water the geraniums. Also, what time was it? Also, Minnie's clothes were dry (though just as navy blue); if Minnie wanted to iron them, she should bring her own iron. "Be right over," said Minnie. Next she attended to the washing machine: its cycles were finished. Minnie unloaded it. Beryl's John's bellows and the parrot's cries competed for third place. John was saying, "I've got a message for you , Minnie. Must be urgent or they wouldn't have faxed it from New York to the University of Western Australia, Physics Department," and the parrot was urging, "Come into the garden, Min," but since both tunes played concurrently, it was a little while before Minnie could decode either. Finally she turned to John and ordered, "You, take the bass line," and to the parrot, "You, try the soprano." In this fashion, with John speaking in a deep, gruff voice and the parrot fluting away in a little high voice, she managed to grasp both messages. John had been so overwhelmed by the sense of responsibility imparted by a fax from New York City and his own role as Bearer of the Fax, that he had been keenly tempted to demand a police escort while he drove it home to Minnie. Minnie took the piece of paper John held out, went into the garden and observed that, as the parrot had in its own inimitable fashion been trying to tell her, the rain had stopped. Then she fished an envelope out of the mailbox.

She unfolded the New York fax. It was from Natalie Barney and consisted of five words:

"Hurry, hurry, hurry, hurry, hurry."

Minnie looked at the envelope she'd taken from the mailbox: franked in London, sealed with red wax in which could clearly be distinguished the imprint of a signet ring stamped with a raven. At the bottom of the seal were inscribed the initials R.V., gracefully entwined. Minnie broke the seal and stared at the letter enclosed. The message consisted of five words:

"Hurry, hurry, hurry, hurry, hurry."

What did it mean? She had never met this person. Of course, she had never met Natalie either, but she had read her books and owed to her every favourite opera. Secretly Minnie believed Mozart must have been a lesbian; nothing else explained that incredible music. A well kept secret. *"Voi che sapete,"* indeed.

"Who's the fax from, Minnie?" John asked eagerly.

"Friend in New York," Minnie mumbled.

"Is she coming to Perth? You must invite her to the party."

"Mmm," said Minnie. Then it struck her about Vivien's initials.

"John," she said, "R.V., that is what they call Vivien, isn't it?"

"Well," said John, "it is a bit familiar. I don't like to myself, I hardly know the gentleman, but he did ask Beryl to call him R.V."

"But doesn't it seem strange to you?" Minnie pressed him. She thought he probably was the same John Beryl had had last time. Same accent.

"Australians are rather fond of initials," John began, then hesitated, "though of course Mr. Vivien wasn't born here."

"Where then?" asked Minnie.

"I do believe he was born in England, but spent much of his time in Paris."

This was a new angle. However, Minnie did not like to wander too far from the original question.

"'R,'" she said.

"'R'?" repeated John, in the interrogative. "'R'?"

"Well, it doesn't stand for 'John,' does it?"

"Er, no," John replied. His wife's daughters often baffled him and he had found that boundless affability was the best approach. "'J' would stand for 'John,' wouldn't it. If you think about it."

"But the initial is 'R,'" said Minnie, triumphantly. John waited.

"Men are called 'John,'" Minnie stated.

"A great deal of men are called 'John,'" John agreed. "It is a common first name in Western cultures. I, for example, am so called."

"And Laura's husband," said Minnie. "And Ingrid's boyfriend."

"Yes," John agreed. "But they can be called anything."

"Oh, no," said Minnie. "They can't be called 'Ingrid,' or 'Beryl,' or 'Laura.'"

"No," John agreed. "But they can be called 'Clive,' and 'Liam,' and 'Hasdrubal.'"

"Theoretically," said Minnie. "Theoretically, they can be called 'Pseudo-Dionysus the Areopagite,' but in actual fact, they are called 'John.'" And before her mother's husband could invent another quibble, she asked the question of questions. "John," she said, "what is Vivien's first name?" In case that was not clear enough, she continued, "What does the 'R' stand for?"

"I don't know," came the momentous response.

Minnie shrugged in disgust. John went off to check the platters he'd left steaming, steeping and soaking.

Since it was impossible to know how long the cloudbreak would last, it seemed advisable to hang the laundry out right away. Minnie thrust the fax and the letter into her dressing-gown pockets and shoved the newly washed clothes into her empty suitcase. She was pinning two pairs of jeans to the line, with a pair of knickers on top to save on clothes pegs, when it struck her that for the first time in ten years she had answered a ringing phone. And how had Nea discovered Beryl's number when Minnie herself did not know what it was? She pushed aside the two flapping left legs to fish more shirts out of the suitcase.

"Called International Directory Enquiries," said an American voice.

Why is it that the most intriguing questions have the least exciting answers?

"I suppose that's why Americans have such a bad sense of geography," said Minnie. "You don't have to know where a place is, you just have to know its number."

"And have you noticed how International Services always has an American accent?" said Milly, for once in perfect concord with her twin.

"Did you remember the iron?" the American voice asked.

The clothes on the line were bone dry, the suitcase was empty and Minnie had left Moira's new steam iron on Beryl's ironing board in Balga.

"No problem," called the voice. "Ranier will have one. Meanwhile, would you mind letting me out of here? You got a little overenthusiastic with the woodpile."

"Hey girl," said Nea, once Minnie had tugged a sufficiency of logs away from the front door to allow it to open. "You look hot in that bathrobe. Real hot, know what I mean?"

Minnie nodded. "It's thick flannel alright. I was having a shower when the phone rang and I picked up the first thing that come to hand."

The thoughts and sensations she'd been enjoying immediately prior to interruption flooded back over Minnie's body. Minnie let the air out again through her half-open mouth with a little sigh. There was a bead of moisture hanging on her bottom lip which she licked off with her tongue.

"Go for it," said Nea. "Everything they told you about San Francisco is true. There's something floating in the air over the Bay and
it's useless to resist. We do sex all the time, every hour of the day
and night: in elevators, in restrooms, in hot tubs, in sushi bars.
Especially in sushi bars. You could do it with me right now if you
wanted."

Minnie smiled. Then she giggled. Then she laughed till she was
bent over, sobbing and hysterical.

"Rose quartz," diagnosed Nea, nodding her head wise-womanly.
"For grief." She went to the bathroom and returned with two large
lumps of which she put one into each of Minnie's clenched fists till
Minnie's hands felt like loaded guns. Nea dug her fingers into
Minnie's neck and began exorcising knots and whorls.

While she worked, Nea crooned, "Hey girl, let go that grief. Let
it go." Over the years Nea had gotten used to female visitation. Her
city was situated on one of the most powerful faultlines in the
world and women were always dropping through. Ranier, her ex-
lover, was one of the most popular dykes in the world and was
always passing women on to her. Many afternoons found Nea
rubbing the shoulders of hopeless cases, though they did not
usually bring their wet laundry or barricade her into her own
house. Nea liked the soft plush feel of Minnie's bathrobe.

Minnie disliked massage. It was sex masquerading as a health
aid. "In my country," she said tentatively, for the fingers were warm
and seemed friendly, "we drink tea."

"Okay," said Nea, "but no sympathy. I'm all out. If you've come
here to sob over how wonderful Ranier is, how much you want
her, how good you could be together, then just remember: I've
heard it before and before and before."

"Ranier is wonderful," said Minnie. "She's got what I need."

"What is this dependency shit? What does Ranier have that you
haven't got?"

"An iron." said Minnie.

Nea went to put the kettle on.

"Nea," Minnie called.

"Go right ahead," said Nea. "It's on the table surrounded by the votive candles. Watch you don't burn yourself. Ranier's number's written on the back of the receiver."

Come mooning around here and all they want is to phone my ex-lover. I should start a dating agency for all her rejects so they can get together, swap Ranier anecdotes and relive great moments, thought Nea gloomily.

"Actually," called Minnie, "it was you I wanted."

At this Nea brightened considerably.

"You just noticed what bright green eyes I have?" she suggested.

"You have beautiful eyes, Nea," said Minnie, "but it wasn't that."

"You just realized what lovely dark curly hair I have," suggested Nea.

"You have wonderful hair, Nea," said Minnie, "but it wasn't that either."

"You just recognised what a deep sexy voice I have," said Nea.

"Your voice is the sexiest I ever heard," said Minnie, "but that wasn't what I was thinking of."

The phone rang. Nea answered. It was Ranier.

"She says she doesn't have an iron but she's on her way to see a lesbian writer in Oregon who's sure to have one."

"Butch or femme?" Minnie asked automatically.

"Butch," said Nea.

"No good," said Minnie. "Femmes own irons."

"What's that neat English word for bullshit that sounds just like 'bulldagger'?" asked Nea.

"Balderdash?" suggested Minnie.

"Balderdash," said Nea. "Femmes wear soft floaty things that drip dry and hang in voluptuous folds. It's the butches who have to make sure their creases are sharp. Ranier reckons she'll be back in three days; she says will you wait?"

Minnie grunted. Couldn't go anywhere with her shirts all crumpled. Pink maybe she could have got away with. But navy blue you had to iron. Through the open door she caught snatches of Nea's end of the conversation. "Castoffs" figured prominently. Minnie wasn't entirely sure they were talking about clothes.

"So, what," said Nea, reappearing with a tray of tea, proud that she actually had some in the cupboard, "were you going to say before the phone rang? And what the hell is it with you and ironing anyway?"

This last came out more aggressive than she intended.

"I like ironing," Minnie replied, finding the second question easier to answer than the first. "It's very soothing."

"More soothing than massage, for example?"

"You have to just lie there and let them do what they like to your body during a massage," said Minnie. "You have to trust them. Whereas ironing, you're smoothing out and flattening down but you are standing up and, if anyone attacks you, you've got a lethal weapon right there in your hand. I always get out the ironing when some man comes to fix the pipes. Looks peaceful and domestic, but you could smash his fucking head in if he tried anything."

"Whoa," said Nea. "It's not men who flock here. Just an endless stream of beautiful, disturbed women."

"Beautiful, disturbed women?" said Minnie. "Well, that's the answer to your first question. Only you can't brand them with a steam iron with quite the same nonchalance you'd use on a man who attacked you."

"You speak from experience?" asked Nea. There was something about Minnie's tone which sounded like a warning.

Minnie shoved her hands into the pockets of her dressing gown. Straight into the two pieces of rose quartz. She grazed her knuckles, winced with pain. Nea was watching her. Minnie looked up, opened her mouth and next thing she knew she had told Nea about Genevieve.

"My lover left me."

"I know," said Nea.

Wonderful words.

"The ultimate betrayal," said Nea.

A touch overblown but Minnie was grateful Nea was trying.

"After nine years spent almost constantly together, I had no friends of my own, no property of my own, no place of my own. I wasn't even half my former self; I was half of Genevieve."

"Rule number one, Minnie," said Nea. "Be careful."

"How could I be careful," Minnie asked, "when I didn't know what was happening?"

"Rule number two," said Nea. "Know what's happening."

Minnie was silent.

"Want a hug?" asked Nea, her eye free of the glint which had lurked in its corner since Minnie's arrival.

"Hug me," said Minnie.

There were two arms laced around Minnie's back, she was held against soft breasts and the breath on her cheek smelt of apples. She closed her eyes, smelling apples, breathing, feeling soft breasts against her. It went on for a long time. She had no wish to move. Nea bent over her; Minnie felt Nea's nose brush her forehead. The arms tightened around her.

"She's going to kiss me," thought Minnie. She tilted her face upward but Nea was too near and Minnie too long-sighted for anything to be more than a blur. She smelt and felt and heard, but she could not see. In a far corner of some foreign field Milly was trying to catch her attention. Poppies grew in Minnie's field, tall and red. And the feeling of being held, and holding, and the swift desire for intimacy, for being touched, and the sharp delight of that touch, the savouring of each moment until the next came laden with more sweet pleasure than the last. The intense, incredible relief, the gratitude for being brought back to life.

"I'm still a lesbian," Minnie murmured into the orange velvet petals of the geranium, her bedfellow. "How wonderful to be a lesbian. I never want to be anything else as long as I live."

"There are advantages," said Nea, whispered breathlessly.

And Minnie the fish swam along Nea's body lapping, lapping

until at last Nea cried out "Ranier" and came.

They lay a while, a tangle of limbs behind the woodpile which Minnie had so thoughtfully transferred to the porch on her first visit. There is a purpose in all things.

"I'm sorry," said Nea.

"Oh no," said Minnie, "oh God no. I don't care, I mean I don't mind. I know you're in love with Ranier. And of course it's indescribably better to have sex with the one you love. But that, just now, was good and kind and the first time since Genevieve. And for heaven's sake it is simply not possible to regret an orgasm."

"I don't know about that," said Nea.

"We're not going to lie here on this extremely uncomfortable wooden porch with tiny splinters entering our soft bodies from all sides and look back on all the orgasms we might have regretted having because we disliked their consequences or their antecedents, are we?" giggled Minnie.

"I have to have a cigarette," said Nea.

"Blimey," said Minnie. "I don't remember how long it's been since anyone said that to me."

"I've given up," said Nea, "I only smoke after an orgasm."

"Nice to see you're keeping your quota up," said Minnie beginning to feel some of her old irrepressibility rise. Then she began to laugh.

"That's awful," she spluttered. "Oh God, that's really awful. Imagine making love with a woman and calling out your ex-lover's name when you come. Jesus, I'm so glad I don't care about you."

Nea stared, hurt flickering in her eyes, then she gave it up and laughed too.

"*Oy veh,*" she said, "*meshugeneh.* Hey Minnie, I like you. Know what I mean, I really like you."

"I know what you mean," said Minnie, "I like myself." She smiled, sadly. "At last, I like myself again."

Nea turned toward her, stubbing the half-smoked cigarette out on the boards. "Hey girl, come here." She put her arms round

Minnie and kissed her softly on the mouth. "Stay any longer and I'll fall in love with you, and then what will you do?"

"Emigrate," said Minnie ambiguously.

Nea sighed. "This must rank as the longest courtship in the modern era."

"Yeah," said Minnie. "All afternoon."

They sat, approximately covered by Minnie's scarlet dressing gown, though one at least among them would have termed it a bathrobe, Nea smoking another cigarette, Minnie drinking another cup of tea. Nea plunged her hand into the pocket nearest her. Out of it she pulled a thin, shiny piece of fax paper.

"What's this?" she asked. "Hurry what? Or should I ask, what does the other pocket say?"

She leaned over Minnie and pulled out the letter.

"What's this all about then?" asked Nea.

"I don't know," said Minnie, echoing John six thousand miles before.

"You want to know if I've heard of Natalie Barney and what I think 'R.V.' stands for?" said Nea. "Ranier's the real expert. I've only got the gossip."

"Much more informative," said Minnie.

"Well," said Nea, "Natalie Barney is *the* lesbian par excellence."

"An excellent lesbian indeed," said Minnie.

"She's good, know what I mean," said Nea. "Not a patch on me, but good, I'll give her that. But she's famous for being a lesbian. And that status she shares with no one."

"Balderdash," said Minnie. "Natalie Barney is not the only famous lesbian in the world."

"Aha," said Nea, "she's the only one famous for being a lesbian. Now, that's something to be famous for."

"Sappho was famous for being a lesbian," said Minnie. "So was Queen Christina of Sweden."

"No," said Nea, "Sappho was famous for being a poet who was a lesbian and Queen Christina was famous for being a queen who was a lesbian."

"You're not just a pretty face," said Minnie.

"Wanna watch yourself, girl," said Nea. "Let your attention wander away from my face, you don't know where it might end up."

"And 'R.V.'?" asked Minnie.

"You have an uncanny ability to stick boringly to the point," sighed Nea. "An R.V. is a recreational vehicle."

"What's recreation got to do with it," asked Minnie, "apart from the obvious?"

"You do kick up quite a dance trying to distance yourself from the obvious," Nea threw back. "All the best things are within reach of your own right hand."

"Do you have to bring sex into everything, Nea?" said Minnie.

"I like to name names, Minnie," retorted Nea. "That's what we lesbians are known for. That and having orgasms. Face it, honey, lesbians and clitorises...."

"Clitorises," said Minnie happily, "clitorises," she said to the benign geranium. "Lesbians and clitorises. 'I simply remember my favourite things, and then I don't feel so bad.'"

"Lesbians and clitorises," Nea continued inexorably, trying not to laugh, "are the only organisms whose sole function is pleasure."

"You're an idiot, Minimax," flapped a semaphore message from Flanders Plain. "You know who R. Vivien is if you stop to think. But you don't want to stop and think. You want to keep asking as though it were still a question."

"Vivien?" repeated Ranier's voice from the other side of the woodpile. "Renée Vivien? She was Natalie Barney's lover. Died an anorexic Catholic at the age of thirty-three. Doesn't everybody know that?"

"Blimey," gulped Minnie. "Thirty-three. She was my age."

"Here's your iron, Minnie," said Ranier. "Sorry to take so long. Nobody in California uses one any more. We're too busy getting in touch with our creases."

As Minnie plugged the iron in and set to work on her collars so she could get out of her dressing gown at last and slip into something uncomfortable, San Francisco faded in the steam and she walked back into Beryl's garden.

John looked up from his pudding basins, which resembled nothing so much as a row of test tubes, and beheld a little rainbow over the swimming pool and a contented smile on Minnie.

"Minnie's lost her funeral mask," he remarked to his wife that night. "The one she's been trying out to see would it go with her epitaph." From which Beryl concluded that cooking was good for John's verbal skills and washing was good for Minnie's melancholy. What would happen, she wondered, if her family were to branch out into other domestic chores.

IN THE BLOOD

⇒ 7 ⇐

*I*ngrid had woken up that morning and decided the time had come to have a baby. She smiled fondly across at Loviebuttons, asleep on a mattress in the second-best bedroom Laura had lent them until the birth. The first-best was Laura's own; she had a strong sense of propriety. Loviebuttons had kept out of Ingrid's bed since the sixth month, though not out of her body; heterosexuals have nonreproductive sex too, as Minnie had recently been so surprised to learn. She had previously assumed that, since they found lesbian sex so shameful and so barren, they only fucked for babies themselves. About five tries each, and that was it for their lifetime. She had been rather pleased, casting an anxious thought over the well-being of her own heterosexuals, to learn otherwise.

"Loviebuttons," Ingrid called peacefully.

"Decided to pop, have ya?" asked her sleepy helpmeet delicately. Not instant emotional rapport but a result of the law of averages. If you ask the same question first thing every morning for three weeks, you will eventually receive an answer in the affirmative.

"It's Lolita's birthday," said Ingrid. "Run me over to Mum's to collect our things."

"What things?" asked Loviebuttons, who was yawning and scratching his chest prior to farting and pissing on the toilet seat. He had his manhood to think of. "Thought you left them all down in Bridgetown. I was gonna hire a van and me and John was gonna go get 'em while you was pupping."

"Just drive me to Mum's, Loviebuttons," said Ingrid.

The Loviebuttons in question stepped into his twelve-day unwashed jeans. "Orright," he said tenderly, whistling for Rot, Bull and Dobe.

Minnie had returned from San Francisco invigorated and full of herself. She was going to solve the mystery of Renée Vivien and Natalie Barney and she was starting right now. Natalie had levered her over to San Francisco, Natalie had introduced her to Nea; if Natalie wanted her, she had only to say the word. And she'd said it five times. All Minnie needed to know was: where was she? The answer would surely be in one of Natalie's books. Minnie had borrowed John's library card. He only ever read physics books and had been so bitterly disappointed when Primo Levi's *Periodic Table*'s only inert gas was helium, not nice neon which he used for his lasers, that he had checked out the video of *Dune* five times in succession and sworn to open no book save those titled *Solar Is Nuclear*, which he had had to go to the trouble of writing himself.

Minnie was looking for a plastic bag in which to carry home Natalie's books. She fished the old W.H. Smith bag out of her suitcase. It had a hole in it. That bag was a veteran. It was in that very bag that she had brought home *The Marriage of Figaro,Famous Scenes and Arias*. But it had a hole in it. It was ripped from just under the front handle, diagonally across the logo, right over to the left edge. Most people are unable to say which is the front and which the back of a W.H. Smith plastic bag, but Minnie had had this one six months which is a long time in the life of a chain-store carrier, and she had got to know it inside out. There is no loyalty in the world if a person can throw away an old bag merely because it happens to have matured into holes. Minnie decided to mend it.

She went into the spare room, where Zebbee and Son slept when their Granny was babysitting, to look for a roll of Sellotape.

There was not a surface in the spare room which was empty of either (a) cooking vessels, or (b) baby requisites. The beds were piled high with little pink fluffy towels, pink fluffy blankets, pink romper suits, pink cardigans and jumpers, pink frocks and pink lacy sunsuits. Someone had either waved a pink wand over the rest of Lolita's life, or they had flung a scarlet flannel dressing gown into the wash with the baby things. The blue shawl Minnie had bought for Ingrid secondhand on the Portobello would be the only uncoordinated item in Lolita's babyhood. The chest of drawers was graced by a large green ceramic bowl containing mung beans; on the top of the dresser stood a hermetically sealed jar containing figs and port; at the bottom of the wardrobe was a wok in which something stirred. The something had claws. Nestling next the wok was a pair of baby bootees. Pink.

"No Sellotape," said Minnie. "Mu-u-um."

"Don't tell me," sighed Beryl. "Another plastic potty or more fresh sumac John's had airlifted in? Honestly, if it isn't Ingrid's baby, it's John's party. The doorbell hasn't stopped since six this morning. Some of us have work to go to."

"Lettuce to eat and boats to wave at," said Minnie. "Mum, I can't find the Sellotape."

"No, well," said Beryl vaguely. As John said, Minnie was looking more like a human being than a visitor at her own wake, positively joyous. It was Beryl's private opinion that what gave most people most pleasure was finding someone to have sex with. A mother feels these things. Good, one down. Now if only Ingrid's baby would put in an appearance, Beryl would be able to relax with Alyona Ivanovna, having a nice chat with young Raskolnikov. She pulled herself together. *The good mother answers her daughters questions patiently. A hasty response might stunt the young person's emotional growth in later life.* Beryl did want to be a good mother, didn't she? No. Being bad merely required more energy. "What did you want the Sellotape for, dear?"

"To mend my W.H. Smith bag," replied Minnie. "All it needs is a strip of Sellotape down the middle, reinforced by another strip on the inside, and it'll be as good as new."

The doorbell rang.

"G'day, Dublin Bay prawns. Where d'ya wan'em?" The delivery man was standing dangerously near the parrot's beak.

"Freezer," snapped Beryl.

The man looked round.

"In the frigging fridge," cackled the parrot.

"Now, now, madam," remonstrated the prawn carrier. "No call for language, no call at all."

He left his burden in a briny heap on the morning papers and departed.

"Why do you want to mend a plastic bag?" Beryl asked as calmly as she was able. "They give them away free in every supermarket."

The doorbell rang.

"G'day, sixteen pineapples. Where'll I stick em?" asked a man in orange overalls bearing the legend "an another ananas."

"Next to the prawns," replied Beryl quickly before the parrot could get in the more usual and scabrous response.

"For the library," Minnie said, once the ananas man had gone.

The doorbell rang.

"G'day, fifteen hand-me-down baby socks," said Laura, dumping a pile of white woolly objects on the morning's paper, next to the pineapples. "The girls at Sweet Sugar High took up a collection."

Beryl did a quick calculation. Lolita's lucky Mummy would not need to wash any clothes for baby for the first three hundred and sixty five days of its life.

"Why does the library need mended plastic bags, Minnie?" asked Beryl.

The doorbell rang.

"G'day," said Ingrid. "Have all our things arrived?" She waddled into the spare room. "Oh good," she said peacefully, "Loviebuttons, fetch." She swayed back into the family room, surveyed the scene and asked, "What are the scampi doing with the pineapples and the bouquet of little socks?" Minnie looked in the direction Ingrid was pointing. No Sellotape.

"How avant-garde," she said. "Is it John's centre-piece?"

"No," said Beryl, "it's still life. Any moment now someone is going to come in and paint it."

"Not very still," observed Laura. "The scampi are getting away."

Beryl's John was excited. He had just found a marvellous cooking tip: "Each day you will fill the syringe with the marinade and inject the contents into the *gigot.*" All that remained was to find out what sort of animal was a *gigot,* to which corner of the world it was native, and order one. Women made altogether too much fuss about cooking. There was nothing to it but organisation. John popped out of the bedroom to check on the figs he had left getting acquainted with the port. The spare room was full of baby clothes and rottweilers were invading the wardrobe.

"The lobster," squeaked John, "and the eggs of lobster."

Whereupon the august assembly of rottweilers (two), bulldog crosses (two), and Doberman pinschers (one, but very big) pounced upon him, threw him to the floor and set about sundering the flesh from his bones so that, in true biblical fashion, nought would remain but the palms of his hands and the soles of his feet. To their slathering disappointment Ingrid, who had stuck her head round the door to see how Loviebuttons was getting on, ordered peacefully, "Dogs, outside. Loviebuttons, you know Mum doesn't like them in the house. They make her John nervous."

At the sound of the beloved voice, the hounds formed a canine column and made a stately, if regretful, exit. There was no one to slaughter in the garden but the parrot, who could fly and was not embarrassed to use this fact to its advantage. There was, they agreed as they shook their salivating heads, no such thing as a fair fight with a parrot.

Beryl's John, having peered into the wardrobe to assure himself that nothing untoward had befallen the lobster in its wok, crawled under the door of the spare room and into the family room. He was a little flattened, but otherwise unharmed.

Beryl had rescued the Dublin Bay prawns and found them a temporary refuge in the sink. The pineapples occupied four fruit baskets. The sock garland Beryl held in her arms for the time being.

"How ever will you keep track of who gave you what, Ingrid?" she asked.

"There's been such a procession of magi and my list is rather sketchy." Blessed Beryl. After twenty-five years as a secretary it would have been quite impossible for her not to make a list of castoffs brought for her granddaughter. But the crowd had been thick, the rings at the door rapid and frequent; someone had to invent a system for numbering in sequence or certain people would go unthanked. Everyone to whom Minnie had detailed Ingrid's plight—no water, no house, no electricity, no gas, no road, no postal delivery, and no shopping centre—from Laura's John's sisters-in-law to the baby doctor in the green silk tie, had come that morning, while all but Beryl slept and left something for the young mother and her newborn babe. Some, further off and hearing only sixth- or seventh-hand, had left a manger made of stained pine on the front lawn next to Beryl's statue of the Genius Loci. The girls from Moira's work would have been terribly hurt if no thank-you note ever came from the proud mother in gratitude for the beautiful whatevers. They knew what was due them.

Ingrid put her lovely head on one side and smiled at Beryl's John. John recognised the gesture. He would have to have been spectacularly unobservant not to. He owed Ingrid something for calling off the dogs and numerical sequencing was one of his minor passions. He sat a moment, gazing at the parrot for inspiration.

"Okay," he said, after a couple of minutes. "This should do it. Weights ten, nine, eight, down to two, then modulus eleven for the check number. Got that, Ingrid?"

"No," said Ingrid smiling peacefully, "but you have."

John went off to locate his graph paper and demonstrate his formula.

"A seven-digit code per benefactor, then two digits for a total of ninety-nine gifts each and a final digit as a check. Mark 'x' if that figure is a ten," John chanted happily as numbers and symbols boiled and bubbled across his page.

Exit Ingrid followed by Loviebuttons and the sulky mastiffs.

"Such quiet dogs," Minnie said admiringly. "Must be very well trained."

"Trained to go for the throat," said Laura. "The reason they don't bark is that Ingrid's John removed their vocal cords. He didn't like the noise. Not peaceful."

The room cleared in a moment. Laura had to return the steam iron to Moira and collect Zebbee and Son; Beryl's John drove to town to patent his sequencing formula and Minnie at last made up her mind to abandon the W.H. Smith bag and make do with one from Today's Supermarket (selling yesterday's food at tomorrow's prices). Beryl decided on a quick hit of Russian poetry (probably that one about the rain which follows the woman into the dinner party) before she had to rush off to the hospital and fulfil the expectations of the maternal role by bursting into tears as Ingrid was wheeled into the delivery room.

Beryl's John met Minnie in the driveway and thought he recognised her. He offered her a lift just in case.

"Ingrid's on the way then," observed Minnie.

"Oh yes," said John. "Er, where was she going?"

"To take delivery of the new baby," said Minnie.

And John nodded. But then, neither one of them was ever likely to give birth.

Several hours later Minnie returned to an empty house, her arms filled with plastic carrier bags. Inside them was a shelf's worth of the lives and deaths of Natalie Barney and Renée Vivien.

"Hurry," she muttered to herself. "Hurry, hurry, hurry, hurry."

Then she opened the books which were to tell her everything.

For the next few hours she sat down and stood up, lay on her bed, kicked her feet in the swimming pool, made tea, poured the boiling water into the rubbish bin, tried to fit the kettle whistle to a gooseberry fool pot and fed cauliflower cheese to the telephone. The parrot watched her progress with the omniscient benevolence of a parent.

"Natalie Clifford Barney," she declared, "I love you."

The tea and the gooseberry fools, much of which she did manage to put into her mouth and not the sugar bowl, were punctuated with little cries of, "On a park bench, Natalie, at seventy-seven! You glory."

The parrot listened to this thunderbolt and waited for the flash of light to measure the distance between Minnie's instincts and her comprehension.

"Oh!" Minnie ejaculated. "Oh, oh, oh."

For it said in the book that Natalie Barney had been taking a stroll along the *Avenue des Anglais* in Nice in the glorious year 1954, when she had spotted a good-looking woman and sat down upon a handy bench in order to observe her at liberty. Whereupon, the object of her interest had seated herself beside our heroine, struck up a conversation which was to lead to twenty-three years of pillow talk.

"Oh Natalie," Minnie bleated, "you must have been there all the time."

"If she was seventy-seven in 1954," chirruped the parrot, "just think how old she is today." The parrot was a long-lived old bird itself and in its revered opinion all one lost with the years were one's inhibitions. It was roused from its reverie on its own expertise (which that ungrateful prude of a water snake never got to taste; the parrot was right off reptiles) by peals of laughter.

"Imagine that," Minnie guffawed. "Just imagine that. Gertrude Stein asks Alice Toklas where Natalie gets all her women from. They are standing right in front of a whole café full of people who are hanging on their every word. So Alice says, 'From the toilets of the Louvre Department Store,' when it was benches all along."

"Benches and horse-drawn carriages, and boxes at the opera, cornfields, and the beds of her men friends..." said the parrot, wondering where its next conquest would come from.

"Naturally Natalie wanted revenge. When people began to ask what was going on between Gertrude and Alice, Natalie would say, 'Nothing. They are just good friends.' A clammy, clucking nothing. She made them sound as though they had no legs, and nothing in between. My mother would agree with Natalie. She says that in order to respect people, you must credit them with an active and exuberant sex life."

The parrot could not repress a sigh. It worked most diligently to deserve such respect; whose fault was it that success was so elusive?

"Hmm," murmured Minnie, oblivious of the parrot's psychic distress. "When Renée refused to see her, Natalie took up position beneath her balcony, accompanied by a famous opera singer, serenaded her with gusto if not passion..."

"Huh," croaked the parrot. All passion and no gusto, that was the story of its life.

"When they had done, Natalie threw Renée a bouquet of flowers arranged around a sonnet Natalie had composed."

The parrot stuck its head on one side, began its swaying little dance shuffle, and gave a convincing rendition of *"Viens poupoule."* It had nothing against lesbians and had been an admirer of Natalie Barney's ever since a migrating cuckoo told it of the time Natalie, dressed only in a white nightgown, had herself delivered to Renée in a coffin full of enormous lilies. In its decadent period, when it had insisted on dyeing its feathers black and wearing World War Two dog tags round its neck, the parrot had even fancied itself Natalie's ornithological opposite number, but John's new slide rule, whom it was courting at the time, refused to attempt a Renée Vivien impersonation. That sour, unimaginative instrument had declared it had nothing whatever in common with the young, blonde-haired poet, that anyone who could discern any points of comparison between any mathematical instrument and a blonde-haired poet was certainly a surrealist, if not worse. The parrot had got a lot of satisfaction the day John came home from the university and declared, "With the mass production of the pocket calculator, the slide rule is dead."

Natalie Barney had accomplished much of which a randy parrot would be proud. At the age of seventeen she had glimpsed that famous, high-class prostitute, Liane de Pougy, riding in a carriage in the Bois de Boulogne. Natalie, dressed as a page, had gone on bended knee before Liane. It is said that she remained in this position, beneath Liane's voluminous skirts, in a box at the Paris Opera, throughout the whole performance. Whatever was she doing under there? The parrot snickered like a school girl. When Renée left Natalie and surrounded herself with a bullying baroness—the parrot was not absolutely sure what a baroness was, it assumed it must be some kind of bulldog—Natalie had devised the brilliant scheme of swapping seats at the opera with a friend at the last minute so she could sit next to Renée and embrace her. All this was excellent in both conception and execution. But the parrot had a fine sense of degree and when Natalie repeated her seat-swapping stunt at a seven-hour performance of *Die Götterdammerung* in Bayreuth, it felt its heroine was no longer gloriously immoderate, but verging on vulgarity. There was very little a parrot could do in the face of such pomposity but hum *"Viens poupoule"* and change the subject. The parrot hated Wagner. No one would ever suspect that one of being a lesbian.

"They all seemed to agree that Natalie had no ear for music," Minnie mused aloud. The parrot flapped and squawked: Wagner was not music, it was early heavy metal. "But then why use *'Voi che sapete'* as a frontispiece?"

"Conoscenti's acrostic," said Milly smugly though, if the truth be known, the natural opioids of Flanders Plain had left her with a terrible headache. It is difficult to say "conoscenti's acrostic" in any tone other than smug. Try it. Try saying it with awe, you sound sarcastic; try it with fear, you sound sarcastic; try it with joy, you know how you sound. "It's all crashingly obvious," Milly continued. The word "crashing" came in at the last moment and had not been planned. It described the headache very well.

"Do tell," said Minnie, sounding sarcastic. She left the book open on a simply ravishing photograph of Natalie at ninety-five.

"Darling, 'Voi che sapete' means as you probably know…"

"You who know," said Minnie, "you know I know."

"I know you know," agreed Milly undeterred.

"You who know I know you know," parroted the parrot.

"Natalie being unmusical," Milly ploughed on regardless, "was primarily concerned with the words. The music of Mozart was an agreeable extra."

The parrot choked on its cuttlefish.

"She used that aria at the front of her book as a secret message which only those who *did* know could decode. The song of a girl dressed as a boy, falling in love with everything in skirts, who wants the ladies already acquainted with love to look into her heart and tell her if that is the emotion which burns there. Now, Minnie, what could that possibly be about? Whose love is continually in question, continually in doubt? Renée died in 1909, Natalie in 1972, but you have recently received messages from each. How is this possible?"

"Post took a long time," suggested the parrot, ignored as usual.

"Clearly Renée knew she would live forever," Milly pursued her train of thought, forcing the headache into a corner. Whenever anyone says "clearly," it signals their intent to lecture. Minnie decided to nip it in the bud.

"I find this cult of nostalgia merely escapist. A desperate diversion from present political doldrums."

"I'm not talking heritage," Milly exploded, "I'm talking vampire."

* * *

Ingrid had been in labour for three hours now. Loviebuttons was exhausted. His best behaviour was a great strain: no smoking, no drinking, no swearing, no scratching his armpits, spitting in the corner or patting his crotch. His mother-in-law had even suggested he might like to throw his jeans in the washing machine. Having been told more than once that his baby boy hadn't been born yet, he decided, "Bugger this," and went off for a drink at Laura's with John. Only John was at work spraying racing cars and the fridge was unaccountably empty of beer. It was thirsty work becoming a father, everyone knew that. Someone must be at home today waiting to sympathise with him.

At exactly what moment it occurred to him that Moira was the ideal person is unclear. He only knew he was hailing a Swan taxi one minute and the driver was asking where to, and the next he had given Moira's address in Victoria Park. As soon as the words were out of his mouth he knew he had done the right thing. Ingrid would never know and he'd be a sight easier to live with once he'd shot his load. No one could expect a bloke to go without for as long as he had. And you couldn't accuse him of spending the house-keeping on whores because, obviously, Moira's time would be free to rellies. Laura's John didn't charge for servicing his car. So Moira wouldn't charge for servicing his privates.

There was an unfortunate misunderstanding at the door. When the driver wanted paying and Moira had to shell out. It did not start things out on a good footing.

"So, how's it goin' with Ingrid?" Moira asked, keeping John on the front veranda.

"She's in labour," John informed her.

"Well I know that, but is she doin' all right? How frequent are the contractions?"

"Oh, that's okay. She's not havin' contractions. She's doin' this natural birth without drugs."

There was a pause. The pause developed into a silence. The silence into a long silence. The door was not opened. Booze did not appear and was not offered.

"So you gonna invite me in then?" John prompted, seeing as Moira didn't know her manners.

"Don't look that way," said Moira.

"Moira," said John, "I'm puttin' it to ya straight. You know what I want and I know you got it."

"And I know you ain't gonna get it," said Moira. "Least not from me."

"It's your job," said John outraged.

"I'm not a public utility. I work my own hours and right now I'm not on duty."

"Aw, come on, Moi, you know you like it. It's no secret I keep Ingrid happy that way."

"It's no secret ya no good for anythin' else."

"Don't be like that. This'll be a friendly. We'll just curl up in a corner somewhere. Just the two of us. Get to know each other. You're family, family should be familiar."

"Family should keep out of each other's pants."

"Now, no need to get coarse." John put his hand out and stroked Moira's hair. Women like a bit of sweet talking before they get to the loving. "You're a shit-hot Sheila, Moi. I wouldn't come to you in my hour of need, and I'm bein' frank here, Moi, I don't just want you, I need you. What with Ingrid laid how she is, I wouldn't come to you if you were just another sleazy whore. But you, you're great. Great tits, great ass…"

Moira picked up one of the dumbbells she practices with, swung it in the air, and smashed it down on John's head. No she didn't. She just wasn't hard enough, that was her trouble. A soft touch through and through.

"You get the fuck out of here, you piece of steaming shit and if you ever lay hands on me again I'll grind every one of your bones into the tar with my Cadillac. And if you so much as think of going to one of the other girls while Ingrid's lying there on that hospital bed, you just watch out when you step off the kerb one of these dark nights because me and the caddie will be on your trail."

No. Didn't say that either. She believed in men's need of her. How else could she go on? Lawyers, doctors, accountants, insurance brokers, they all came to her, along with professors and mechanics and policemen and millionaire financiers, every ugly, paunchy, jowly, short-assed one of them. And they each left her feeling that little bit better about themselves. She saw the inner man, the weakness, the fear, and she made it better. Many of them sent her sweets, flowers, perfume, inexplicably sentimental about their spilled sperm on her bottom sheet. Not even inexplicable really. It's only possible to feel sentimental about bottom sheets if you don't have to clean them. So instead she said, "Go away, John. Sober up, or get drunk, whichever. I'm not working today and I don't do family." She paused. "I'll call you a cab."

"Don't bother," said John, "I know when I'm not wanted." Then he reconsidered. He still didn't have any money. "Orright then," he allowed graciously, "I'm gwine a Laura's." A drink, that was what he needed. No one could grudge him a drink.

Moira watched the taxi drive off, her twenty dollars in the driver's hand. An expensive afternoon.

"G'day, Moira," called a cheery voice.

"G'day, Mrs. Morgan. Hello, Mr. Morgan. Real beaut, isn't it."

She poured herself a Coke from her immaculate fridge, knocked some ice cubes out of her immaculate ice tray, and went and sat a moment on the front veranda. The identical backsides of Mr. and Mrs. Morgan swayed slowly away up the road. What was it like to get gradually more like someone over the years? Moira gazed at the strelitzia, the bird of paradise plant, which decorated the front yard. She often looked at it, alone, brightly coloured; everyone got pleasure from it, they only had to look its way. What would Laura say if she changed her name to Strelitzia? Different from her whore name, Jackie. She clinked the ice cubes in the glass, idly. A small wet patch appeared on her thigh. She clinked faster, the Coke spilled faster, the ice crashed, leaped from the glass, thudded to the wooden boards of the veranda and skidded away under the seat. Moira was furious. And she'd run out of tranks. Meant to get some more at work but she hadn't been in today. It was dangerous to get angry. She hated him, she bloody hated him. She wanted to cut his frigging head off. And she'd calmly paid out for his taxi fares. What was wrong with her? He treated her like a street lamp. There must be something else she could do, something involving small intricate cruelty. Little pinpricks of pain and a lasting reminder. Needles. Golden needles. Strelitzia's Tattoos & Teazels. Sounded good. Sounded ugly.

Beryl's John was disappointed but not discouraged. He had been down but not out; only that made him feel like an American pugilist which, he reflected, was asking for trouble. He had rushed his new serial code formula in to the Patents Office, sat on an orange plastic chair to wait as instructed, picked up a copy of *S Is for Space,* turned it over to read the back-cover blurb, glanced at the spine and felt hot and cold and all the fine web of emotions attributed to the heroine of a gothic novel when she discovers the bloodstain is wet. For there before him, in gold block, was a perfect example of a ten-digit number. Where you or I might have shrugged at the coincidence, Beryl's John knew that something was seriously amiss. He opened the inside back cover expecting the worst. He found it, for there was a list of titles each with its own ten-figure figure, easily identifiable as a series, as Beryl's John's own patent series. Could one sue for anticipation? He thought not. He was forced into the melancholy conclusion that his new system for ordering the hand-me-downs given to an expectant mother by which gift and giver could easily be identified, with a special check digit so that one could ensure the number in question was indeed valid as part of the series, his system was already in use in international standard book numbering. It was awful. He would go home and drown his sorrows in covered cock with cumin, a classic of the French kitchen.

On the way back to Balga he thought he recognised his wife's youngest daughter's boyfriend outside a house which reminded him strongly of his wife's middle daughter.

"Going my way?" he called politely.

"Got any grog?" asked Ingrid's John from Laura's driveway.

"Only what the figs are marinating in," said Beryl's John.

Rum blokes, these Poms, thought Ingrid's John, dickheads the lot of them.

"Wanna quick stubby down the Balga Tavern?" he suggested hospitably. Something told Beryl's John that his figs would not be suffered to marinate peacefully in their excellent port if the young man came, drinkless, to the house. Unfortunately, nothing told Beryl's John that a session at the Balga Tavern would endanger more that the figs.

Minnie and Milly were diving between each other's legs, turning somersaults in the water and retrieving pebbles from the bottom of the pool. Minnie had left her bikini tied to the steps, a costume Beryl's John had crocheted during a previous enthusiasm. He had threatened to become disappointed when it looked very much as though no one would wear it. Beryl had noticed, however, that it was navy blue in colour and would therefore suit Minnie who never knew what she was wearing except that it had to be blue. The crocheted bikini had an unfortunate tendency to abandon its wearer at the slightest ripple and Minnie felt deliciously unclut-tered without it.

Minnie was superbly happy. She had rung the hospital and to no one's surprise, except perhaps Ingrid's John who did not know yet, busy as he was getting plastered with Beryl's John at the Balga Tavern, Ingrid had been delivered of a a nine-pound baby girl named Lolita. Minnie was welcome to visit in the morning, meanwhile Ingrid was weary from her labours and should see only her mother and husband. Minnie had called Interflora and ordered an enormous bunch of orchids to be sent to her sister's bedside. There was the little matter of how she would pay her credit-card bill, but things seemed to be turning up at such a rate that she trusted the money would surface from somewhere too. After that she rang Laura, who already knew, having assisted at the birth.

"I told Zebbee and Son," said Laura, "and Zebbee wanted to know all about it. Only she couldn't pronounce the name Lolita, so d'you know what she calls Ingrid's baby?"

"What?" asked Minnie. The weight of that single syllable was immense as the sudden possibility of "Lorelei" flashed into her mind.

"Lollipop," laughed Laura.

Lollipop. Of course, Lollipop. Little Lollipop's new Aunty Minnie laughed in defeat; Zebbee was a worthy victor. Then she went back out to the garden, dived into the water to get on with her job of being happy, a skill she was planning to perfect.

Minnie had, she felt, a natural propensity for happiness. It used to be, before dreadful London and beastly Genevieve, her greatest attraction: wild energy, intense enthusiasm and irrepressible bounce. An American woman she remembered, the soft Southern accent if not the name, had once ten years ago begun to pat her softly on the head, pushing her ever so gently downward, then releasing the pressure so that Minnie, being responsive, had indeed started to bounce. She bounced in massive leaps and drops so that eventually the Southern woman, who was not tall, could no longer reach her and Minnie bounced on her own momentum alone. What had Genevieve done to her? She had seen that wild energy, that "piece of air with lightning in it," and while not understanding it had yet tried to harness it, for energy can only be converted, it cannot be created or destroyed. Now that was over; the restricting coils of the transformer had been wrenched from their iron core and the suffocating, static Minnie had been released to a more kinetic future.

Milly harangued her from the sidelines. "…Bleeding wound," she was saying, "Christ crucified a clumsy reference to the menstruating woman. Think of all those beautiful female heads rising superbly from between their lovers' thighs, mouths dripping with menstrual blood. Triple taboo: no oral sex, no sex during periods, no female to female sex. Who is it sucks blood from the neck of a supine virgin? Who lives forever? Who confers immortality on her own blood partners? Who flies in the window, flitting like a bat to the heroine's bedroom despite a welter of crosses and garlic wielded by a desperate husband?"

"Well," drawled Minnie lazily, "I guess from your tone of voice the answer's not Christopher Lee or Vincent Price."

Minnie swam, a naked body in warm, perfumed darkness, the evening breeze blowing in softly from the ocean. She smiled to herself.

"Well, maybe so. Maybe so."

"Strelitzia's Tattoo & Teazels," chirruped Moira when the phone rang. She had written it out on a paper doily in italic and copperplate. One of her regulars had taught her calligraphy. It had been his passion to have dirty words written all over his body in elegant strokes. Fortunately he had not cared about spelling, just as long as it was filthy. Moira would run out of new insults and genital jargon and have to make them up. Foreign place names were good, she'd found, they always sounded lewd. "Vladivostok," she would write, and "Bugrino," and when her john asked what it meant, she would assure him it was real sexy stuff, but don't ask her to say it out loud, she didn't want to sully her mouth.

What?" said Laura's John. "Oh, sorry. Must have the wrong number." As soon as she recognised his voice Moira was tempted to say nothing and let him hang up. She was disgusted. How could there be two of them in one day? Did childbirth give men a hard-on? And she hadn't thought Laura's husband was like that.

"Okay John, it's Moira."

"Aw, you had me fooled good and proper. I was just about to hang up."

"What can I do for you?" Drop my Cadillac on your head?

"I, well, it's hard to explain. Maybe it's not really appropriate, you bein' Laura's sister'n all."

"Oh don't let that stop you."

"What's that? Look, does Laura talk to you? Tell you things, I mean. See, I don't think she's very happy and she won't tell me what it is, so I thought maybe…"

"She feels unappreciated, buy her a new dress. She's bored, encourage her to get a job. She wants to get her hair done, take the kids out for the day."

"Aw yeah, that's a good idea."

"Which was the good one?"

"Well, Beryl's John's throwing this big party after Ingrid's baby's born and now that Minnie's here, and I'm sure Laura would like some new clothes and a trip into town and everything. Maybe I could take the kids to the zoo."

"Maybe you could, John. Maybe you could."

"Yeah, thanks a lot."

"For just being here when you called?"

"That, of course, and for listening."

"Oh, listening too."

"Anything I can do for you any time, you let me know."

"Just so happens I'm about to go into business. You could come along and fill the waiting room."

"Oh sure thing," said John a mite uneasily. "What business?"

"Tattooing," said Moira. "I'm setting myself up in a tattoo parlour. You tell me your troubles while I stick pins in you. Like ladies at the hairdresser."

* * *

Everything was going splendidly down at the Balga Tavern. Ingrid's John had three pints lined up in front of him, with five empty glasses on one side. Beryl's John had had two martinis and was beginning to feel sleepy. The two men had nothing to say to each other but, since that did not prevent either from speaking, it was no great loss.

"I'm having a baby," said Ingrid's John. "It's gonna be a boy. Gonna be the strongest, brainiest, cockiest little bugger out."

"I've invented an international serial numbering system," said Beryl's John. "They're going to use it on all the books that get printed."

"He'll be a great man when he grows up," said Ingrid's John. "Could be the next state premier. Could be as big as Mick Jagger or even Muhammed Ali."

"You'll see it everywhere," said Beryl's John. "Everywhere there's a book, there'll be one of my numbers on it."

"He'll be big, my boy, my son," said Ingrid's John. "Anyone who says different's a liar."

"Might not seem like a big thing to you," said Beryl's John, "but the whole classification system will depend on it."

"Is big," Ingrid's John insisted, "I just told ya."

"Well, I suppose it isn't very big in terms of size…" said Beryl's John.

"You askin' for a fight or what?" said Ingrid's John. "He's very big, biggest size they got."

"Who is?" asked Beryl's John who, compelled by the stimulus of Ingrid's John's fist in his face, had found himself listening to the man's last assertion.

Laura's John, who had just nipped out for a quick half, bought himself a drink and came over to their table. A toast was in order. The whole pub had toasted him when they heard about his first kid.

"My son," Ingrid's John was saying, "my little boy." Then he got confused and tried again, "My new baby."

"What's he called, then?" Beryl's John was saying. "Your son, what's his name?"

"John," replied Ingrid's John without any hesitation whatever. That bit was quite clear. Any son of his would be called after him. He felt a sentimental glow.

"Congratulations," said Laura's John. "Nine pounds, screaming and kicking. That's one big bouncing baby."

Ingrid's John beamed. "One more for the road, then we'll introduce the little shit-kicker to its proud father."

Laura's John remembered something and laughed. "My Zebbee calls her 'Lollipop.' Isn't that cute?"

"Lollipop?" growled Ingrid's John. "Your kid's got one wallop of an imagination. My son's called 'John.'"

"What son?" asked Laura's John with a worried frown. This was not the time to bring up little infidelities left back in Queensland. 'You just told me I got a nine-pound baby boy."

"Girl."

"Boy."

"It's a girl, John. Roolly cute little baby girl."

Ingrid's John stared at Laura's, his half-finished stubby halfway to his open mouth. "Lollipop?" he said, in a daze.

The other two men looked at him, noted the bottle in his clenched fist, the muscles swelling dangerously in his arms, the sinews standing out on his neck. They better get him out of the tavern before he started breaking the place up.

"Let's go on home," said Laura's John.

"Yes," Beryl's John backed him up, "time to go home."

They bundled him out the door so fast he had time only to smash the bottle on the counter and overturn the table they'd been sitting at. When the barman muscled over to place a strong reprimand, they explained, "He's just had a baby."

The barman nodded sympathetically. "Girl? My wife had one of them."

As they drove up to Beryl's, that being the nearest place to offload

the drunken, outraged John, Minnie was just swimming one last
lap in the blissful, naked darkness and the parrot was flapping
overhead.

The parrot, while not positively friendly toward Minnie, was not
positively antagonistic either. An attitude it bestowed equally on
the rest of humanity. It liked to wait and see, sit on the garden
fence a while, see which way the feathers ruffled. Today its own
feathers had been grievously ruffled. Equivocal toward humans, it
was passionate about music and loyal to its own. The suggestion
that the music of the genius Mozart could be a mere extra had hurt
the parrot deeply. But silly people might say what they liked, sensible parrots scorned response. The parrot had for some time been
working on its scorn; it was lonely and it felt this loneliness might
be in some way connected to its habit of rising above whatever
distressed it. Rising above is second nature to parrots but the ac-
companying scorn needs careful handling. The parrot had taken a
genuine interest in Minnie's conversation, would have squawked
her the opening bars of *Voi che sapete* because, of course, it *did*
know, so the unprovoked attack on beloved Mozart came as a di-
rect hit, causing the parrot a good half-hour sulk.

Sulking in the afternoon, however, was as nothing compared
with the inarticulate fury which had seized the parrot that morning. It had been chased by dogs. By two rottweilers, two bulldog
mixes and one large Doberman pinscher in the grounds of its
home. That, at least, was natural and, since the parrot could fly, no
great threat. It expected on these occasions to be warned in advance by the barking, panting and shuffling hullabaloo such dogs
kick up when they mean to tear a defenseless creature from limb
to limb and spread its entrails on the ground.

The parrot had not been warned; there had been no barking,
only a hoarse hiss such as a cobra parades before a fatal strike.
Cobras not being native to Western Australia, the parrot had paid

no mind. Probably just that inflatable water snake trying, too late, to attract attention. It was not, therefore, until the five unbaying hounds were nearly upon it that the parrot had soared off into the lemon tree. It had lost a bright green tail feather in the upset. From its vantage point in the clear blue yonder it had mused upon the recent event and concluded: that if the dogs were not barking, this was due to incapacity not lack of desire; that some human had interfered with the proper working of the dogs' throats; that the only human capable of such brutality (here the parrot had laughed; it meant, of course, capable of such humanity), was the one who had bred them in the first place. The dogs were dumb beasts, double-dumb; what fitter creature to punish their loss than a talking parrot?

Who but a parrot with an aerial view of the proceedings could forestall, or even foretell, the horror ("unpleasantness," as Beryl was later to call it) of what was about to befall? Not Laura's John. He could not understand a fella absent from his wife's bedside the night she gave birth. He'd been there round the clock when Zebbee and then Son were born, amazed, overawed by how tiny Zebbee was. Those toenails, little pearly drops like dew on a rose, but even dew was bigger. He often brought the kids along to the garage, saying they wanted to see the new sunburst Daddy was working on. But the reason closest to his heart was that he burst with pride in them; he liked his mates to see what wonders they were. Not Beryl's John. He was, though too shy to say so himself, not good with people. He was fond of them, found the abstract theory much to his liking, and his patent sequence for hand-me-downs was an offering of pure goodwill. But, truth to tell, Beryl's John found physics a great relief and relatives a strain. Not Minnie. She was happily oblivious of the danger. She had remembered a line from a poem by Olga Broumas that was quite perfect: "Like amnesiacs in a ward on fire we must find words or burn." It had all the mystery of Emily Dickinson's "I found the words to every thought I ever had but one," but rather more urgency. A woman who is thinking about words little imagines that her brother-in-law is about to attack her.

Ingrid's John was in a terrible rage, and his rage was terrible. Someone had tricked him, someone was laughing at him. When he found out who it was, he would kick their fucking head in. He would smash their teeth down their throat. He would take a chainsaw to their kneecaps.

"Spoiling for a fight, aren't ya?" he said to Beryl's John who was trying to get him to sit down.

"No, no," said Beryl's John. "No."

"Well take your bloody paws off a me, ya poofta." Ingrid's John glared around the room for the source of the whipping fury which was flooding his body. He caught sight of his own jeans. "Thinks I'm dirty," he burst out. *"You're welcome to drop them in the washing machine.* Too right, I'll drop them. No worries." With which he proceeded to pull his jeans off and run around in his underpants looking for the washing machine.

"Put your pants on, man," Laura's John ordered him.

"Shut ya mouth," bellowed Ingrid's John, lunging, but Laura's was too quick for him, having drunk nothing but three sips of Swan lager he had managed to get in before they had had to leave the tavern. Laura's jumped out of the way, and Ingrid's, finding no brittle nose to crack, no bony jaw to smash, no soft lip to split, fell forward onto the ground.

"I'm off to bed," announced Beryl's and ambled away muttering.

Laura's surveyed Ingrid's, who lay half-naked on the rug, his face bloated and his mouth slathering in spit.

"See ya later," he said and walked back to the tavern where he'd left his car.

Moonlight flooded the garden. Minnie climbed out of the pool at last and was bending to untie the crocheted bikini from the steps when she noticed someone standing in the shadow of the house under the pergola. There was a sudden noise behind her, something winged brushed her shoulder and shot off into the sky. One fleeting moment a shadow passed across the moon, the garden was engulfed in the darkness of enormous wings which belonged to no earthly creature. From this darkness came an inhuman cackle, for all the world like a parrot laughing. The disembodied laughter roused the figure under the pergola whose face was obscured by a night-flowering cactus. It appeared to be a man, who appeared to be watching Minnie. He appeared to be naked, drunk and moving.

"And as for you," he appeared to be shouting, "you're gonna get what's coming to ya."

For one so drunk he appeared capable of enormous speed. Aggressive men were so far from Minnie's current preoccupations that she failed to respond correctly, take out her submachine gun and shoot him dead. She had forgotten that it is both illegal and sinful for women to remove their raiment anywhere but the close confinement of four walls, a locked door and a bathtub.

"Stuck up little bitch, think you're better than I am. You're nothing but a dirty whore. Got more respect for Moira, least she's honest 'bout what she is. You, you're just a hole."

It occurred to Minnie that the house was empty, John and Beryl must be still at the hospital, and the neighbours, hearing screams, would shrug and vow to make an official complaint about those noisy pool parties, until sleep pulled them back under and by morning they had forgotten all about it. There was no one to help her.

Minnie had forgotten the parrot. It had flown round the garden and was now waiting in the protective custody of a bottlebrush bush whose bright red bottlebrushes and green leaves were ideal camouflage for a red and green parrot. The bush stood by the pool steps by which the drunken John must pass.

While on land John's advantages, including a six-foot body and pumped iron muscles, must have subjugated Minnie, yet in the pool Minnie reckoned she stood something of a chance. For example, she could swim and John could not. What happened when she grew tired, or when the brilliant idea of dropping rocks on her head glimmered in John's mind, had no satisfactory answer. It was, however, less frightening to have a weak plan than to have none, Minnie argued, and fear was her worst disadvantage.

John's sense of wrong mounted as he stumbled toward the pool. It was those fucking bitches, laughing at him, sitting up in the trees mocking him. They were all the same, women. Turned round and had daughters just to spite you. Wasn't gonna happen again. This time he was going to have a son if he had to keep pumping all night. His foot hit a rock lying on the path, nearly throwing him spread-eagled to the ground. Once he'd recovered his balance he picked the rock up. "Smash the bitch's head in. Don't want no lip." He had by now reached the side of the pool and was raising the rock above his head when a shrill whistle blasted his eardrum. He dropped the rock and turned toward the noise. Then a terrible thing descended upon him, scratching his face, tearing at his hair. He opened his mouth to shout but the thing caught his lips and held him. The piercing pain wiped everything else out of his mind. He lashed the bushes with his hands, trying to wrench his assailant off, but his fingers closed over bottlebrushes which fell apart at his touch. The more he pulled away, the tighter the thing held on. Like a hook in the gills of a fish, like the jaws of a bulldog with its teeth in a thigh, something bit through his lips, pinioning him to the spot.

The parrot enjoyed its revenge which was, from the moral standpoint, a piece of pure altruism since John had not harmed the parrot itself. Human lips were soft and fleshy and much chewier than a cuttlefish. After a while the parrot felt it had made its point and was preparing to let John go and reflect upon the misery of being physically prevented from giving voice to pain. It craned its neck over the pool, checking that Minnie had the sense to scarper while John was distracted. The young woman was nowhere to be seen but over the roof of the house came the most extraordinary beings the parrot had ever laid eyes on. And, having laid eyes on them, it felt that it never wished to lay its eyes elsewhere.

The sky was full of birds, great black ravens flying in an enormous V against the light. Their feathers appeared at first to be black, but a closer examination showed them a very dark blue; no, dark green; red, surely, a deep flashing blood red; but there were dashes in the red of light yellow, a pale half-ripe lemon yellow; no, indeed it was a strong, vivid fluffy-chicken yellow. How many were there? They blanketed the sky and the rushing of their wings was like thunder. They landed on the roof, on the lawn, in the lemon tree, hovered over the swimming pool, beating up the water into spinning tops. The parrot's heart was uplifted; among these proud beauties it would find its mate, the sweet companion who would forever banish scorn from its crest, the cherished darling whom to admire was to adore and to adore was to love and to love was to be loved in return.

Minnie, from her hideout below the bottlebrush bush, looked up into the sky and beheld the two most beautiful women she had ever seen in her life. One was young, slim, blonde, and boyish of figure, her long straight hair fell in a fine curtain to delicate shoulders. The other had the appearance of an old woman of ninety-five with white hair pulled back from her face stroking the tip of her ear and exposing the lobe. She had such a look of vitality in her eyes, such a burst of good humour playing round her mouth, that it made Minnie happy simply to look at her. And as she looked, she saw that what she had taken to be an old woman was at closer examination a young girl whose golden halo of hair lit up the sky. Minnie thought she had never seen eyes so blue.

The Dublin Bay prawns crawling at the bottom of Beryl's kitchen sink peered out the window, their eyes swivelling on their little stalks as the sky turned to seawater teeming in microscopic animalcules invisible to the human eye but all bearing flags saying "Dinner, dinner, dinner" to a Dublin Bay prawn.

The lobster lounging in its wok was unable to see the sky due to the heavy karri doors of the wardrobe but it felt, in all the orange craters of its shell it felt, that out there was something very nice to pinch.

In the carport where they had been locked, the rottweilers and the bulldog mixes and the large Doberman caught the glorious fresh blood smell of helpless creatures about to be beset by the gnashing teeth of nightmare hounds. They wished to offer themselves for the part of the hounds.

Even the discarded W.H. Smith carrier bag shifted in Minnie's wastepaper basket. Somewhere out there was the blob of crude oil which could be cracked and polymerized into that exact brand of plastic which can make a W.H. Smith bag feel that it has been moulded and sheeted all over again.

For such is the power of the vampire that she appears all things to all creatures and holds sway even over the inanimate, so that each feels her to be the very thing their heart most desires.

Without a word from the beautiful beings in the sky, each respondent knew exactly what it was called upon to do, as though daily drill had synchronised each action. The dogs ripped through the piece of rag which closed the carport ever since Beryl's John had invented a unique locking device but forgotten the unique key; they raced over to the pool steps where the parrot held the drunken John captive, their tails knocking open the kitchen screen door as they ran. Through the netting crawled the sort of procession which must inevitably remind one of Sartre, Pound, and de Nerval: a rock lobster followed by two dozen Dublin Bay prawns. Needless to say, without even time to exclaim, "Don't come the raw prawn with me, mate," the drunken, violent, abusive John was nibbled to death by prawns, squeezed to death by lobster, mangled to death by mastiff, pecked to death by parrot, and, as if that wasn't enough, smothered by a W.H. Smith bag with a tear through its logo. It should be pointed out, however, that he was not drained to the last drop of blood by vampires. These were lesbian vampires and they had their pride.

IN THE BEST OF BURLESQUE

⇒ 8 ⇐

Beryl lay as still as an Egyptian mummy in an Egyptian tomb. That being the only kind of mummy which ever got any rest, it was the only one which could stand the comparison. Beryl expected at any moment to be arrested for unmummylike activities and so was preparing her defence in advance: she was reviving an ancient custom which dated back to the pharaohs. Actually, she was scheming. The list she kept stored carefully in her mind of all the members of her family, all their little hopes and distresses, all the small services which should be performed to smooth the way to their achieving the former and avoiding the latter, with asterisks next to those which must be done urgently, ampersands for those which she could afford to delay, and circles for those which might need to be queue-jumped at a moment's notice, a system which, while not in the least mathematical—Beryl knew that if once she demonstrated a head for figures, the household bills would become her private property—was far more elaborate that any mere ISBN, since it had to accommodate so many more variables, human beings not yet having succumbed to the rigours of the B format; and Beryl had worked her way to the bottom of her list. If any person, knowing the existence of this list, had informed Beryl that she might one day come to the end of it, Beryl would have been shocked and not a little shaken. She was continually promising herself titbits for when the list would be finished and everything crossed off, but that does not signify that the possibility of an empty list ever really entered her consciousness. For an empty list is a list with nothing on it, it is a nonlist, a list which no longer exists. The titbits were tidily fitted in between listed activities, or doubled up with routine essentials like baths and emptying the compost.

Beryl went through the items of the old list (she spoke these last two words much in the tone of a French aristocrat invoking the *ancien régime*) checking that what had been ticked deserved ticking and that what had been crossed deserved crossing. When she reached the end she felt much as a logger must on discovering that the branch he has been sawing with such gusto was the sole support between him and a twenty-foot drop. Thus she lay very still while she plotted lest the tree discover that the branch was no longer connected and see fit to let it go with a thudding crash to the ground, and her upon it. Beryl had been worried about Laura and her John, but they were cosy again and having barbecues. She had been worried about Moira, but that was a bottomless pit of all too nameable horrors and she had scratched it off the list before it could take hold. She had been worried about her own dear Loviebuttons, but since the physics had taken and he had been going to Physics Evenings, socialising with physicists, he had even begun to recognise members of the immediate family, though names still often eluded him. She had been worried about Minnie, but her eldest daughter had left that dreadful woman—of course she must make her own choices in life, but Beryl hadn't liked the sound of Genevieve—and had obviously found a replacement somewhere. Beryl had no more idea of where Minnie found her women than Alice Toklas and Gertrude Stein had of Natalie Clifford Barney. She supposed there must be a pool of them somewhere into which one dipped when one wanted a fresh one. Beryl had been worried about Ingrid and Lolita, but mother and baby were doing well. Lolita was perfect, had all her fingers and all her toes—Beryl had not been able to stop herself counting—and would soon be putting her feet in her mouth and spitting spinach with the best of them. Beryl had been worried about the lack of baby things, but baby things had materialised out of the ether of Western Australian benevolence. She had been worried about the lack of water, house and other amenities, but that, Ingrid had peacefully informed her, had all been put right.

Beryl lay next to her somnolent Loviebuttons and let her mind go blank. Whereupon it filled with Dostoyevski and Tolstoi, Chekhov and Gorki, the Winter Palace and the Summer Palace, the Odessa steps and Dersu Uzala, the lions of Leningrad and the gigantic Dom Knigi on Nevsky Prospekt where all those timeless classics were for sale. She would stay in bed all day immersed in the Cyrillic alphabet and if anyone wished to bother her they would need to come laden with a pot of tea and quite three lettuces. She would limit each audience to ten minutes and from two till four in the afternoon she would not be "at home" at all.

The other member of the household revelling in new-found content was the parrot who had at last discovered its parrel, its parrock, or whoever it is that parrots long for all their lives. The parrot sat on its perch in the aviary gazing fondly at the W.H. Smith bag who had come into its life in so romantic a fashion the previous night. It should perhaps be remembered that the parrot was not the most faithful bird in the world; its infatuations were short-lived, though all-encompassing in their season. Next week perhaps, or maybe even tomorrow, it would go off the W.H. Smith bag like a ton of bricks, it would wonder what on earth it could have seen in a piece of torn plastic, it would feel even a little embarrassed and hope no one would mention their two names in the same sentence. But for the moment, for this early morning rising fair and blue, the parrot saw only the grace and beauty of the W.H.

Smith bag's folds as it flapped in the breeze. It thought that it would never see a billboard lovely as that logo.

Beryl's John had a hangover. It was his first hangover and he would like to have been able to boast of it with the rest of the blokes and say interesting things like "hair of the dog." But he had acquired his hangover on two martinis and this, he felt, might not establish his reputation as a hard-drinking he-man. He would have preferred, like Minnie, to drink orange juice. But anyone seeing him with a Fanta in his hand would assume he was a sober alcoholic. So he would just have to go on drinking to prove he wasn't. Life outside the periodic table was awfully hard. Beryl had found Minnie's teetotallerhood a larger pill to swallow than her daughter's lesbianism. She would pour out a discreet measure of orange in a wineglass and announce, "Your usual, dear." John might have found life easier in California where everyone had been reclassified alcoholic so that no one should be made to feel bad. Those who did not drink could relax to discover themselves the adult children of alcoholics. Those who were neither the offspring of drunks, nor drank themselves, were clearly co-alcoholics, dependent on the habits of others to bolster their confidence that they too had a place in an alcoholic universe. Where Minnie would have fit in this scheme of things is not recorded. She had given up drink at a party, sipping her first glass of wine for over a year, realising that this was indeed her first glass of wine for over a year and she never would have noticed if she hadn't just been passed a glass. Probably her regular consumption of fifteen cups of tea a day would reassure the locals that she was a substance abuser in her fashion. Knowing Minnie as we all do, she would have been so fascinated to discover the new California verbs "to co," "to deal" (dredge up anything nasty that ever happened to you and offer it to a new lover as a pledge, replacing the old exchange of pinkie rings and charm bracelets) and "to work on" (meaning to bore everyone else with), that she would have smiled prettily and looked thoughtful. Beryl's John, however, had too many strikes against him. He was not an addict, poor man; he did not live in California; he rarely drank tea. In short, he was doomed. Doomed to drink martinis and suffer ignominious hangover.

Minnie was talking to Laura. She had not waited the night before to witness the drunken John despatched severally. As soon as the silk of vampires had departed the sky, the spell was broken and Minnie had fled like, well, like a bat out of hell. Fearing to pass through the house, she had slipped into the laundry room, pulled the Swiss army knife from the shelf, slit the mosquito netting on the window, and crawled through into the front garden. From there to Laura's was but a terrified step in the dark. Thus the fifth bedroom, overlooking the reticulated lawn, came into occupation. By morning the bed in the fifth bedroom was graced by three bodies; one asleep, two wriggling. For Zebbee, who always knew what was going on, had run to tell Son that there was a new visitor who should be bounced on without delay. And Laura, seeing both children's rooms empty, the bathroom void of the floating dolls of the night before, the garden unmolested by hover-mower or chain saw, the family and lounge rooms free of attack by Hoover, concluded that her offspring were entertaining and dropped in to join them.

Beryl's lie-in was brought to a halt by a sudden thought. Had the night-flowering cactus flowered that night? She had been watching it closely and it was very near its time, then Ingrid had gone into labour and Beryl had pushed everything else to the back of her mind. Beryl rolled over and put one foot out of the bed. From that moment she was lost. Loviebuttons groaned beside her; Beryl responded automatically, "Poor darling, let me make you some coffee."

Poor darling, let me make you some coffee, such an innocent expression to bring about so total a downfall. For then Beryl had indeed to go and put the kettle on, check the cactus—which had bloomed and wilted overnight and would not flower again for another seven years, but which, Beryl consoled herself poetically, had heralded the delectable Lollipop—and thus she discovered the previous night's destruction.

"What on earth did you get up to while I was at the hospital?" she demanded of her husband.

John moaned and looked pathetic but since his face was hidden in the blankets, this did him no good.

"Nothing," he replied.

"Well who was here last night?" Beryl persisted.

"No one," said John.

"No one and nothing have between them bashed in the screen door, slit the mosquito netting in the laundry room and crushed my lovely Venus-flytraps which I'd put under the windowsill for a change of air."

Loviebuttons grunted something from which Beryl understood that he had been for a drink at the Balga with an unspecified number of unspecified Johns. He added, hopefully, that he had one helluva hangover. Beryl was as stone.

She rang Laura.

"Hiya doll," chirruped Laura. "Isn't Lollipop a poppet?"

"Yes," said Beryl.

"In case you were worrying, Minnie's over here."

"Perhaps she can explain what went on last night," said Beryl.

Minnie was handed the receiver.

"Mum," shrilled Minnie.

Beryl was in no mood for shrilling.

"Well," she said, "I'm waiting."

"Mum, it was awful," said Minnie, and she began to tell her mother about the strange man who had appeared in the garden intent on rape and murder. She described how she had been saved by the intervention of the vampires but, unfortunately, Beryl was constitutionally incapable of hearing the word "vampire," so her daughter's explanation sounded as full of holes to her as her husband's had. She decided to cut it short.

"Minnie," she said, "did you slash through the mosquito netting in the laundry room?"

"Yes," said Minnie, "but…"

Beryl interrupted, "Since you are thirty-three years old I can hardly threaten to take it out of your pocket money. The least you can do is pay for the netting to be replaced."

An apology and a box of chocolates would help. Beryl gathered there had been some kind of minor break-in while Minnie was in the pool. Still, could have been worse: nothing had been taken. Why did Minnie have to be hysterical about every little thing? Made an emotional drama out of an old plastic bag.

"Jesus Christ," Minnie burst out, "that woman. She's more concerned about her precious mosquito netting than the safety of her precious daughter."

Beryl sighed in remembrance of that little glimpse of peace. Why had she been vouchsafed even so much? Better to have lived her life in ignorance; now she would be forever hankering. She went into the laundry room to assess the damage and whether she might repair it herself. Her path was blocked by a foreign suitcase. Closer examination showed it to be full of freshly ironed clothes, all navy blue.

"This is a bit much," thought Beryl. But then, it was all a bit much.

"I'd better take it over to her."

When she reached Laura's no one seemed to be around. She rang the doorbell but there was no reply. She left the suitcase in the driveway next to the garage so that it was hidden from the road but clearly visible from the house. No doubt they had just popped out to Cole's for loo paper.

"Don't run over the suitcase, Mum," said Zebbee as they returned with the loo paper.

Minnie stared. Her suitcase had been dumped on the driveway. She jumped out of the car to retrieve it. Inside were, neatly folded and ironed, all the clothes she had brought to Australia and dried out in San Francisco.

"I don't believe it," she said, aghast. "Mum's disowned me."

"Don't take it so hard," soothed Laura. "It's the ones who wave politely and wish you every success in the future that you never see again. When they drive off in a fury dumping your suitcase on the road you know there is unfinished business." She paused, considered, and added, "'Spect she'd like some time to herself. Come camping with me and the kids up at Raven Rock."

Ingrid smiled peacefully at the infant Lollipop sucking at her breast. She turned and smiled peacefully at Loviebuttons as he showed her photographs of her new home. He had worked very hard, the precious treasure; he deserved her smile. Overnight, it seemed, he had got that old shed over to the land in Gunderdin, erected it, strung electric cables out from town, extended the pipeline to provide water from Mundaring Weir, had the ground graded to allow four-wheel-drive access, fixed up a post-office box, and dug trenches for the drains.

With all the rain they'd had lately, the rain barrel had looked after itself. There was, as yet, no shopping centre, but Ingrid had complete confidence. Outside the new house five dogs gambolled in the dirt, barking with enough full-throated ease to scare off any intruders who might have found their way to that pleasant glade. Ingrid yawned. After one had gone to the trouble of wanting a thing it was most satisfactory to have it provided. For Ingrid lived at the centre of a dualistic world in which women's forte was desire and men's the satisfaction thereof. Erring menfolk, violence to women, and cruelty to animals were no part of this world and Ingrid would not countenance them.

* * *

Beryl's John groaned once more but nothing happened. He coughed, first a throat-clearing little gurgle, then, when nothing more happened, he harrumphed loudly. He swung his arm out from under the bedclothes and over to the nightstand, located his coffee mug and decided to make the best of things. There was something odd about the cup but the exact substance of that oddness did not occur to him until too late, until he had swigged a sip, gulped, choked, sat up and spat it out. His mouth had been invaded by murk. The coffee was cold. The coffee cup was cold. It was not a lovely cup of freshly ground coffee with warm milk made especially for him by his loving wife. It was his Nescafé of the night before. He peered at the nightstand. There was no other cup on it. His wife had not made him any coffee that morning. She had offered it, but she had not made it. Better clear this up right away.

"Beryl," he called. "Beryl."

But Beryl came there none. Only the tapping on the window of the citriadora, the "pretty pollys" of the parrot out back. What does a man do when coffee, the bedrock of family life, is offered but not made? Beryl's John was not a lazy man, he was not a greedy man, nor a philandering man. He did not leave all the housework to his wife, he did not expect a hot meal ready for him on the table when he came home, which was lucky because on Russian nights he would have had a long wait, but he thought they had an understanding about the coffee.

John could not get out of bed without he had first drunk a cup of freshly ground Kenyan with warm milk. It was their little joke that coffee was his sole humanizing factor, his only need, the one thing which tied him to the economy of production, cultivation and transportation. If he had not been dependent on the Kenyan coffee workers to plant and weed and pick, on the shippers to ship and the shops to sell, he could have dispensed with his own kind altogether and gone to live in the wilderness with his fibre optics. From his need for coffee sprung all his socialization. The exploitation of the Kenyan coffee workers by international capital, the impoverishment of the African soil consequent upon over-harvesting, the impoverishment of the African economy consequent upon too many cash crops, the starvation of many of its children consequent upon so much arable land devoted to inedible luxuries which were then shipped abroad, all this formed the key to John's politics. While it might be preferable that people understand the ways of the world from an abstract, philanthropic standpoint, in fact we find it much easier to understand things which affect us daily. Coffee was John's daily paper, his current affairs, even his career motivation. And this morning he hadn't had any.

He reached again for the cold coffee cup. This time he drank and as he drank he collected himself up: there was an adjustment he must make to the police equipment; the radar was picking up only the speed of the front cars; he could make some alterations and it would be able to distinguish individual vehicles. Then there was the electronic gate down at Mr. Vivien's which, he was told, was not user-friendly, well it was hardly meant to be was it? And then there was the party food which was proceeding according to plan, but the plan had missed one important variable: John's puff pastry would not puff, and it was essential for the truffle turnovers.

In little short of half an hour John had set both his arms and his hair and his wife's kitchen counter and his wife's mixing bowl in a gooey plaster cast of damp dough. It had a pleasing texture, like childhood plasticine before they brought in Lego and Meccano and other hard-edged toys, but even with his scant knowledge of social mores, John knew that the party guests would not touch it.

Three hours later John was back in business. He had made his alterations to the radar scanners using his home terminal and a nifty piece of electronic mail. The police would be pleased. John liked people to be pleased with him. Mr. Vivien's electronic gates were another matter. John sensed a battle of wills going on between his wife, who liked gates left open, and her boss, who liked gates shut tight. John was sure Beryl would come up with either an equitable compromise, or more likely, a cast-iron reason why she was right.

This time, before he went back to the pastry, which was beginning to seem like a long job, a tinge of "How can truffles turnover possibly be worth it" was creeping like a thief into the back of his mind. He decided to get help. He would do the sensible thing. He would ask a woman. They had been baking perfect pastry for centuries. There was only one problem. Beryl was out. John rang Laura, and the problem became two problems: Laura was away at Raven Rock. John knocked on Minnie's bedroom door and the problem became three problems: Minnie was not there. John thought of ringing the hospital and asking to speak to Ingrid but he was certain to be told she was resting and would he like to call back in an hour or so? He might throw himself upon the mercy of the ward sister but he felt his enquiry, important though it was to himself, might rank rather low on a scale of human urgency and that childbirth probably came above it. He tried Simone at Sweet Sugar High who giggled and said of course there was a secret to making perfect pastry and as the bakery owed its reputation to its close guarding of that secret, she was hardly likely to give it away, now was she? John agreed that she wasn't. Simone suggested that he come on in and choose something delicious from their display if he had a sweet tooth, it was bound to be better than whatever he was making at home, now wasn't it? John could not agree that it was. It might very well be true, but he could not agree to that truth. Finally, he phoned Moira.

"Strelitzia's Tattoo & Teazels."

"It's about the pastry," said John, "I just can't get it right. Well, to be honest, I can't seem to do it at all. It's for the truffle turnovers for the party, you see."

"No."

"Er? What do you mean, 'No?'"

"I don't see."

"Well, they're a sort of underground mushroom, hugely expensive, and they have special dogs which go and root them out with their noses. They're absolutely delicious."

"And what made you think that a tattoo parlour was the best place to seek culinary advice?"

"Isn't that Moira?"

"Who is it wants to know?"

"John."

"Oh, yes," said Moira.

"I'm," John paused, drawing the same teetering family tree that Minnie had engineered in the bath foam, "Beryl's husband, and Minnie, Laura, and Ingrid's stepfather, and Zebbee and Son's grandfather, and John's father-in-law." He felt he'd done remarkably well.

"You're nothing to me," said Moira.

"Oh, don't say that," said John. "Surely every individual has their own contribution to make."

"Hrm," said Moira, an echo of her sister Laura. "Go on, then. Make one."

"I wonder if you'd like to try some shop-bought pastries with me and help me decide which ones to use as a prototype for my own cooking."

"You mean you can't make pastry and you want to buy yours in for the party?"

"Well," said John, "yes."

"What had you thought of?"

"Sweet Sugar High," said John, "Ye Olde English Sweete Shoppe, Miss Irmgard's."

The names tripped off his tongue as though to the manner born.

"Sounds reasonable," said Moira consideringly, "we should do the Cinnamon Bun and Kylie's Tearoom."

"I'll meet you at Miss Irmgard's, shall I? That's not far from Victoria Park."

"Alright," said Moira resignedly, "but if this is just an opportunity for you to collect sympathy over territorial squabbles at work, then don't bother. I don't do sympathy any more, I do pins and needles."

"Territorial squabbles?" enquired John.

"Who gets the biggest laser, whose computer works fastest, whose hard disk lasts longest." Moira had had physicists before.

They found a seat at Miss Irmgard's.

"This is specialty Viennese," said Moira. "You must try the himmeltorte."

But John was not listening. He could see the dark roast black beans waiting in the grinder, could almost smell the drugged scent of fresh coffee.

"Oh," he said. And like a miracle the waitress walked toward them with an enormous pot and, without asking, poured out a fragrant cupful.

"Could I trouble you for…" he began.

The waitress set a jug of warm milk on the table.

"Ah," John sighed.

They ate and they drank. The cake shop grew crowded, a man approached them.

"Is this seat taken?"

He sat down. John recognised him, after a minute or so staring and blinking. It was the police radar man he'd spent the whole of the previous afternoon with.

"I fixed the equipment," said John. "Had you noticed? It can individuate between speeding vehicles now."

"Yes," said the policeman, nodding, "Very good. Excellent in fact. Double the solved crimes figure." Then he looked at Moira. "Seems to me I know this young lady too." He looked back at John with a mixture of scorn and approbation.

"Allow me to present my daughter, Moira," said John.

It is possible he had grown confused; who else could the young woman be since she was not his wife or his colleague? It is also possible he was being gallant, though gallantry had been a mystery to him hitherto. Either way, Moira appreciated the gesture.

"Thought your name was Jackie," murmured the policeman suggestively.

"Oh no." John was categoric; when he got a name right, he got it *right*.

"This is Moira, Laura's sister."

The policeman looked from one to the other and shrugged. He made a note to mark Jackie's file "RR" for "respectable relations."

After he left, Moira turned to John.

"Thanks," she said. "I'll give you a free session in the parlour, soon as I'm set up."

"That'll be very er…" said John, "very…."

"Permanent," said Moira. "You'll look good with a tattoo. Way of making your mark."

IN THE BATTLEGROUND OF THE SOUL

≫ 9 ≫

Raven Rock: so called after the remarkable flocks of these impressive non-native birds that gather in the extensive coastal dunes once a month; it is said that their visits coincide with the full moon and are accompanied by bats, blood-letting and blood-curdling cries. The superstitious amongst you will want to keep well clear of the area north of the camp site as far as the two black rocks on a moonlight night. Those of more scientific bent will enjoy fossicking in the dunes where they will find many intriguing limestone formations, much like those of the Pinnacle Desert but in miniature. These formations are said by some to resemble the towns and villages of an ancient civilisation." Minnie read from the leaflet Laura had left on the dashboard.

"Sounds spooky, doesn't it," said Laura. She had swallowed two No-Doze caffeine tablets and was buzzing. It was a long way to Raven Rock and Minnie could not share the driving. The four-wheel drive was insured through the garage and the policy only covered John and Laura. "I'll be awake all night with this stuff running around my brain. Fancy dropping in on the ravens?"

"Cynics suggest both bats and ravens are attracted by the noxest perpetua cactus which flowers around the time of the full moon and flourishes in the sandy limestone soil. The cries are the shrieks of the bats as, having sated themselves on perpetua flowers, they are impaled on the cactus spikes," Minnie continued.

"First the roses then the thorns," thought Laura. Was nature invented by the Gideon Bible people?

Seeing that they were two lone women with two small children, the campground owner felt it necessary to help with the tent. Which meant allowing him ten minutes to get the ropes tangled and the poles in all the wrong holes, feeding him a credible exit line involving: a queue of campers waiting to register/a missing washer on one of the shower taps/an unleashed dog barking viciously near the ocean, before Laura could position everything correctly and hoist the tent. It was the only one Minnie had ever seen with two storeys and a balcony. Then Minnie set off for a walk and Laura took the kids to the beach. Minnie had just time to cover five miles inland, get hot, thirsty, and tired, realise that if she'd gone five miles in one direction then another five awaited her on the way home, even though they were the five she'd already walked, when she spied the dust of a car coming toward her and wished it would turn out to be a nice safe lady who would offer a lift, have kids with her and therefore a cold drink.

"Want a Coke?" asked Laura, as Minnie clambered in beside Zebbee.

"Haven't had Coke for years," said Minnie appreciatively.

"Kids drink the most disgusting stuff," said Laura. "Any weird tastes you have, you blame on pregnancy before and the kids after. It got too windy on the beach so we decided to go round the coast to where the river meets the ocean. It's sheltered on the south side."

They swam in the ocean, they jumped the waves, they splashed in the rock pools, they gazed at the fish, they found one pool which was exactly Zebbee- and Son-size and warm as a hot tub with sand like caster sugar. Laura scraped oysters off the rocks with a sharp stone and they ate them, sand, sea water and all. God, they were delicious. They tasted of sunny days on the beach with laughing children and indulgent adults.

"You and Ingrid friends again?" asked Minnie. "If you were there for the birth 'n' all."

"Aw, yeah," said Laura. "We quarrelled, then we made it up. I mentioned one of Ingrid's ex-Johns to her current Loviebuttons and she got mad. She said I brought him up all the time. I only said what a dickhead the last one was, who used to get drunk and pick fights. But you know how it is: you can't talk about a previous boyfriend to the new one; they throw a jealous fit and sulk for the rest of the day."

"Do they?" said Minnie, fascinated and amazed. "We're always dying to know all about each other's previous. In case we've slept with them as well; in case their ex's have slept with our ex's; in case somebody is somebody else's acupuncturist; in case our ex is someone they fancy; in case everyone is invited to the party and they want to know who's who."

"Sounds a bit too cosy for me," said Laura.

"Better than losing someone just because you're not sleeping with them any more," said Minnie.

"You still friends with Genevieve then?" asked Laura.

"I never want to see her again for the rest of my life," said Minnie fervently.

"Hrm," said Laura. "You're no different from the rest of us."

"Hrm," echoed Minnie.

"But you keep telling me you are."

"Do you know there's a world movement toward homogeneity?"

"What's that? Something you do to milk?"

"It means everyone is getting more like everyone else."

"Eating the same breakfast cereal, watching the same TV programme at the same time each night, telling the same joke?"

"Like that."

"Most people want to be treated as unique individuals."

"They want to be treated as unique individuals who wear the right clothes and buy the right brand of ice cream, just like all the other unique individuals who watch the same commercials. I mean," Minnie added, waxing eloquent, "what's the first thing a mother does when her newborn baby is handed to her by the midwife?"

"Sees is it a boy or a girl," said Laura with a practiced eye on her own offspring, now neck-deep in sand like characters in a late-night play.

"Oh, no," said Minnie, "the midwife tells her as soon as the little thing gets out, 'You have a fine baby boy/girl, Mrs. Thingy.' No, the mother checks to see that the baby has all its fingers and toes to make sure it will be like everyone else."

"To be sure it's not handicapped," Laura protested. "That's only normal."

"It's all only normal," Minnie sighed. "Normality: the height, length, and breadth of our ambitions."

Laura's fine baby boy/girls were now busy holding each other's heads underwater to see how long they could stay there without drowning. She felt it her duty as their mother to put an end to the infant experiment; it might warp their enquiring minds for life, but at least it would keep them alive. They were not, as it turned out, unduly perturbed, only rather breathless for a while. But perhaps a probing therapist would dredge out the story twenty or thirty years later—"the bitter moment when my mother forced my head out of the water. I've been addicted to Perrier ever since." Only therapy can discover these things.

"There was one woman I slept with recently..." Minnie said, oblivious of the warping of vulnerable psyches taking place before her.

"How recently?" Laura enquired curiously.

"Few days ago, why?"

"Mum said she thought you'd found someone."

"Mothers always know."

This was an afternoon for oysters and rock pools. Minnie did not wish to discuss her mother. There was probably a time in her life when her mother had saved her from drowning too. One never gets over these indignities.

"Anyway, this woman, Nea, she came, and when she came she was moaning and groaning and then she called out, 'Ranier,' which is the name of her ex-lover."

"Strewth," said Laura. "How embarrassing. What did you do?"

"I burst out laughing. I mean, it has its funny side."

"Reckon that's easier for us," said Laura. "If a girl cries out her boyfriend's name in bed, she doesn't have to worry about getting it wrong. One way or another, he's bound to be a John."

"Something to be said for homogeneity, then," said Minnie.

This time they both laughed.

"So where is Nea? Why don't you invite her to John's party?"

"She's Californian," shrugged Minnie. "She lives in San Francisco."

"Oh Minnie," said Laura, with half an eye on the large shell Son had found, in case the occupant proved to be in residence and came out and bit him. "The last one was either schizophrenic or manic-depressive and the new one lives twelve thousand miles away. Why don't you find someone nice and local who'll treat you right?"

"Why don't I find someone nice and local who'll treat me right? Know the formula, Laura? Because if you do, you'll make a mint."

"Why don't you go and live in San Francisco, then?" asked Laura. It was fun, now that her own life was sorted out into an ordered if boring pattern, to make wild plans for Minnie. Soon, she supposed, she'd be living through her children. No, she wouldn't. What nonsense. But so easy to slip into with all those dissatisfied housewife stories on the TV. "Darling, I'm leaving you. I need to get in touch with the inner me." They hadn't had inner me's, her and Moira, when they were little.

"Because I'd have to get married or they wouldn't let me stay." Minnie was answering the question Laura had forgotten she'd asked.

"Married?" repeated Laura blankly. "Can women marry in California? I guess if they can do it anywhere, they'd be doing it there."

"Not to a woman, Laura," said Minnie. "To a man."

"You? Marry a man? But you can't," Laura was shocked.

"A marriage of convenience."

Laura imagined Minnie married, leaning on the arm of a charming young man, herself and Ingrid as bridesmaids. No. She could picture Minnie as the groom. She could not picture her as the bride.

"Oh," said Laura. Then she thought for awhile. "If you have to have babies too, so they'll let you stay—babies of convenience, I mean—then you can give them to me to adopt."

"Why, thank you, Laura," said Minnie solemnly. "I think that's one of the nicest things anyone has ever said to me."

She meant it. While someone else might be implying that she was incapable of bringing up children properly, Laura, Minnie was certain, simply knew that no baby would ever be convenient and that she was well established to look after a third. Laura had a thoughtful look on her face which said that she was even now planning which room Minnie's child should have.

It was hot in the tent and stuffy. Zebbee had insisted that the zip be closed against the bat-black night. Minnie's sleeping bag was a plastic sachet of offal boiling in a saucepan. Coated in sweat, Minnie kicked at the sachetskin and the sleeping bag bunched at her feet like trodden grapes. She snorted, snorkeled and turned over; repeated the series in the opposite direction, a corkscrew pursuing a rotten cork deeper and deeper into the bottle. She was standing on the pavement outside her flat in London. Beloved objects were flying through the window and smashing at her feet: her cassette recorder, her collection of opera tapes which disemboweled themselves in the road, her freezer full of gooseberry fools, even the bath oysters bounced off her boot and landed in the gutter with the bath octopi. Genevieve appeared from behind the curtain, panga in hand, shouting, "Think you can lock me out? You close the door on me, I'll come in the window. You bolt the window, I'll crawl down the chimney. You cut the branches off the chestnut tree, I'll shin up the drainpipe. But I'll come, and I'll keep on coming." "You do that," Minnie shouted back. "You shin up the drainpipe. But do it because you like drainpipes, or because you like shins. Here's the keys, Sweet Sugar Heart, I've signed the tenancy over to you and you can spend all day long looking for ways to get into what's already yours. As for me, I do not dwell in your house anymore." Genevieve loomed at the window, her face purple and yellow with bruises, puffed up with drugs, a red scab over her eye; she stared out at Minnie and her face melted back to the one Minnie had loved better than all others; then Genevieve jumped and a sheet of glass cut through her body severing every artery. Before Genevieve's arteries could fold into Ingrid's severed foot, before Beryl could shrug over Minnie's violated body, "You should have been wearing your bathers," Minnie was awoken by a loud hooting. She lay on her back in her navy blue pyjamas, in the hot salt bath that was her body, gazing at the plastic green above her and listening to the soft breathing all around. The sleep of small children is a comforting sleep. Minnie's heart slowed to a thud, calm but wide awake. She crawled through the tent flap, then rezipped against Zebbee's bats.

The hoot came again, louder, nearer now. Minnie got to her feet. It was cool in the fresh air; she breathed in softly through her nose so she could smell the tang of the night cactus, then great mouthfuls: enormous gulps of air taken for the pleasure of being alive and free. She yearned for the sight and spray of the ocean. And the ocean was there, the other side of those sand dunes. Minnie set off, walking, then striding faster and faster until she was running hell for leather over the dunes, over the beach, filled with longing for the vastness of the water below, the vastness of heaven above. At last she stood with her feet in the waves, her hair in the wind and the horizon beckoning everywhere she looked. The moon was bright, so bright that Minnie wondered whether it had indeed been full the previous night, it seemed not to have waned at all. The odd hooting caught her ear again and she bent her gaze away from the stars and out to sea. The moon shone a platinum path leading to the cleft between the two black raven rocks; it was from that direction that the hooting came.

Minnie could not walk on water but the moonlit path was a causeway, a living bridge, and Minnie trod on the backs of a million luminescent sea creatures gathered by some force, some great joy in each other's presence. Without a backward glance, her second thoughts echoing her first and urging them on, Minnie crossed the causeway with the stumbling speed, the weak-kneed urgency of a woman going to meet a lover she has never seen but wants more than anything else in the world. She reached the black rock, slipping and sliding on the blanket of seaweed which swept its volcanic surface like long green hair. Under her bare feet little blisters in the bladder wrack popped, squirting a spray of salt water at her ankles. The light, porous quality of the boulder she grasped to pull herself up surprised her. The earth round there was limestone, no volcanic eruptions recorded in the area. Were they due for a new one?

What she saw once she'd achieved the summit surprised her even more, for there, anchored amid the chopping waves, was a yacht. It flew under the ensign of the black raven on violet ground, upon its prow was painted the name "Natalie Barney." Minnie could hear Zebbee announcing solemnly, "That's my Dad's boat," herself laughing with Zebbee-like delight. She sat on the black rock and gazed at the yacht. She sat like a woman who has waited a month, two months, six, hovering round her own letterbox each day, accosting postmen in the street, accosting people who are not postmen, watching people who are postmen climb the stairs to other people's letterboxes, watching people who have received post open their letters in the street; she sat like a woman who has waited, impatiently, and who has received and who prolongs the pleasure of receiving by placing the letter on the towel rail and brewing a cup of tea before looking at the contents. She is not caught by sudden fear that the letter will prove unworthy of the wait. She knows the letter will contain everything she wanted. She knows it will say, *Come. I must meet you.* Minnie knew, gazing at the yacht from the black rock, that she had been waiting for it, and for she who sailed upon it, all her life; that everything she had ever done had been leading inexorably to this moment. Therefore she savoured the moment. The sea spray blew in her face, unprotected by the rock; the exhilaration of the waves swirled at her feet; from over the water sounded the five notes of *The Magic Flute,* which Minnie had mistaken for a bird hooting. She listened; one, two, three, four, five.

"And now," she decided, "I will swim to that yacht and meet my destiny."

There was no question of slipping into the water and striking out in a firm breaststroke; she had only to let go the rock and the waves would pick her up and deposit her in the drink where she might sink or swim surrounded by their infinite indifference. She tugged off her pyjamas, which would have filled with water and hampered her movements, then tied them to the rock, as one who would mark her passing through an alien place. They whipped in the wind like twin navy flags. She swam at first as one might walk through crowded streets a distance too far to run, with an errand urgent and possible, requiring a firm and steady pace. But the distance between her and the yacht did not seem to be narrowed, though she moved further from the black rocks with each thrashing leg and flailing arm. Was a rip swelling and sweeping her out to sea? How close would she come to the yacht? Close enough to call? Close enough to wave? Must she watch the green light on its starboard for five years, bobbing in the water? It was cold. Cold and bracing, cold and terrifying. Her body was owned by this boundless, bloodless, nerveless entity which need not even say "jump" but threw her in the air, turned her round, plunged her into its salt depths and spun her out again, upon whom her pummelling fists made no impression. One thought kept her buoyant: that one had died from time to time, but not for love, and since she did this all for love, it could not drown her. So she swam, when she could, steering a path between the troughs and peaks, the perpetual motion, diving through the breakers to keep some sense of level progress. Thoughts entered her head from nowhere. She had fled London and Genevieve, taken refuge in her mother's house only to flee from there and on to Laura's . This headlong leap toward Natalie had the inevitability of a body thrown from a tall building, but was it hope or fear, this raging impulse which it pleased Minnie to name "destiny"? She longed for peace and safety, and she sought it in the everchanging sea.

The caffeine still surged through Laura's veins as she sat in front of the tent, gazing at the stars. What if? What if? What if? Minnie had still not returned from her midnight bathe. Should Laura go and look for her? Zebbee's silken head lay on her mother's lap, her small feet in her mother's warm, caressing hand. Laura could have woken Zebbee and all three of them might have bathed; the waves would be so beautiful, their luminous foam frothing in the moonlight. But inside the tent Son stirred and coughed a little in his sleep. The world becomes a different place when your first child is born and you find yourself that institution: Mother. This is a commonplace of responsibility and woman's role. What they do not say is that the world changes again when your second child is born, for then there are two of them but still only one of you. You are outnumbered by your own motherhood. It was easier, Laura had found it easier, to mother after the second, but so much harder to unmother even for a few hours. Oh, John had been as helpful and delighted with two as one; it wasn't that. This was about her, not him. Minnie was out there, having a good time, and Laura wanted to talk to her.

Minnie was lost in infinity: unseen, unnecessary, irrelevant. It is not, after all, the feet which distinguish men from women, though this is a good rule of thumb (or toe) for transsexual-spotters. No. It is the attitude, the feeling each has about being absolutely alone which is the real test. Men imagine, when walking in some isolated beauty spot alone at dusk, that women do not enjoy themselves when by themselves. This is because men more frequently encounter women in groups and not upon their solitary walks. They wonder at this, between a contemplation of the view and an address to the board, and conclude that women are not there because they have no wish to be there. Men do not imagine they themselves might be the cause of women's absence; that a lonely twilight hillside with a solitary man is not a place where a woman can be alone. The man himself begins to think of supper, of expounding upon the beauties of nature snugly surrounded by four walls and central heating. If the loneliness and hillside continues for too long, he begins to feel a kind of awe, a dread, an unaccustomed insignificance; he feels the stars up in the firmament shine neither for, nor despite him, but are oblivious of his small progress by their light. It is a kind of terror which besets him now; he longs for a homely woman's face, a face to tell him that he does exist. It was, on the other hand, the very absence of this man which granted Minnie her longed-for dalliance with infinity.

At the end of this long journey into night Minnie's numb fingers grasped the metal ladder which gave access to the yacht. She was, she noticed, blue with cold, which was at least interesting. Her skin stung so much she wondered had she swum through a swarm of jellyfish until she realised it was the prickling of extreme cold and a reassertion of red over blue. She felt both utterly exhausted—the energy required to bat an eyelid was energy she resented expending—and a tremendous vitality. More than anything in the world she wanted a hot bath. A thought at odds with the ponderous truth of the waves. Was this hysteria? Minnie wondered, like a concerned onlooker.

As she boarded the yacht, Minnie had the strangest presentiment that she would find herself once again walking up the driveway, past the car with its "Love Your Mother" and "Fat Jewish Lesbian" bumper stickers, the thriving velvety geraniums, and onto the porch to dally a while behind the woodpile. She almost looked around for her suitcase. Was even her subconscious a product of American imperialism? She expected at any moment to be declared the fifty-first state. But there she was, naked aboard a yacht, wet and cold and expecting a fatted calf. She knew nothing practical about boats like: where do they keep the woolly jumpers and where is the hot soup for the swimmer come in from the sea? She had the usual layman's useless commonplaces: "Port out, starboard home" and "There is no red port left in the bottle." Finally, her confidence gave out and since there were no facts whatever to boost her up, save the five-word letter and the enigmatic fax, gravity took its tithe and deposited her, a small puddle on the deck, where she lay at the mercy of whoever, and whatever, came across her.

She did not stay there long for the swaying and keeling of the boat caused the puddle to trickle down a runnel and collect on the ceiling of the cabin below. Before she could turn into a stalactite and finish her life a geological curiosity, a voice she had begun to recognise called her name aloud with warmth and not a little satisfaction.

"Minnie," Nea glowed, "I thought I'd find you here. And now I get to bring you back to life."

Nea's method of defrosting and revivifying Minnie has been described earlier. You probably remember: it begins with hugging her very tight, proceeds with kissing and biting her neck. In this case, however, the hugs were chaste and medicinal. The door swung open; Minnie and Nea were wrapped respectably in towels, giggling because they felt like ghosts in shrouds and because Nea had sneaked in a chaste and medicinal backrub.

Before she looked directly upon the face of she who is famous simply for being a lesbian, Minnie studied the air around the woman's body, as though a careful appraisal of where Natalie was not were the best foundation for seeing where she did stand. By this method it did not take long to realise that another woman stood by her side.

"...looks like an effete long-haired girl." said Beryl's voice. "Sickly and graceful. Like a spot of gardening would do him no harm at all. And I don't mean any of that decadent, opium-eating, tortoise-killing nonsense with the lilies and white violets. Digging turnips, lifting potatoes, turning the compost. Lets me landscape lettuces up in Dalkeith because they have such pretty pale green leaves, though I have to steer clear of anything robust and vulgar like cos or webb. When I suggested a vegetable garden he said magnanimously, 'Granted. Whatever you like provided it's black.' I explained that unless it was an aubergine, a black vegetable was a vegetable in process of decomposition. His eyes lit up."

IN THE BEATING OF HER HEART

⇒ 10 ⇐

Well, my dear," said an ordinary, pleasant-sounding voice with an ordinary pleasant American accent. "You look like a drowned rat. Would you like a hot bath? There is so little one can offer people now that the necessities of life are mass produced. The great gush of naked maidens in need of saving from the foggy foggy dew has decidedly fallen off."

Minnie looked at the mouth from which the voice issued. It was a pleasant, ordinary bow with full red lips, smiling decorously. The nose above it was high-bridged and fleshy, the nostrils seemed naturally to flair. The cheeks were Slavonically bony, a healthy pink flush caressing them as though Miss Barney were a little out of breath, called to the door in the heat of some domestic task: kneading dough, perhaps, or making batter. A downward glance at the cleanly tapered fingernails, the soft palms glimpsed behind the tender curl of the fingers declared that no household flour be-smirched these hands though some regular, even hearty, physical exercise maintained their elasticity and dexterity.

From the hands, held in front of Miss Barney's formal grey suit, Minnie's eye wandered over the somewhat portly figure, the soft

rise of breast checked by the firm bodice, up to the very determined lines of the neck, half hidden in the folds of a silk lavallière.
Only then did Minnie dart her attention to Miss Barney's eyes.
They were warm and kindly, and piercingly blue, but not obviously sexy.

"Yes, that is to say, no. The bottom's dropped right out of naked
maidens," stuttered Minnie idiotically.

Miss Barney smiled indulgently. "I'll have them run a bath for
you."

She disappeared from the cabin. Minnie turned for the first time
toward Miss Barney's companion who stood stiff and pouting, like
Son about to hurl himself upon the ground, kick the floor and bite
the carpet.

"You got here," said the thin blond pout.

"You told me to hurry," said Minnie.

"I wanted to get it over with," said Miss Pout. "Natalie's affairs are
a complete bore from every point of view save hindsight." Nea sat
up and nudged Minnie in the ribs. "It's been fun, Minnie, real fun.
I've had a nice day, ya know, but I got a heavy dose of separation
anxiety from San Francisco and I think I better get back to my
roots. Like, nobody round here would even know what rebirth
acupuncture is, let alone which star signs are best suited to it."

Renée Vivien surveyed Nea with eyes like cold wet fish.

"What's that?" she asked, glacially.

"Oh, that's Nea," said Minnie. "She's from California."

"It's the process by which you relive your own birth trauma,"
said Nea. "They stick little wooden needles in pressure points all
over your body, then they set light to them. You do a lot of con-
trolled breathing. Helps you let go of the dead wood you've been
carrying around."

Minnie was too awed by her surroundings to enquire whether
your mother was required to undergo your birth a second time as
well, for the sake of authenticity.

"They stick lighted needles in your bare flesh and you are re-born?" said Renée Vivien.

"Sure," said Nea.

"Acupuncture is an old tradition of the Orient," Renée Vivien informed her.

"Okay," said Nea, "you're right. So it's a bit more complicated than I said...."

"I would like to know all about it," said Renée Vivien.

"I'd love to tell you. I'd just love to. I mean that most sincerely, but I don't think I have time..." said Nea, feeling increasingly awkward. Renée Vivien was staring at her with the white fixity of trout's eyes about to pop out of the skull in the heat of the grill pan.

"You have all the time in the world," Renée Vivien assured her.

"Right on," said Nea, "I'm right with you there. I believe in taking time. I mean, we are steamed through the pressure cooker of the rat race. We are the purée of a decadent society. I mean, America is *through*, totally degenerate. We have to start dancing to a different drummer, a different drumbeat." All the time she was speaking Nea was edging closer to the door, the white sheet tied firmly at her shoulder like an Indonesian sarong.

"You look like the altar maid of an Eastern temple," pronounced Renée Vivien, taking hold of her elbow as she passed. "I believe we have much in common," she continued. "Tell me, do you write poetry?"

"Oh, all the time," said Nea, squirming, "literally, all the time. Believe me."

"I myself have translated the complete works of Psappha," said Renée Vivien, a streak of satisfaction passing under her heavy-hooded eyelids.

"Yeah?" said Nea. "I'm off my head with excitement for you."

Renée Vivien acknowledged the compliment with a slight bow.

"I have a room," she announced. "We will not be disturbed."

"I couldn't," said Nea emphatically.

Renée Vivien brushed objection aside. "You will find in it everything your heart can desire. I had it gift-wrapped and forwarded from Paris, 1900." Pride flickered across Renée Vivien's prominent brow. "We will listen to the music of the Aeolian harp."

"Is that wimmin's music?" asked Nea, "I really don't go for rock. That male, thrusting beat, that rutting pelvis."

"The Aeolian harp is plucked by the pure vibrations of our sister, the wind," replied Renée Vivien gravely. "We will fill our nostrils with the scent of incense. You will recite your poetry, and I will show you my Buddhas."

"Oh boy, do I wanna see your Buddhas," said Nea. "Girl, I am wetting my pants I am so fascinated by your Buddhas."

And with that Nea Naomi High Priestess Orisha of the Crossroads and Renée Vivien, poet and translator, passed out of earshot.

Leaving Minnie with Natalie Clifford Barney.

"Your bath's ready," called Miss Barney.

The bathroom to which Minnie was led was so spacious, so high-ceilinged, so elegantly windowed, so marbled, so well appointed with salts and powders in blue glass bottles (glass which would glint so prettily with the morning sun shining upon it, though on this bathroom no sun shone), the towels so soft to the cheek and enveloping, the bath itself so like an intimate tongue. As she lounged and stretched, pouring soap upon soap, heaping foam upon foam, Minnie wondered at the silence. But "silence" was too general. This was a most specific lack, an absence. Something she expected, nay, took for granted in these circumstances. She looked around. The hot tap was dripping, little droplets forming on its metal rim till they became fat and soft as juicy grapes, all rolling into one and tumbling into the water. The foam, heaped over her body like whipped cream, crackled and popped in her ears like a breakfast cereal. The shutters rattled in the same light gust which, seconds later, was to stroke her neck, leaving in its wake a trail of goosebumps and a not unpleasurable shiver, as though on some hot day an icicle had stalked her spine. Ah, music. It was music that was missing. Minnie's baths were accompanied by opera and surely it was *The Magic Flute* which had guided her to this place. Perhaps, in doing that, it had done its job, its duty by her, and was now playing somewhere else, for someone else. Perhaps all baths past were mere precursors of this wet tongue, this eight-handed octopus, this froth-and-foam, skin-tingling grand luxe.

Natalie knocked at the door.

"I've had them rustle up something for you to eat," she called. "I'm sure you are hungry.

Minnie felt a twinge of panic and incomprehension. Wasn't Natalie supposed to slip into the bath alongside her? Natalie rarely did what she was supposed to. Breakfast, on the other hand, once Minnie had stilled her breathing, gulped a sufficiency of gulps, calmed her beating heart, and commanded her legs to quit shaking, was a good idea.

The toast had not got cold; it smelled warm and yeasty. It was spread with butter and a thin layer of gentleman's relish. The orange juice was freshly squeezed and the tea was Minnie's favourite, Darjeeling. Under a green china cover sat a hot plate full of bacon and eggs, fried sausage and tomato. Miss Barney took up position on the other side of the table and watched Minnie eat.

"I do so love a healthy appetite," she said with something like regret.

"Aren't you having anything?" asked Minnie. "Shall I pour you some orange juice?"

"Oh, I can't drink that stuff," said Miss Barney. "I have a special tipple of my own in the drinks cabinet."

She strolled to the icebox and ran her eye over the shelf, over a series of bottles labelled, in faded brown ink, "Type O," "Type A," "Rhesus+," "Rhesus−."

"Rhesus positive," she murmured. "Think I'm developing an allergy to that. Good glug of '0' should do the trick."

She returned to the breakfast table with a large glass of thick red liquid. Minnie glanced at it, wondering. Looked like a Bloody Mary but there was no smell of tomatoes. Blood oranges, Minnie decided. She wanted Natalie to make a move soon, swiftly and irrevocably. But the irrevocable gestures—marriage, maternity—are not for vampires. Minnie felt she had known Miss Barney all her life, that when once she held her in her arms she would declare, "You're not strange, I know you," for the weight and size of Miss Barney's body would be as familiar as her own.

"That's better," said Miss Barney, smacking her lips. "Now if you've finished we could sit somewhere more comfortable."

Minnie followed her glance. The most prominent item in the room was a low narrow bench which looked extremely hard despite the velvet padding cushioning it.

"Not there," said Miss Barney quickly, "I wouldn't sit on that if I were you."

"Why not?" asked Minnie innocently.

"Oh," said Miss Barney, "it's ugly, uncomfortable, and inhibiting. These dual-purpose furnishings end up inadequate to either role."

"Dual purpose?" repeated Minnie. "This doubles as a…"

"You can sleep in it during the day," Miss Barney explained, "if there's a guest staying over."

"Oh," said Minnie, "a sofabed."

"Coffin, I think, is the word you are searching for," said Miss Barney primly.

"You sleep in a coffin?" said Minnie. "Sounds more than a little morbid. 'The grave's a fine and private place but none, I think, do there embrace.'"

Miss Barney was profoundly irritated. Poetry bored her and she hated Marvell and his coy mistress. She knew that Minnie knew. She knew, what's more, that Minnie was consumed with curiosity and a frankly sexual fascination. She also knew that Minnie would not bring the subject up herself, as though the very word would sully her pretty mortal lips. Minnie expected an itemised confession followed by grand, physical passion, to be initiated by Miss Barney, which she could enjoy without committing herself if it "didn't take." She would swim home afterwards and declare to the world that she knew she was normal because she'd tried it with a vampire and had lain there simply yearning for a mortal. Miss Barney had half a mind to stab her saber-toothed canines into the silly twit's neck and suck all the blood from her body. But the freezer was already full and Renée had made her join the League Against Blood Sports. Miss Barney suppressed a sudden sigh. Minnie's interest in her stemmed entirely from her books; how could she tell the young woman she hadn't written a thing in fifty years?

"Miss Barney," said Minnie, interrupting her host's reverie.

"Oh really," said Miss Barney, "since you have already stripped me naked with your eyes, I think the time is well past due for you to call me Natalie. Don't you?"

"Yes," said Minnie, blushing to the base of her skull. "Natalie, do you have any communicable diseases?"

She said this in exactly that tone of voice in which one usually requests an aspirin. Natalie was halfway to the bathroom cabinet before she turned and said, "Communicable? What, pray, is an in-communicable disease? One which doesn't bear speaking of, like piles? Or one which one doesn't dare to speak its name, like ho-mosexuality?"

Minnie was about to object that piles were called hæmorrhoids these days and homosexuality had been struck off the disease list, but she experienced the now familiar sensation of dizziness which meant either that a situation was beyond her or that she would shortly find herself in San Francisco. She decided to throw a rope out and pull herself back to the subject.

"I mean there are some diseases which are commonly passed from one person to another, during sexual intercourse for ex-ample," she said.

"Oh," said Natalie with a flicker of amusement. "Do you carry a list of all the possibilities so I can tick off which ones I have now, which ones I picked up in Tangiers, to which I have developed an immunity and which ones I ought to try and contract so I won't catch them in pregnancy?"

Minnie was not so easily put off. "Have you had an AIDS test recently?"

At this Natalie threw back her head and laughed. "I'm a vampire. How could I have AIDS?"

"It's not a laughing matter."

"I'm not mocking the pain of the victims," said Natalie gently.

Minnie looked pious. The great gale of laughter had, however, unlocked some of the knots of nervousness Natalie would never admit to. Her life had changed almost unrecognisably the day she became a vampire. They fled from her who sometime did her seek. Surrounded by friends and lovers, ever ready with a witty sally, what had happened to her since 1972? And to those friends, vampires themselves now for the most part, living on in isolated corners of the world, looking back with bitterness perhaps to the days they had spent together in the Temple of Friendship, wishing they had spent them otherwise, accruing wealth, good health, material things, which would be more use now than memories? Of them all, only Renée remained with Natalie, her first great love, but love had died fifty years ago and their current ties were clear and commonplace: Renée needed an attentive nursemaid and Natalie needed Renée's money. For Natalie's inheritance died with her and even her bed, which should have been a holy grail of lovers, was sold ignominiously at a yard sale. Whereas Renée had that uncanny knack with stocks and shares.

All this Natalie had piled up to say to Minnie. She wanted to speak after the long silence. Something in Minnie's letter, the attention to her books, the glittering comprehension, had made Natalie believe that Minnie could bring her back to life, inspire her with desire to write again. This vampirehood was living death: Minnie would be her Lisbon *Traviata,* for like Maria Callas, Natalie would perform again more stupendous, more beloved than before.

But what they had in common was Minnie's present and Natalie's past. How could this meeting stir anything more than nostalgia in Natalie? If only Minnie could make some effort toward a bridge, some recognition that a bridge was needed. Natalie ploughed on politely, hoping that the right moment would come.

"I have lost some good friends to the AIDS virus," she said.

"I thought you said vampires couldn't get it," Minnie persevered stubbornly, no more able to change the subject than Natalie.

"Certain sections of the population were virtually wiped out."

"You just contradicted yourself."

"Minnie, you ought to know from popular movies on the subject that virtually wiping out a vampire is simply not good enough. As long as our hearts still beat we can restock the old arteries and make the most stupendous comebacks. It gives us pause for thought, that's all."

"I don't follow."

Minnie, clad in the towel in which she had consumed breakfast, lounged on the sofa as provocatively as she could. The small indecencies of naked thigh and flash of naked breast were at best a television memory, but she arranged herself in a makeshift display. Manifestly it was not working; Natalie patted her ankle with an absent-minded regularity. Minnie was reminded of the exercise where one strives to pat one's head with one's left hand while rubbing one's stomach with one's right. Natalie found the lounging suggestiveness an irksome cliché.

"...some things change. I bought that coffin as a sex toy, had myself delivered to Renée in it. Now, with the new light-proofing, it's just a piece of furniture as necessary and as unaesthetic as your English wainscots."

"I thought it was a vital piece of your equipment. I thought the first rays of the dawn's early light would transfix you, shrivel your body to graveyard mould."

"Don't gloat, dear. I understood in these liberal times a more tolerant attitude toward minorities was fashionable."

"You're out of date; liberals are being trampled under a stampede of convention. And even old-guard liberals might draw the line at an oppressed minority who demanded the blood of a virgin every night."

"You never know. They seem to have accepted the removal of eighty million clitorises on grounds of holy tradition."

Minnie made a dismissive grunt, about as convincing as a mouse caught under the paw of a cat, an Ancient Briton sneering at Caesar, "Yeah, you and whose army?"

"Most people would rather die than turn vampire," she said.

"And die they undoubtedly will," said Natalie, "most unsatisfactory."

"Because you can't feed off them?" Minnie wondered suddenly whether Natalie was hungry.

"To put it bluntly, parents can't become vampires."

"Whyever not?" Minnie demanded, as though Natalie had just refused them car phones or state welfare payments.

"Breeding."

"Babies?"

"Babies. The vampire, male or female, is irreversibly sterile. The DNA code is altered by the intrusion of vampire blood into the nuclei; those parts of the DNA spiral dealing with heredity and propagation are chemically altered toward immortal personal survival traits, as opposed to species survival."

Down among the Buddhas and the incense, Renée and Nea were getting along famously. Renée had offered Nea a glass of thin green tea and, since the flavour was brackish, the aroma unpleasant, Nea had assumed it was free of any claim to stimulating the taste buds and must therefore be homoeopathic. She had drunk it down with restrained enthusiasm. She felt very much at home in that room draped with heavy oriental hangings, seated on the low

cushions which, apart from an ancient samovar, were the sole furnishings. The flickering candles reminded her of the rituals common to the San Francisco Bay. At any moment, she felt, Renée
would put a new whale song on her CD player, arrange her crystals in a powerful hexagon on a piece of black silk, and commence
summoning the energies of the geological substrata. Renée was, she
was sure, a natural at channelling. It came as no surprise to Nea
when Renée, pacing the room like a captive spirit, declared,
"Sometimes I feel as though I had strayed into this modern age. I
believe I am an exile from Mytilene, my eyes filled with memories
of that unknown world. My pagan soul seeks its harmonious
motherland in vain. I am of all ages except the present day."

"Oh I know," said Nea. "In my past life I thought I was the high
priestess of an Inca temple. I went to this really terrific guy, an
intense medium, a real healer. He passed his hands over me, two
inches from my body, you know, polarity healing, and I felt this
sensation of total peace in every fibre. He told me I was blocking,
in denial, you know. That something bad had happened to me in
a previous life and I was still grieving for it. Well, it took a high
colonic enema to get it all out. All the shit I'd been collecting. And
it turned out I wasn't the high priestess at all. I was the victim and
the priestess ate my entrails as a sacrifice to the Sun God."

Renée smiled soulfully, closing her heavy hooded eyes, "That can
be very upsetting to a sensitive organism."

"Now I'm a Yoruban priestess," said Nea.

"I'm a Hellenic pagan," said Renée. "I was a Catholic..."

"Oh don't give me your lapsed Catholic story," said Nea. "We've
read the book. Or your Catholic girlhood. I know all about it: you
bathed in a long white nightie in the dark and they told you to
wash between your legs very quickly, one wipe, with a facecloth,
just before you got out so you wouldn't contract impure thoughts."

"That's not the case," said Renée, remembering her hasty
Catholic conversion three days before her last death.

"Yeah, I know," said Nea, "I'm trivialising. It was a hard life but kind of sensuous too and it instilled in you a lasting sense of values plus how dare I criticise another woman's ethnic background. Right? Well hey, I'm not a WASP either. I'm a Jew. I don't even eat shellfish. To me a prawn is an insect." Renée was lost in reverie.

"If it is true that the soul is reborn in several human forms, I was once born on Lesbos. I was only a sickly and graceless child when an older companion led me into the temple where Psappha invoked the Goddess. The luminous memory will never fade through the years nor yet through the centuries."

"Honey," said Nea, "you got any crystals?"

Renée turned toward her as though returning from a place long distant. "Crystals of what?" she asked. "Are you suggesting that all this is a drug-induced hallucination?"

"No way," said Nea, "but you seem pretty hung up on this Sappho chick…"

"Psappha," Renée corrected her. Renée's ears could hear the absence of a mute "p" at a thousand paces.

"This Sappa dame," Nea continued, "and I want to tell you that I am right with you, every step of the way. And if you want to enter into deep psychic communication with your spirit guide, I'll be only too happy to provide the third angle to ground the cosmic forces of the triangle. But you need crystals." Renée studied Nea's face and, seeing only avid curiosity, left the room in search of what was needed. She returned before Nea had time to complete her reading of the *New Woman's I-Ching*. Nea never travelled without a set. Renée stood in the doorway a moment, looking triumphant. She strode in, holding a bulky something in the skirts of her toga. Into Nea's lap she poured a fountain of glass which sparked blue, red and green flames as it fell.

"Sweet shit," yelled Nea under the crystal cloudburst, "this is the most beautifully cut stuff I ever saw in my life. They're flawless. My God, they look like diamonds. Wherever did you get them?"

"I will be able to speak to Psappha?" Renée asked anxiously.

"With these babies to channel the energies we could put a call through to God. Don't you feel the power pulsating?"

"I do."

"So tell me your secret. Where did you dig them up?"

"They come from the Octagonal Gallery. I dismantled the chandelier."

Minnie was now snoring so loud and so nasally you could have built a railroad to Peking on the soundwaves. She was having a dream about a demonstration. Thousands of nuclear families had taken to the streets and were waving placards saying "Count Dracula Was Our Forefather" and "Civil Rights for Parents: We Demand to Be Vampires Too."

The noise of Minnie's snores reached Balga, four hundred miles away. Milly felt embarrassed, attempted to cover the sound by humming a little tune.

"Pa pa pa," she hummed, "pa pa pa," growing louder and more determined as the snores crescendoed.

"I wish you wouldn't," cawed the parrot crossly.

Milly was mortified. She and the parrot had, she thought, reached an understanding. The parrot had told her how helpless it felt, born and bred for captivity, yet constantly yearning for the open bush, the pleasure of swooping down in a flock of other parrots upon some unsuspecting fruit orchard and ripping every tree to shreds. It asked her to imagine how humiliated a parrot might feel on being taught to gabble "Pretty Polly, pretty Polly" and "Who's a good boy, then" when no one it knew was called Polly and the inhabitants of the household were uniformly unattractive. As for being a good boy, it had told her, it would have much preferred to be a thoroughly evil parrot. And Milly had told the parrot how perfectly ghastly it was to be the alter ego of a lesbian feminist, to be someone else's conscience, to deliberate on worldly affairs using her frame of reference, no matter what your own leanings might be.

"I don't know how they decide which alter ego goes with which conscience," she had moaned. "I think they write everyone's name on little scraps of paper, throw them over the banisters and whichever scraps hit the ground at the same time they pair up for life. Just because you have the same specific density as a person does not mean that you want to spend all of your time with them, having their arguments and snubbing their friends."

After which they had sat a while in the comfortable silence of perfect accord. The world was a sad and bitter place and they were most hard done by.

"If you could come back to earth again after you die," said Milly dreamily, "and you could be anything, anything in the whole world, who would you come back as?"

The parrot thought for a long while, ticking over all the creatures, animate or otherwise, that it had ever envied. There was that exquisite blue glint in the old medicine bottle which was mistakenly thrown onto the compost heap. Did it want to come back as a blue glint? Or there was that lovely tune Beryl's John played sometimes, the parrot had never caught the name. Would it like to come back as "Po po po pom"? If the truth be known, the parrot felt rather parochial; the circumference of its worldly experience was that area of the globe which fell within a ten-yard radius of Beryl's front door, the perimeter being Beryl's garden fence. You saw a lot of life within that compass but, the parrot could not help feeling, there must be more outside.

"I would like to come back as a wild parrot," it said firmly.

"I would like to come back a full person and not an alter ego," said Milly.

They had looked at each other and felt the warm glow of a common bond. The parrot wondered. "Maybe," it thought, "maybe." Milly was a little incorporeal, but then some of its greatest loves had been on the skimpy side. The slide rule, the inflatable snake and the W.H. Smith bag had turned out, each in turn, to be all body and no brain, so maybe Milly, who was all mind, would prove to be just the thing. Milly, who had never been in love before, was taken by storm by this new emotion. She felt like singing. Something about an elusive creature in love with a parrot. Her agile mind came up with a splendid ragbag of songs celebrating kittens ("snowdrops on"), tigers ("I'm a tiger…"), alligators ("See you later alligator"), even vampires (*"In der Stille mit die Vampire,"*) but there was only one song she could think of that had any parrot associations. Thus when the nasal ferocity of Minnie's snores reached Balga, the tune which Milly hummed to block it out was, inevitably, "Pa pa pa; pa pa pa."

"I, I, I," she stammered, unsure what had angered the parrot, but certain an apology would help, were she able to get one out.

"That is my song," said the parrot soulfully. "It is not a little ditty to be hummed on a whim. For me that song is a hymn to life, to joy, to love."

When the parrot uttered the word "love," a thrill shot through Milly such as she had never before experienced. *"Voi che sapete che cosa é amor, donne vedete s'io l'ho nel cor."* Could this be love?

"Then," she asserted bravely, "my singing it is entirely appropriate."

The parrot knew now. A spirit might make an odd bedfellow, but better a kindred spirit than one more beautiful, inert lump.

"Oh pa, pa, pa," stammered Milly, intending to imbue the word "parrot" with all the loving tenderness it could contain.

"Pa pa pa," echoed the parrot in exultation.

And so they sang:

Parrot: Pa Pa Pa Pa Pa Pamillina
Milly: Pa Pa Pa Pa Pa Parrotina
Parrot: Are you now entirely mine?
Milly: Now I am entirely yours.
Parrot: Then be my darling turtle dove!
Milly: Then be my darling little parrot!
Parrot and Milly: What joy it will be, if the gods are kind to us,

and reward our love with children, such dear little children!

Parrot: First a little Parrotina!

Milly: Then a little Pamillina!

Parrot: Then another Parrotina!

Milly: Then another Pamillina!

Parrot and Milly: It is the highest of the emotions, if many Parrotinas and Pamillinas are to be their parents' blessing. It is the highest of the emotions, Parrotina! Pamillina!

Beryl tossed and turned in her sleep. She was dreaming about her list and crossing off the various family members as they disappeared from the travails of this world. Minnie was drowning in a midnight ocean; Laura and the kids were being seized by a giant raven who would carry them to its eyrie in a weird limestone formation; Ingrid, Lollipop, and the current John were getting caught in a flash flood up at Gunderdin; Beryl's own John was falling into a giant vat of shellfish whose claws he kept trying to measure; Laura's John was about to be overcome by the fumes of a new metal paint he was using to finish Mr. Vivien's portrait; Mr. Vivien's property was being impounded by a new ordinance outlawing v*****ism as undermining family values; Moira was getting engaged to a Russian sailor who would make an honest woman of her provided she never learn to speak Russian, for her great charm was that the sailor did not understand a single word she said. Then Beryl was alone in the world. Then she slept like the woman who has everything.

Beryl was rudely awakened by the screeching of the parrot and the voiceless but nonetheless powerful droning of Milly, who was as unmusical as her better half. The two creatures Beryl had neglected to finish off. Next time she dreamed she would be more comprehensive. The alarm clock on her night table poured her a consoling cup of tea, brushed her teeth, turned the radio on to

"Sounds of the Sixties" and told her it was 6:00 A.M. Time to drive down to Dalkeith and clear up after whatever revelries Mr. Vivien had enjoyed the night before. More dead tortoises and broken chandeliers, no doubt. Although officially a secretary, Beryl had agreed—for a substantial remuneration—to clean those rooms which the more superstitious domestics refused to enter. They complained that there was an old lady who haunted the place, slept in a coffin during the day and enticed hapless maidens to their doom. The domestics were people of the world: hapless maidens and haunting old ladies were an occupational hazard these days, and every single one of them had a tale to tell of an employer who slept in a hot water tank which would periodically spill over and bring the ceiling below down on someone's head, usually a small child with its whole life still before it, and compared with that a coffin was a nice, dry, cosy affair. But sleeping during the day, they drew the line at that. They did draw the line at that. It set a bad example to the tweeny maid who must get up before dawn and scrub the grates and polish the flags. Everyone should be out of bed by midday or their rooms could not be aired and unaired rooms were bad for a maid's complexion. It is well known that food consumed before noon has half the calories of food eaten later, that early risers are high achievers and those who rise will shine. One day Mr. Vivien and Beryl, both bored out of their minds by the complaints of the domestics, put their heads together and decided that Beryl would be responsible for the state of the Long Gallery, the Octagon, the marble staircase and Mr. Vivien's 1900 Room. Which is to say that Mr. Vivien made the decision and Beryl worked out how she might profit from it.

As she threw on an old cardigan, shuffled the keys, and headed for the carport, Beryl caught the last chorus of "Pa pa pa."

"Harrumph," she snorted uncharitably, "how can a parrot and an alter ego have a baby?"

Nevertheless her own caretaking streak was so strong, she left the Perth Metropolitan Phone Directory out on the kitchen counter, open at the display ad for the Perth Metropolitan Fertility Clinic. Let them sort it out.

The midnight call of the ravens came not for Minnie alone, she was simply in the most propitious place to respond. Laura had sat for some time in the tent flap, Zebbee's feet in her maternal hand. She had sighed. Laura had long suspected that the family's changed fortunes were entirely Beryl's doing. The arrival of Mr. Vivien had been too fortunate; blessed was nearer the mark. Minnie did not know about those days because she had not chosen to know, but they had been ragged, cheerless, and dreadful. Ingrid's accident had come out of nowhere. As accidents must. Beryl had lost her job, needing to be constantly on hand to Ingrid; her John had just finished his Ph.D. but there was as yet no money. And the dream house had nearly slipped through Laura's anxious fingers. Then something had happened, and they had agreed to call it Mr. Vivien. But who was he, exactly? A shadowy man who kept to himself and only ventured forth after sunset. A young blond financier, supernaturally good, a self-made millionaire who had money while everyone else had gone to the wall. But no one knew where Vivien had come from, he seemed to have no personal life though Beryl seemed to be in on his every move.

Laura lay Zebbee gently on the tent sheet, wrapping her lightly in a towel; it was a warm night. Influence was the key, it seemed. Beryl's John was bound to get a job once his Ph.D. was under his belt, but it was odd the police had contacted him, an ex-taxi driver without a particularly distinguished record. Ingrid's compensation too. Of course it was never in doubt, but the extent of the award made you imagine some benign and powerful hand behind the scenes. Laura thought a while, adding things up in her head, taking nothing away. If you are certain of something completely crazy, and convinced that it is, somehow, not crazy, does it make you certifiable, or does it make you right against tremendous odds? Laura shrugged to herself. There was no Mr. Vivien, Beryl had invented him, dressed him, bought him a house, spoke to the police and to the courts and to the property dealers in his voice. In their moment of need, Beryl had suddenly seen that all it took was influence, and she had gone out and got it. The place in Dalkeith was a tremendous confidence trick, but a trick which had worked, which was working every day.

Laura felt a twinge, a shiver down her back. Soon Beryl would dispense with Mr. Vivien and all his trappings, send him on somewhere else where his influence was unknown. It was frightening. Was it? And what exactly frightened Laura? Realising her adoptive mother's tremendous power? Beryl had never used it for herself, only for her loved ones. And Beryl had brought Minnie back. One day none of them had heard from her, the next there she was again with her suitcase and her funny ideas and her still unspoken sadness. Oh, there was the dream of a lover. Well, everyone dreamed of a lover, same as they dreamed up millionaires. An author, what was her name? Natalie Barney. Didn't mean anything to Laura. Yes it did, that was what John had had to paint on Vivien's yacht.

Laura shivered again. Had Mr. Vivien become somehow real, had his friends started coming back to life through whatever hole his arrival had created? Laura imagined an immense filing cabinet in which all the index cards were filed "dead," a partition door with a cupboard across it to prevent it being opened, someone pointing toward the door, indicating the "dead" cards behind, saying "Oh, but they're not dead. They're only sleeping. Some day soon they will wake up." She was furious. Why should the dead awake? They'd had their chance; why should anyone live forever? What about the children? She glanced at Zebbee; it was their turn now.

"Still awake are ya?" called a voice softly. "Know where I can get some fresh water? I've only just arrived and I'm parched."

Laura looked up amazed. She had been alone for hours on a rock in the middle of the sea, or so it seemed. The speaker was a man, young, tanned, good-looking. A tall dark stranger, in fact.

"They turn the water off after midnight," she told him. "Midnight till 6:00 A.M."

"The witching hours," laughed the young man.

A third time, Laura shivered.

"Aw, are you cold? You should get back in the tent. I'll look around for myself."

"No," said Laura. "It's okay. I can let you have some water, if you want. Or a beer. Would you rather have a beer?"

"You're right there, I would. Mind if I join you?"

"You can sit down if you like, but talk softly or you'll wake the kids."

Kids. Mother, Married Woman, Keep Off. Oh, why did it have to be like that? Why couldn't she be like Minnie, pick people up in hot tubs.

"Oh yeah? Husband inside asleep too, is he?"

She didn't need to hide behind John for protection.

"No, he's not. He stayed in Perth. I came with my sister."

They talked for a while, in soft voices in the soft moonlight. About this and that. There were looks and glances, sighs, smiles, muffled laughter. When he finished his beer he looked at Laura. There was a question in his eyes.

"Got another? I'll restock your supply in the morning."

Laura shook her head slowly. "No," she said.

"That's my lot, is it?" he said.

"That's your lot."

"He's a lucky fella, your husband."

And the young man disappeared into the night, like a gift offered and gently refused.

About this time of the early hours of the morning, Minnie found herself washed up on the beach at Raven Rock. Laura, Zebbee and Son stood in a semicircle around her.

"Fuckwit," said Laura, "next time you go for a moonlight dip either leave a suicide note or invite us along. And if you think I've brought a flask of hot tea you've got another think coming."

"I've got one," said Zebbee.

"And I spilled it," said Son.

IN THE BUBBLE AND SQUEAK OF LIFE

Beryl had just wiped up the last of the tortoise and thrown its remains in a body bag when the phone rang.

"It was dreadful and it was my fault. Sheer bloody-minded, insensitive boorishness. She is my perfect beautiful darling and I treated her shamefully." Beryl's cue to settle down in the winged leather armchair in Mr. Vivien's office, yearn for a hot cup of tea, and say, "Now, Natalie, bloody-minded, insensitive and boorish you may be, dear, but you usually manage to live with yourself."

"She'll never want to see me again."

"Why? Whatever have you done?"

"I can't tell you. I just called to say that I am about to do the honourable thing. I am going to open the shutters and let the hard light of day show me up and shrivel me up as the monster I truly am."

"I wouldn't do that if I were you."

"Why not?" A suspicion of hope glanced across Natalie's heart.

"Once you're gone and your body is a heap of dust on the deck you will never be able to speak to her, make amends." Beryl was still rather out of breath from the thirty-yard sprint through the

Octagonal Gallery, over the marble staircase and up the vanadium spiral. She had not yet managed to convince Mr. Vivien that a telephone in the conservatory outside the 1900 Room would not be an anachronism as long as they were careful and did not abbreviate its name to "phone." Telephones, she argued, had been around since at least 1837. Whereupon Mr. Vivien would succumb to a bad dose of spleen and the matter would not be broached for another fortnight.

"I would tear the heart from my body. I would wring the blood from it and present it to her on a silver platter. I would cut it up with a knife and fork and swallow it."

The extravagance of her language was a salve in itself. The operatic bleakness a reminder of past glories.

"I don't think she'd like that very much. Come away from the shutters and sit down on your cosy old sofa. Not on the coffin, Natalie. It'll only make you morbid. Help yourself to a long cool glass of Rhesus on the rocks. Now, tell me."

"*Era per me un'angela, una creatura di sogno. Era la mia tesora.* (She was my angel, my dream, my treasure.)"

"I expect she still is."

"You're very calm."

"I think that's my role, isn't it. That's why you rang me."

Even vampires look to mothers for emotional support and since their own have almost always died before them, and since as Natalie explained to Minnie, breeders cannot become vampires, one often finds respectable married women servicing a small coterie of the undead.

"She wrote to me, she came out of nowhere, she admired my work. I told her 'Come. I must meet you.' I begged her to hurry. She came halfway round the world to be with me. She swam out to my yacht in the high seas. She was weary, nay, exhausted. I had them run a warm bath, I spread a table before her. She ate and drank and then…"

"Yes?"

"Oh I falter, words fail me."

"Come now. I'm sure you've told me far worse about your past."

"She was sitting on the sofa, right where I am now. I still smell the essence of camellia from the bath oil. There she was, beside me, her plump soft arm almost touching mine. And I..."

"Yes?"

"I talked to her. I don't know what got into me. I talked to her for hours. I used her as a sounding board for everything that was on my mind. I meant to make love to her, you must believe me. I meant to be the best, most attentive, athletic lover she ever had. But I was so engrossed in my own thoughts that somehow I forgot the purpose of her visit."

"Natalie, you can save the situation. Genuine sentiment will win out over mere clumsiness, or the literature of the world is in jeopardy. Here is what you should do..."

"Yes?"

"Ring that poor young woman up and invite her out on a proper, old-fashioned date."

"A date?"

"Yes. Today you will send her a five-pound box of chocolates and some roses."

"A bouquet of lilies and orchids, a spray of violets, a sweet-smelling nosegay of lilies of the valley, a soprano to serenade her."

Before Natalie could orchestrate a repetition of her more famous romantic feats, Beryl cut her short.

"No. Today roses and chocolates. Tonight an invitation to go dancing.Tomorrow a corsage the colour of the lady's dress. The heyday of the classic date was circa 1955. You will need a tuxedo."

Beryl set to work rethreading the crystals on the chandelier. Fortunately none were broken but it was a fiddly business. She was worried that the sharp sides might cut her fingers, but if she wore gloves she couldn't feel the little hooks and match them up with the little holes. She turned the radio on for something soothing while she worked.

"We interrupt this broadcast to announce that in a secret late-night session the state legislature decided that in line with the rest of Australia, it is no longer lawful for a local authority to intentionally promote v*****ism or to support the publication of any literature which might be considered to present the v***** lifestyle as an attractive alternative to the nuclear family. As the state premier explained, 'We in Western Australia have always prided ourselves on being geographically isolated from the worst of the corruption and vice now sweeping the eastern states. We have until now had no v***** laws because, like Queen Victoria before us, we have not believed that v*****s existed. Many people will be puzzled as to the implications of the new legislation. As a guideline to the areas affected I would like to give some prominent examples and set everybody's minds at rest. Certain films now on general release will be withdrawn forthwith: *Brides of Dr*****, starring Christopher Lee, *The Hunger*, starring Catherine Deneuve and David Bowie, *Daughters of Darkness*, starring Delphine Seyrig, and *Velvet V*****. All books by the author Bram Stoker will be removed from the shelves of the state libraries.'

"Glad you could join us, Premier. A report just in from London says a group of anti-v***** protesters have torn down a blue plaque commemorating Bram Stoker's Chelsea home. Meanwhile we have been asked to warn listeners that if any of you suspect that you may be living next door to a v*****, please, please be careful; do not approach the suspect, do not accept any invitations from the suspect such as offers of a meal or coffee, do not lure the suspect into a deserted glade. Many people believe even in this day and age that v*****s may be killed by running water, the smell of garlic, or the sight of the True Cross. This is superstitious twaddle and poppycock.

"V*****s should be pulled out of their coffins and exposed to the light of day but, we repeat but, only by duly authorised personnel wearing rubber gloves, mouth-guards and dental dams, in case of accidental contact. If you see or hear anything irregular, contact the proper authorities immediately but remember: a person who sleeps all day is as likely to be an invalid as a v*****, the presence of a great space between the upper median incisors, an exaggerated development of the incisors compared with the canines, and a growth of hair on the neck may all be perfectly normal signs of masculinity; sexual intercourse within the hallowed confines of the family can include some lovebites, so if you see your next-door neighbour suddenly wearing a long silk scarf round her neck to conceal those telltale hickeys, she may well have been to bed with her husband."

The rest of the broadcast gave details of the new measures in process to impound all property belonging to proven v*****s. Beryl shook her head. Her dreams were so often prophetic.

Beryl moved on to the Octagonal Gallery and set about dusting all those pictures. Then she would smear them with Windowash. Then she would wipe the Windowash off. Mr. Vivien had instructed her to use old newspapers and shine up with vinegar and water. Beryl had refused. She knew a bit of damp newspaper was the best thing ever invented for cleaning glass but if you let go of one mod con, they would find reasons to deprive you of all the others. That lovely furniture polish that you simply spray on and wipe off, saying goodbye forever to strained wrists and aching forearms, was damaging the ozone layer and contributing to the greenhouse effect. Beryl liked the greenhouse effect. The new detergents which ate dirt and stains that other powders left behind were nonbiodegradable. John had taken it upon himself to explain to Beryl, not once but three times, with diagrams of molecular formations, what nonbiodegradable meant. He could have saved it for his students. Beryl had known the first time she heard it that nonbiodegradable meant convenient. In the same spirit, convenience foods stunted children's growth and the blessed television warped their minds. Beryl paused a moment in the polishing and

imagined a forest full of warped and stunted children. Why hadn't
she thought of it sooner? The more stunted, the less lip. She should
have stuffed them with hamburgers; she should have pumped
them full of Valium; she should have chained them to the TV. She
could organise a Housewives' Spray-In in the middle of the Stunted
Children Forest. Each woman would bring along her favourite
banned household product: toxic oven cleaner which poisons the
Sunday roast; double-strength Monster-Glue whose fumes cause
hallucinations; Soakoe, the washing liquid, into which you plunge
your understains and two minutes later they're clean, and the fi-
bres are so rotten you have to buy new ones—show me the woman
who seriously resents a new pair of soft white satiny knickers and
I'll show you the terminally ungrateful. Could it be that
Windowash injects a secret psychedelic into their product, a secret
ingredient so addictive that Housewife X will do anything, say
anything to protect it and her use of it despite the well-known fact
that Windowash is tHe most lethal bleach and should it come in
contact with your pretty peach and plum curtains, you are going
to have to dye them white because you will never get the stain out,
and overnight the Pink Room will have to bow to expedience and
change its name by deed poll to *"Blanche Neige."*

Beryl had reached the fourth wall of the Gallery. She sat down
under the portrait of Elizabeth Báthory, the Blood Countess, and
admired the vista of gleaming glass to her left, the dingy dust to her
right. There was no difference. All the glass sparkled with cleanliness, not a speck of dirt marred the horizon. On the floor below
the far wall was a single red leaf which had blown through the recently opened window. It looked like the juvenilia of a minimalist,
before he got really minimal, and would not have looked out of
place at the Tate Gallery in London. The truth is that a gallery
unfrequented of the sticky-fingered public collects dust at a sev-
enty-five percent slower rate, the principle ingredient of dust being, as we all know, dead skin. Mr. Vivien liked to know who were
his equals and who his inferiors. As long as Beryl had a broom or

an old rag in her hand she was firmly planted in the latter category.

"There is enough real dirt in the world without make-work," said Beryl, silent but determined, "I have had enough."

The beautiful room was empty. The ceiling towered twenty foot above Beryl's head, the far wall, with leaf, was fifty feet away and nothing but empty space filled the middle. One might inhabit it with the lurid outcrop of one's imagination. If it were hers, and she had plans, Beryl would take down those endless portraits of women in their heavy gilded frames and put up something sexier. Such an array of necks and cleavages, one might as well be in the skin room of a beauty parlour which specializes in collagen treatment and wrinkle remover. When Beryl came into her own, she would leave this cool calm room with its long white walls, its echoing roof, its white marble floor, quite bare save one sudden slash of colour—it was the errant leaf which had put this in her mind—a full-colour blowup of Mick Jagger's lips. They would draw you in from a great distance. At first they would appear a mere speck on the horizon but with each step they would get bigger, redder, wetter, till you were close close up and the excitement of that thick muscular tongue lurking behind those pearly white teeth would be almost too much to contemplate.

In moments Beryl had arranged the whole property to her most particular liking, as on a country walk the tourist cuts down hedges at will, prunes back maples and plants begonias, knowing so much better than the owner how to order the grounds. The opera singers must go; theirs was a false and straining sound and why bother when pop music is available at the flick of a radio? Beryl would replace them with a lifesize replica of Alice Cooper's scar, Jerry Lee Lewis's grin—so much sexier than that damply suggestive Elvis: as the Beatles to the Rolling Stones was Elvis to Jerry Lee Lewis—and Rod Stewart's gravel. When you opened the door Mick would moan, "Can't get no satisfaction"; when you closed it he would declare, "Brown sugar, you know it tastes so good." Beryl had been buying brown since the sixties. It made her feel wicked.

She would lay the garden out in a series of green and grey, blending and highlighting the natural Australian landscape instead of fighting and concealing it. She would have low dark plants near the house, getting taller and lighter as the eye refocused for distance; midprospect would be a clump of those heavenly pink and grey eucalyptus culminating in the stark white of ghost gums by the parapet. After that the waves would pile up on the horizon, green, grey and white with a touch of yacht sails. Beryl felt like the artist who at last has a studio large enough for the giant canvas she wishes to paint.

In this outburst of creativity Beryl had absentmindedly dropped the economy size bottle of Windowash she had been holding in her hand. The thick white liquid had oozed out of the new stay-clean cap and was making an oleaginous puddle on the floor. To air the room Beryl had raised the shutters and the West Australian heat came gusting through the windows. In the consequent fumes a tiny army of Housewives X were camping out in Warped-Child-Wood, covering each other's backs with Windowash and cooing, "Your skin is so translucent, my dear, I thought you were a window." Then they would giggle hysterically and wash it off. It is to be hoped that Mick Jagger took his turn at the scrubbing. As the fumes evaporated and euphoria turned to a dull, throbbing headache, the housewives trudged home and covered their husbands with paint stripper. "In case of contact with eyes or skin, rinse immediately with plenty of water and seek medical attention."

Mr. Vivien would, of course, take his 1900 Room with him wherever he went. Beryl would plant kangaroo paw and strelitzia and maybe some giant agave where it used to stand. In the middle of this pleasant fantasy a disagreeable but virtuous thought struck her. Her own dear youngest daughter, Ingrid, and her own dear youngest granddaughter, Lollipop, and her own dear son-in-law, Loviebuttons the twenty-third, needed a place to live. And this had everything. Only the stingiest crone of a mother fantasized beautiful houses for herself to live in without a thought for impoverished youth. Why should healthy, strapping Loviebuttons the twenty-third go out to work when his mother-in-law could provide for him? Why should poor Ingrid get into a moither and a sweat searching up affordable kindies for Lollipop, accessible jobs for herself—like Beryl had had to do when her kids were young—while her own mother was hale and hearty and still had a good ten years work in her?

For a second Beryl imagined the smiles of gratitude she would receive when she showed the little band round Dalkeith. Then reality reclaimed her. Gratitude only went one way: from mother to daughter. Everything the mother gave the daughter was the daughter's by rights and probably should have been handed over earlier, as soon as the daughter expressed an interest. Anything the daughter gave the mother, on the other hand, was to be greeted like a prince's ransom, which it probably was if rarity of gift is taken into consideration. The only event a mother could truly look forward to in her daughter's life was the day the child had a baby in her turn. Then the young woman could join the ranks of the commiserating mothers and cavort with Mick Jagger in Warped-Child-Wood.

This reflection did Beryl a world of good. It taught her the great ugly sin of Selfishness. It told her to keep the beautiful house to herself, to let no one come near, save John on conjugal nights, and perhaps one humdinger of a special event to show the place off and rub their noses in what they were about to miss. It would teach them all a perfect lesson if she cut them out of her will and left the house to Mick, the only one who came when called, gave satisfaction on demand, sang like a fallen angel and danced like the devil. All that remained was to gain custody of the house. A mere detail for a woman used to making winter blankets out of torn shirts, turning cardigans into jackets by lining them and padding them with nylon stockings.

The phone rang. The extraordinary acoustics of the house meant that you could hear the phone ringing in every room and from any angle. You could hang upside down like a bat in the turret, with the full force of the flag flapping in your ear, and still hear the phone. Which was fortunate considering what some of Mr. Vivien's business associates got up to.

"It's over. I'm finished. Do you hear me? It's all over."

Beryl was just scribbling down the wording for her ansaphone message; she wanted every detail ready for the day she took over; "Say what you want and why I should give it to you. Make a good case for your continued existence."

"Sorry, Mr. Vivien, did you say 'over'?" said Beryl busily, as though settling down to dictation.

"Haven't you heard? It was on the wireless. They've outlawed vampires."

"I think you mean v*******."

"Whatever they call us, they're impounding our property, seizing our goods, reallocating our real estate."

"Reallocating your real estate?" Beryl began to pay more serious attention.

"As cowardly as pillage, as brutal as plunder, as bloody as a massacre. What are we going to do?"

"We?"

"Beryl, I need your help as never before."

"Well now, that's what you said when you asked me to clean the Octagon. What's your friend Natalie doing? Can't she sail you away on her yacht with priceless jewels in every orifice?"

"She's somewhere in the fifties looking for figs."

"Dates."

"That's it, dates. I've tried Tangiers and Casablanca but there's no sign of her."

"Pasadena 1955, it's a sure thing."

"Beryl, I got your daughter compensation for her foot injury."

"And I swept up your dead tortoises, Mr. Vivien."

"I got your son-in-law his yacht contracts, thereby saving the new house with five bedrooms and reticulated lawn."

"I rethreaded your chandelier."

"I gave you a job so you could put your John through his Ph.D."

"In fact everything you've done for me has been for someone else."

"Please."

"Alright. But I want the house."

"For Ingrid and the child?"

"For me. For Beryl-the-Bloodyminded."

"You're not in the least bit bloodyminded." Renée Vivien bridled as only a true v****** can bridle. If Beryl had tendencies toward the blood, surely this would have surfaced before.

"This is my inauguration." Beryl smiled as she remembered the portrait of Elizabeth Báthory, known as the Blood Countess. Perhaps she would let that one stay on the wall. Beryl might grow fearsome by association.

"I want the 1900 Room," said Renée Vivien.

"Granted."

"And the bench, *Avenue des Anglais,* Nice 1954."

"Granted."

"But where will I go? How will I get there? What will I do with the vast fortune I have amassed?"

"Indeed," said Beryl.

Ingrid had been thinking. She did this as little as possible. It was bothersome and usually unnecessary. She sat on a fallen trunk which Loviebuttons had planed into a seat, and nursed Lollipop. There were fewer flies at the top of the incline and she could see down to the soak a farmer had dug in the paddock. There were sheep dotted around and some cattle drinking. Ingrid was thinking over a conversation she had had that morning.

Along the newly leveled driveway had come a Land Rover which parked under a tree and from which two persons emerged, a man and a woman. The woman walked purposefully toward the newly constructed shed. Ingrid, gazing peacefully from behind the yellow striped curtains, recognised the gait of a district nurse, or something medical who felt it had a right to be disturbing the dirt on someone else's land. Ingrid had a twinge of uncertainty. She opened the door with something like apprehension.

"You must be Ingrid," said the person in the shape of a nurse. "I was telling my husband about you."

Ingrid nodded noncommittally.

"The place is looking really good," the person continued. "You must have worked very hard."

Ingrid nodded again. She was much taken by the green silk tie around the person's neck. "I like your tie," she said.

"Thank you," said the person, "your sister commented on it too. I should introduce myself. I'm Dr. Grebe, and this is my husband, Professor Grebe."

Ingrid looked at the other person, who stood in the doorway a little behind the first. Lesser crested: no silk tie.

"Yes," said Ingrid, as though corroborating their identities. It was hot and airless inside the shed and it smelled of engine oil. Loviebuttons said it had been used as a machine room before he dragged it onto the lowloader.

"Would you like to sit outside? I'll bring us some ice-cold beer." She pointed up the incline toward the planed tree trunk.

"My husband is Professor of Physics at the University of Western Australia," said the person who called herself Dr Grebe. "But when he comes home at night he's a volunteer fireman."

"You must have lovely times together." Ingrid was wearing her faded blue Madonna dress. "Madonna" as in the old virgin, not the new floozy. And "faded" as in sunbleached, not former. She hoped she was having the right effect: poor but worth saving, like depression glassware.

Doctor and Professor smiled. "We were hoping you could help us." Usually they wanted you to help them to help you, which meant practicing clean living and wholesome attitudes.

"Why?" said Ingrid. "Have you lost your way?"

"Oh no," said the person whose husband must be mute or muted, "we want to dig a well."

"A family project?"

Professor Grebe took over at this point and issued a detailed description of the absolute necessity of him digging a well right here, on Ingrid's land.

"Right here?"

"Underneath the bungalow."

"Aren't you meant to train me to dig my own well?" asked Ingrid. "Like in the charity poster."

More detailed, longer description of the absolute necessity for the well to be dug by students of physics under the tutelage of Professor Grebe.

"Oil?"

"Water. Clean, fresh well water in bounteous supply."

"What's the catch?"

"The catch is," said Dr. Grebe, "they will have to dig up your bungalow and build you a new one that corresponds to government specifications."

"First you going to build me a bungalow and then you going to dig me a well," said Ingrid. She considered the proposition.

Professor Grebe repeated his explanations which, now that Ingrid was hearing them for the third time, contained many references to rock, sediment, pressure and metal ores. There was mention of a ten-year study requiring that samples be taken monthly. This meant, Ingrid realised, that a bountiful supply of young men would be driving out to her land who would most certainly be happy to change her light bulbs, empty her rubbish bin, retile the roof and slap on a new coat of paint as and when. How many West Australian physicists did it take to change Ingrid's light bulb?

"Orright," she said, "but under one condition."

"What's that?"

"You tar the road. It's gonna get all rutted with your trucks and vans coming up and down."

"It's a deal," said Doctor Grebe.

Then they had swallowed down their ice-cold beer, walked back to their Land Rover and driven away.

Ingrid learned from this encounter one important fact about the world: everything comes to she who waits. Seated now on the fallen tree, with Lollipop in her arms and Lollipop's little mouth snuffling and sucking at her breast, Ingrid taxed her mind with the question of Loviebuttons. What was he for? He had given her Lollipop, he had transported and erected the shed, he had connected the shed to the town mains. He was good in bed, or up against a tree, or in the back of a panel van. But Lollipop was born now, and most satisfactory too, and Ingrid did not want another. And God had sent rain to fill the barrel. And soon there would be a new bungalow and a well, sent by a new god called a physics department.

There were many gods in Ingrid's life and they all smiled upon her. There was a god of right feet which had provided enough money to buy land for cash in exchange for causing Ingrid to limp a little and sit down a lot. Ingrid liked to sit down. She found it peaceful. There was a god of old cars whom she had discovered by accident. Loviebuttons had a very old, very battered panel van which had been registered in Queensland. The reason that its plates still said Queensland, although Loviebuttons had been in Western Australia for two years now, was that it never would have passed the state road test. Any passing policeperson observing Loviebutton's panel van would instantly have reached the same conclusion, impounded the vehicle and fined its owner. The police had, Loviebuttons said, an unreasonable prejudice against him. They systematically discriminated against white trash white rastas in floral sarongs and bare feet. They told him to drop the sarong, suspecting drugs, then arrested him for indecency. It was preferable, therefore, if Ingrid drove since she was a chick and owned a driving licence.

Ingrid was driving into town one day when she saw in the rearview mirror that another car was speeding up behind her and flashing its lights. The first time this had happened to her was on the Mitchell Freeway. She was in the outside lane doing ten k's over the speed limit. Naturally, she had slowed down but the other car had only come on faster, flashing like a madman. Ingrid, certain that this was the signal considerate drivers gave you that a police speed trap was lurking ahead, slowed down even more. In the rearview mirror she saw the other car getting very big and very close, as though any minute it would crash into the boot. Then she saw it swerve dramatically and overtake her on the inside lane, blasting its horn to boast its skill and grace. Loviebuttons had nearly had a fit when she told him about it afterwards. He had called her a fuckwit and a drongo. He said that when a car comes up behind you very fast and flashes its lights you must either speed up or move over into another lane. Thus, when Ingrid noticed the car flashing its lights as it followed her into town from Gunderdin, she speeded up since she was on a small country road without lane markings. The car behind speeded up as well and turned into an unmarked police vehicle. Ingrid thought this unfair. The police vehicle waved her over and ordered her to pull in. It always took Ingrid a little while to change gears, especially when she wasn't expecting to, consequently she parked rather close to the police vehicle's bumper. Without leaving his car, the policeman took a loud hailer and ordered the driver of Ingrid's car (which, Ingrid calculated, must be herself) to get out on the passenger side with her arms up and lie face down on the ground. This seemed quite wrong to Ingrid since the ground was dirty and they said at the prenatal classes that she might experience some discomfort if she lay on her belly during the later months of pregnancy. "Move it," shouted the policeman through the loud hailer, "if you're not out of there in ten seconds I'll blast your head off your shoulders. M***** f*****."

The policeman watched a lot of late-night California reruns and had been longing for a chance to shout m***** f***** in an appropriate context. He was as yet unsure whereabouts in the sentence m***** f***** should go. At the beginning: "M***** f***** move it!"? After the verb (rendered in the imperative): "Move it, m***** f*****!"? He didn't really like it stuck at the very end, as yelled at Ingrid, but he wasn't sure why. He would practice some more that night into his tape recorder.

Ingrid moved as fast as she was able, which was not very, and clambered out the driver's side feeling flustered. Instead of the long-haired yobbo drug addict wanted in three states for manslaughter, sheep worrying and related offences, the policeman was confronted by the sight of a hugely pregnant young woman in an enormous faded blue Madonna frock. The young woman swayed heavily and looked at the red dirt dubiously.

"It'd kill the baby," said Ingrid, shaking her head.

"No!" growled the police officer, who was a family man himself. "No, don't do that. It wouldn't be right."

"Orright," said Ingrid, "I won't."

The police officer stared at her. Poor, beautiful thing with her lame foot and enormous belly. Fella who did that should be ashamed of hisself. He reached over onto his dashboard for one of the new milk chocolate Mars bars he kept there and, before he knew what he was doing, he had offered it to Ingrid.

"For the baby," he said.

"Aw gee," said Ingrid, "that's roolly sweet of ya."

The policeman shrugged bashfully.

"Is that what you stopped me for?" Ingrid asked, "Or was there something else?"

"Aw, yeah. Did you know that one of your back brake lights is not functioning properly?"

"Not functioning?" repeated Ingrid. "No worries. She'll be right, mate." And she smiled peacefully at him so that for the next three and a half hours he had no worries.

Ingrid attributed the gift of the milk chocolate Mars bar to the god of old cars. She peacefully expected that the world was full of such benign deities who attended one in adversity and the reason that she was unfamiliar with them was that adversity came so seldom. Lollipop burped sleepily and had to be settled in a sling on Ingrid's back. Ingrid struggled to return her mind to the matter at hand. Loviebuttons's principle functions were now complete and his generic function, sex on tap, could be provided by a local John with no building skills whatever. One of the physics students would probably do. Ingrid would look them over.

And so, the conclusion was reached: Loviebuttons was obsolete.

While Beryl was cleaning up in Dalkeith and haggling over property values, and Laura was camping at Raven Rock with two small children and a standard-size lesbian, both of their respective Johns were sitting in the waiting room of a new tattoo parlour which had just opened on William Street. It was called "Strelitzia's Tattoo & Teazel" and rumour had it that the proprietor was a former prostitute. The walls were painted white and sported full-colour photographs of black widow spiders, piranhas and scorpions as well as the more familiar roses, love hearts, Mums, anchors and butterflies tattooed on naked arms, backs, thighs and buttocks. There was a woman who seemed to have had herself dyed blue, every millimetre of her skin sported a tattoo. There was a smiling traffic cop with a smiling snake circling his wrist. There were so many pictures of sailors whose left biceps declared that it loved "Mary Jane" that the series might have been signed, "Andy Warhol." In every other respect Strelitzia's waiting room looked exactly like a dentist's. The hard chairs and ancient copies of Woman's Way with the free doily offer, the exhortation that you declare any contact with contagious disease before commencement of treatment and the muffled cries of persons currently undergoing "treatment," produced an atmosphere which stated as bluntly and as internationally as a road sign that this was the Anteroom of Pain.

"Next please," called Strelitzia.

"After you," said Laura's John to Beryl's.

"No, no," said Beryl's. "I insist. After you."

"I think I'll just watch," said Laura's hopefully.

"I don't allow spectators."

"I only want a very small dot," said Beryl's.

"I don't do dots," said Strelitzia. "Nothing smaller than a rectangle. I've got some great dodecahedrons. Or I could do you a beaut of a rhomboid."

"Some other time," said both Johns at once.

"Hummingbird under the armpit? Porche emerging from the buttocks? Rude words in Russian?"

The two Johns left the tattoo parlour an hour later. Beryl's John's inner left thigh now said "NORWICH." Laura's John's said "VLADIVOSTOK."

IN THE BACK SEAT OF A RED CADILLAC CONVERTIBLE

→ 12 ←

*B*ut this isn't what I ordered," said Beryl's John to the lad from Interflora. He braced his legs in the classic pose of a nineteenth-century boxer. It would have been more effective if he had been wearing more than a towel round his loins. The lad from Interflora was not to know that John's legs were braced wide apart because the flesh around John's tattoo was swollen and the chafing of thigh on thigh occasioned much pain. The lad from Interflora saw a suburban male householder who answered the door in a skimpy blue towel and, when he realised that the caller was a young man, spread his legs in one swift gesture. There was no question in the lad's mind about what this John thought he had ordered. The question was whether or not the lad would give it to him. When the skimpy blue towel slipped gracefully out of the knot John had tied and fell in a soft heap at John's ankles, the lad from Interflora expressed no surprise.

Beryl peered through the open doorway. Her husband was standing on the front veranda in the nude and a young man was offering him a box of chocolates and a bunch of red roses. Years of motherhood had taught Beryl that any inquiry as to why a child is naked on the front veranda invariably receives the reply: "Minnie does it"; "Simone's mum lets her"; "The teacher told us to" (delete where inapplicable). Years of marriage had taught Beryl that the rules for children are the same for husbands, with the addition of tact.

She addressed the lad and ignored John.

"Who are those from?"

The lad read the label. "For Minnie, my melting moment, from an Admirer."

"I'll put them in water," said Beryl, wresting flowers and chocolates from the lad. "Shall I bring you your dressing gown, dear?" she asked John solicitously. "You wouldn't want to catch a chill."

John smiled a very masculine smile and gave his wife a very masculine nod.

"Sorry about the towel," he said to the lad. "I was in the shower when the doorbell rang."

The lad shrugged. That's what they all say when their wives discover them.

Thus any household curiosity which might have been aroused by the anonymous gift to Minnie of a five-pound box of chocolates, all soft centres, and two dozen red roses was eclipsed by Beryl's irritation with John and John's tattoo torment: was it worth the pain? had he picked the right one? would Beryl like it? The irritation and the torment were intensified by their owners' efforts to conceal their existence and, in John's case, the effort to conceal his left thigh also. Minnie accepted the gift in complete silence. She had a nasty sore throat caused by a nasty lump she did not want to discuss.

Next time the doorbell went it was John's fresh okra. Minnie had gone back to bed. Beryl had gone to Dalkeith to gloat. The house returned to normal. Late afternoon the phone rang. Someone else had heard of Directory Enquiries.

"You get that," yelled John. "The party will be starting soon and I'm not half finished."

"It's two days away," croaked Minnie.

"I have every ounce of preparation timed down to a fraction of a second and I cannot waste a moment with home phone answering."

Minnie picked up the receiver and croaked, "I'm sorry, no one can come to the phone right now, but if you'd like to leave your name, your number, the date and time of your call and any message you may have had, we'll ignore it along with the others, in strict numerical sequence. You are number two hundred and thirty-three." She hoped it was someone important like the police with a new kind of laser for John.

"Minnie," said a voice which crept into the pink inside of Minnie's ear and walked up and down her backbone, the voice which had caused the lump in Minnie's throat, the knots in her stomach, the unbalance of her mind. She had a vision of herself lying asleep on Natalie's coffin, mouth open, snoring her head off. She felt embarrassed, but embarrassment was merely the emotion her mind found most presentable and so placed on top, squashing down a seethe of others.

"Natalie?" she said tentatively, as though her own articulation of the name could make of it what she wanted, as though Natalie herself were not already formed.

"Please let me take you out. Tomorrow. Dancing."

Next day a corsage arrived, red, to go with the 1957 red Cadillac El Dorado Biarritz with whitewall tyres and ostentatious chrome which she'd brought over from Pasadena. It just happened to be the colour of Minnie's evening dress, the one Beryl had lent her along with the strapless bra, the charm bracelet, high-heel slippers, lipstick, powder, pearl ear bobs and three crinolines.

Ingrid was coaxing Minnie's hair into the right sort of ponytail. Minnie looked at herself dubiously in the mirror.

"Frocks. What do women wear frocks for?"

Beryl, Laura and Ingrid looked at each other and shook their heads in a line, sitting on the white candlewick bedspread on Beryl's bed. They might have been about to leap up and mime to Diana Ross. Ingrid made an attempt to instruct her retarded older sister.

"So that when their partner takes them out on a date..." Ingrid always remembered to use the word "partner" when talking with lesbians. "They can stroke their thighs without encountering any obstacle."

"I feel like I'm in drag," Minnie protested. "Why can't Natalie wear the dress and I wear the tuxedo?"

Many a promising date has foundered on just such shifting sands.

There was a loud vroom in the driveway. Laura lifted up Beryl's net curtains and gazed at the Cadillac and at Natalie who was walking toward the veranda in a white dinner jacket with broad shoulders, black peg-legged trousers, white buck shoes with crepe soles, a black tie and a black orchid boutonniere which Minnie had sent her. Natalie's hair was slicked back with pomade into a D.A.

"Strewth," said Laura. "When me and Ing got taken out on a date we were lucky if the bloke washed his feet before putting his thongs back on. Skivvy and cut-offs and the great smell of Brut."

"Quick trip to the drives and a Coke if you got in the back with him," added Ingrid.

"Where's she taking you?" asked Laura.

"Entertainment Centre. There's a fifties revival."

"That's been booked solid for weeks. Fifty bucks a head with dinner."

"What did you eat in the fifties, Mum?"

"Ration books and milk tokens."

Natalie drove along the coast road heading for the fifties revival at the Entertainment Centre.

"I thought we could go up to Ocean Reef and watch the waves," she said like a thousand voices before her and a thousand voices to come.

Minnie began to unthaw, warmed by annoyance. "Pull over," she said, "I'm taking this stuff off."

Natalie complied. Minnie peeled off dress, petticoats and other paraphernalia and threw them onto the back seat. "I feel more dignified in my underpants."

"I'm sorry," said Natalie.

"I wrote to you because I admired you, your books kept me going through a long tunnel. Your reply sounded urgent, even enthusiastic. And then…" Minnie paused, "then I fell in love with you."

Natalie watched Minnie's face closely.

"I know it sounds silly, like romantic escapism, but here we are in a car together. I mean…"

"Minnie," Natalie interrupted her, "I know what you mean: what can there be between us, given the enormous gulf? We were born in different centuries, on different continents; we know nothing about each other."

"Can a modern-day lesbian find happiness with a one-hundred-year-old vampire?" Minnie smiled wryly.

"There were things I hoped you could give me too."

"Were?"

"Are you still willing?"

"We haven't tried."

"I've been lonely for a long time, wondering where my friends went, knowing and not liking it. When the publishers reissued all my books, it seemed like a new way of killing me off—making me a classic, a fossil. What could the present generation of eager young women see in my work of relevance to them? And then I got your letter. Somehow it pushed its way through my extremely intricate defence system only six months after you'd sent it."

"And here we are."

Natalie risked a hand on Minnie's arm, light, hesitant. Minnie looked down at it, then up at Natalie, and smiled.

"It must have seemed a long delay to you, but I wrote back as soon as I heard from you. I thought if I didn't write immediately, I never would."

Minnie put her hand up to Natalie's face, stroked her cheek with one finger. Natalie caught the finger in her mouth. Minnie recognised the overtures they were making yet still she hesitated and heard herself ask, "Natalie, what do you miss most from before you became a vampire?"

Natalie shifted in the seat so that Minnie's head was on her shoulder as she spoke.

"Breasts in sunlight. Walking in a cornfield at the edge of the sea with the sweet smell of lavender wafting through the air. Opening an enormous picnic hamper. Offering carefully chosen morsels to the woman beside me. Waiting until our hostess suggests a bathe, then making it clear to my companion that I would like to converse with her alone. Telling her what beautiful eyes she has. They all have beautiful eyes, one's female companions. Stroking her delicate white hands, advising her to seek some shade lest she burn. Watching her discomfort in her tight bodice, offering to untie it for her since we are well hidden from the eyes of men. Her turning her back toward me, lifting the weight of hair off her shoulders. I love the way women put their hair up so I can loose the pins and let the hair fall. Her neck but inches from my mouth, I can see the fine down as I begin work on her bodice laces. One by one, I untie those tight white cords until her full, soft breasts are free. She lies back, relieved of the constricting garment and I cover her with my hands. Sometimes she laughs or asks if it is quite the thing. I tell her she is charming and I am charmed. She smiles and raises her arms above her head for a pillow so that she may best enjoy me. All afternoon I caress those breasts, now with my hands, now with my fingers, now taking a nipple in my mouth."

Minnie breathed again, which had been difficult while Natalie spoke. "Come on," she said. " Let's get in the back." And so they did. And they did.

And so it was they failed to reach the Entertainment Centre and the fifties revival which Natalie had imported for the occasion. And the little time spent in their red evening dress and peg-legged trousers would scarcely have justified the purchase price.

"Why did you call me your 'melting moment' on the card you sent with the roses, Natalie?" asked Minnie, snuggled into Natalie's side. This was, of course, not a real question but a little girlish wriggle, a verbal wiggle to entice Natalie into further blandishments.

"I knew," said Natalie, "I knew that you would feel like hot wet velvet in my hand. Momentous."

"Momentary?"

"Are you asking for eternal love from a vampire? You want to think about that a minute."

"What are you saying? Have you...? Am I...? Have you made me a vampire?"

"Hardly. That was sex, Minimax. Eternal life takes a little longer."

"You scare me. You won't disappear, will you, like a bat in the night?"

"We're lying enlaced in each other's arms and this one conjures visions of tragic parting." Natalie smiled lovingly and for that moment she could not imagine a life without Minnie beside her. "They're making life difficult for us vampires. If I had any sense and was not mooning around with some slip of a mortal, I'd set sail tonight and get back into international waters before the persecution mounts. But Renée is hanging around trying to think of some way to take it all with her."

"Don't put yourself in danger because of me. I thought you were alright because you're not an Australian national and Renée is so rich. The rules are usually different for the rich."

"Usually. But I've lived through all this before. These people mean it. If Renée flees they can carve up her worldly goods amongst themselves."

"When the authorities realise how many of their writers, artists, lawyers, politicians, judges, doctors, university professors have been driven out, they'll see what a mistake they made."

"By then half of us will have been destroyed."

"Let's sail away together."

"Yes," said Natalie. "Let's sail away."

They laughed, at the uncharacteristic wistfulness in Natalie's voice, at their own bright hope, at the thought of anything daring to go wrong.

"And now," said Natalie, "I'd better run you home before my wrinkles set."

Had she been there, Renée would have told Minnie that Natalie was at best a fickle person, full of operatic passion and theatrical gesture. She would have told of other women left by Natalie in concert halls, women trotting off to buy vanilla ice cream and returning to an empty seat; of women sleeping on her doorstep throughout a long cold New York winter; of women Natalie stepped over to walk out through the door. "You are not the first," Renée might have said, "and you will not be the last woman in the world to fall in love with Natalie." Natalie loved the idea of women, especially the idea that she could have them, but she could not love their need for sleep and peace and very soon each new and shining lover bored her, sending her ravening for another. That is what Renée would have said.

At the moment the woman Minnie wanted was Natalie, and that wanting would admit no obstacle the mind could send.

Meanwhile, back in the 1900 Room, Nea and Renée were discussing geography.

"We have millionaires in San Francisco too. It's considered a very respectable profession. Why don't you cut your ties and relocate?"

Renée raised her long lashes an instant then returned to the main business of the day which was sulking. Business was booming; she had bought controlling interests in three Japanese companies at rock-bottom prices because of some government sex scandal and she wanted to stick around and watch the unit price rise.

"You can do all this phoning and writing down numbers and adding them up anywhere in the world."

Renée sniffed, shrugged and examined the carpet which was uniformly black. Nea sighed, glanced at the Buddha on the mantelpiece and was tempted to wink. Solemnity always filled her with a juvenile iconoclasm.

"The East is very in on the West Coast," she said instead.

"I am an outlaw and an outcast," said Renée finally. "To my self-generating, virginal grace, they prefer conjugal rutting and hideous maternity. It is not the loss of my wealth nor the impounding of my property: I remain inconsolable at the destruction of an ideal of purity."

"Well yes," said Nea, wondering how Renée could still call herself a virgin the morning after, or why she wanted to. "San Francisco is a laid-back, dog-eat-dog place. A vampire could feel right at home. There are so many ethnic minorities, sexual minorities, linguistic minorities that the worst a light-shunning, blood-sucking, long-living, coffin-dwelling minority has to fear is that it would get bought up and turned into a Coca Cola ad."

"They would permit me life, liberty, and the pursuit of happiness? They would allow me to sip the pure blood of their blood banks?"

"Hell yes. Why almost everybody there is drinking chem-free."

There remained only the problem of how to move Renée and her worldly goods to the United States. The obvious answer was Natalie's yacht. There was however, a difficulty, small but insurmountable. Renée got seasick on long voyages. In desperation and habit Renée turned to Beryl.

"Don't fret," said Beryl as she sifted through the faxes which had arrived in the night from various parts of the world. "I'll fix it."

"You have my undying gratitude," pronounced Renée.

"Gratitude is nice," said Beryl. "But I want the title deed."

IN THE BEST OF ALL POSSIBLE WORLDS

*B*eryl looked at the long list of guests John was inviting to his party. It would take the best part of a day to phone them all. Then she would have to ring back and check that all the people who promised to pass on messages had passed them on, that people who had been out first time round were now in, that people with ansaphones had played back incoming calls. It is a universal law that phone calls breed phone calls. There was no other way to make sure everyone on John's list learned of the change of venue, for the party was that very night.

Beryl carried the phone down the vanadium spiral and out to the marble staircase, courtesy of a ten-metre extension lead John had given her. Such a simple device; Beryl must have seen them advertised a thousand times. Why had she never thought to get one? This was no time to berate herself. From the top step Beryl surveyed the comings and goings of vans and personnel from Sweet Sugar High she had paid to ferry the garageful of food which John had prepared, out of Balga and into the kitchens at Dalkeith. Somewhere below stairs came the steady vibrations of an industrial strength vacuum cleaner and the industrial strength cleaning woman who drove it. Soon the woman would want tea, and Beryl knew for a fact that there were no biscuits to eat with it and that the woman would insist on a packet. It was going to be a long day. It was going to be worth the effort: Beryl had something to celebrate. How many housewife-secretary-cleaners get to inherit the boss's wealth without sitting on his knee and before he's even dead?

By evening all was ready, except John, who was still cooking. The many heavily laden tables filled him with pleasure; not, however, that of providing delicious mouthfuls for hungry people, but chemistry on a grand scale. Chemistry and physics and biology combined, overflowing test tube or tank, with almost instantaneous results, as his fellow organisms either did or did not eat the nutrients set before them. Like Beryl, John felt that now at last he had found scope vast enough for his canvas.

The gates, with their bas-relief ravens and electronic switches, were left open at sunset. Beryl did not want the guests confronted by an intelligence test before they even entered the house, a test which, she knew, many would not pass. Gate-crashers were welcome; there was food in plenty and Perth was so small no crasher could survive ten minutes without encountering an intimate friend among the invitees. The flag, the new Vivien arms, Beryl had taken down and packed away, ironed and neatly folded, in the 1900 Room which was, as the first guests arrived, being loaded onto Natalie's yacht. Aside from those small details, all was as it had been under the old dispensation, Mick Jagger's lips not yet having arrived.

The guests came in two by two, oohing and aahing at the gardens and the house and the period features, the Octagon Gallery and the vanadium spiral. At anything, in fact, except each other. Simone and Lex were not speaking because Ingrid had done Simone's hair in a "one" the way Minnie had told them she used to have hers. Lex responded with strong, silent peevishness. She liked a girl to look like a girl. Laura and her John were not speaking because of the ornamentation on John's inner thigh. No amount of pleading was going to convince Laura that "VLADIVOSTOK" was a Russian port, and she would not speak to John until he told her the truth. Doctor and Professor Grebe were not speaking because the professor did not open his mouth except about physics, of which there was none on the horizon, and the Doctor was tired of talking to herself. Milly and the parrot were not speaking because they had failed to find any plane on which they could communicate save the purely intellectual, and that had begun to pall. Renée and Nea were not speaking because their immediate physical circumstances did not permit it. Zebbee and Son were not speaking because they were asleep and had been put to bed in a guest room in the vain hope that they would stay there and not bother the adults. Natalie and Minnie were speaking, but they were not there. The last two couples Beryl recognised before the surge of partygoers became a wave and she had to stand back and let things take their course, were Moira and the lad from Interflora on the one hand, and Ingrid and the projectionist from the Omni Theatre on the other. These two sets were not speaking because they had not been introduced and so did not yet know they were a couple, or rather two couples.

Beryl's resolve to become the Australian byword for bloody-minded nearly came a cropper right then. She was on the verge of making the necessary introductions; showing Professor Grebe into the kitchens where the thermometers and oscilloscope were bound to make him feel at home; reassuring Laura about Russian geography; scolding Lex for being as sullen as a v******; and engaging Doctor Grebe in spritely conversation about home births and radical midwives, about which she personally knew nothing and was certain the Doctor would know a lot. At the last moment—some would say after the last moment, for she had already opened her mouth and called Ingrid's name aloud—Beryl's mind filled with the memory of a sink piled high with the dirty dishes of a wholesome family dinner. Salutary, timely vision. Beryl shut her mouth again as swiftly as she had opened it. When asked by her youngest daughter what she wanted, she patted her on the head and told her to see whether John needed anything in the kitchen. Ingrid was so surprised to be ordered to do anything that she complied without demur. Fleetingly, Beryl wondered what Ingrid had done with Lollipop for the evening but thought it better not to ask.

There was one item Beryl must see to before she gave herself over to fun and frolic. In the last of the fleet of Sweet Sugar High vans, uniformly painted pink and green with scallops and cupids thrown in, reposed Renée Vivien's coffin awaiting transportation. After the party Simone would drive the van home with the crockery and cutlery Beryl had borrowed, ready for work Monday morning. Meanwhile, the van was going to the airport. Nea was writing out a label; she looked up as Beryl appeared.

"Just finished. Listen, let me read it back to you: 'No movies, no headphones, no duty free, no courtesy slippers, no drinks, no champagne and positively no meals.' Covered everything?"

"Sounds like it."

"Do you really think if probable they'll have in-flight service in the hold?"

"You never know. This is travelling by Concorde. Got the certifi-cate?"

Nea held up an official-looking form attesting that one John Loviebuttons had died of natural causes including a broken neck and multiple stab wounds. There was another of a different colour stating that Miss Nea Naomi Flipper, High Priestess of the Cross-roads, of San Francisco, California, was given licence to bring her brother's body home for burial.

"Broken neck and multiple stab wounds," said Nea, reading the license aloud. "That's what I call thorough."

"When Ingrid stops smiling peacefully she means business."

"Now pray the anti-v****** riots don't stop the plane leaving."

"They won't stop the Concorde. Certain parties have great inter-est in ensuring Mr. Vivien reaches America in good condition. They've heard he has a hot tip on the Thornton Tiger Fund which he refuses to divulge anywhere but a San Francisco hot tub. There's a Brinx Mat van picking you both up at the airport."

"How about my ticket?"

Beryl handed Nea a flimsy piece of paper. "This is the portion of Minnie's ticket that covers Perth to San Francisco."

"Doesn't she need it?"

"She is sailing to New York on Natalie's yacht. And since I paid for her round trip, I might as well make use of her castoffs."

"Isn't that a little precipitate?"

"Oh, for heaven's sake. My daughters have got to learn to stand on their own two feet."

Beryl turned from the van and surveyed the life of the party. Ingrid was smiling peacefully at the projectionist. Beryl could almost hear her explaining how her boyfriend, her baby's father, had been brutally murdered; feel the projectionist's sympathy and quickened interest. It was like watching an old movie one has seen many times before, whose ending one knows even before it begins but because the story is so vivid, so touching, one feels as moved by the telling and as shocked by the end as if this were one's first viewing. On the second floor Laura was silhouetted against the light, bending over a fuzzy blond head which Beryl knew was Son's. Any moment Laura's John would come softly in through the door and beg Laura's forgiveness for anything she liked to accuse him of. Laura would tell him he was a dickhead for getting himself tattooed but she would allow him back into her bed. Then Beryl caught sight of Minnie scurrying hither and thither, up one staircase, down another. From her speed and distracted motions she seemed to be desperately seeking something.

"I brought my daughters up to consider themselves uniquely wonderful and irresistibly desirable. I hope they will never forget it," Beryl murmured like a spell. She turned again to Nea. "You'd better be going."

The last fleet of vans from Sweet Sugar High drove out through the open gates, unnoticed or at least unremarked, in the general party traffic.

While Beryl had been making the mountain of arrangements necessary to transfer the party from Balga to Dalkeith and airfreight Renée Vivien to San Francisco without government intervention, Minnie had been with Natalie. They had, it seemed, spent twelve hours talking—about themselves, about each other, about the new life they would make together. It could not, however, have been quite that long because that would have left no time for the gentle slide of Minnie's body over Natalie's; the kisses which would never end were it not for the necessity of breathing; the arms, legs, breasts and bellies which would never disentangle were it not for the desire to sit up and gaze into each other's eyes. Minnie declared that if this was sex, then she had never had sex before. Such tender hope, such milky adoration.

"Will you come with me, then?" Natalie had asked.

"Wherever you go," Minnie replied.

All day, all week, all year or all the years of her life, how long did Minnie spend with Natalie? It was so long, a lifetime, could Natalie have performed some vampire trick to give them more than the hours in one day? Did the promise of forever infuse each moment with eternity? That must be it.

All too soon the lovers had to prepare for their departure, postponing further pleasure till the yacht was launched on the high seas. But they enjoyed the packing, the buying food for Minnie to eat and Natalie to watch, the putting things in cases to be unwrapped delicately on the journey. Natalie ordered a mauve silk nightie for Minnie and a bra and pants to match. It arrived while Minnie was changing after bathing and she was moved to try it on right there and then, though she had never owned such a garment in her life and was not certain she approved. This led, as Natalie knew it would, to a fond return to bed and a delay in preparations.

The safe carriage and storage of the 1900 Room demanded serious attention. Because it was still daylight, Natalie could not leave the yacht, so Minnie fetched and carried for her, leaving and entering through a kind of diver's chamber to prevent the light from striking her lover's body. Many things had to be deposited on the shore to make space while the room was loaded. They piled up, like furniture by the roadside on moving day waiting for the truck. There was help, a group of burly men in hard hats and shorts who picked up in their arms objects Minnie could not begin to drag. Possibly there was a crane also; Minnie could not remember, for most of all there had been Natalie.

At last the yacht was ready.

"Think now," Minnie said. "Have we left anything behind? Is there anything else I should get for us before we set sail?"

Natalie shook her head, looked around the room, then started. "Good God," she said. "Where is my coffin? It usually sits right there beside the sofa. Could you have taken it out while they were loading the 1900 Room?"

"No. At least, I don't think so."

"Oh, but where is it? We can't go without it. What if some of the lightproofing was lost during a storm?"

They searched the yacht but the coffin was not on board.

"It must be on the shore," said Minnie at last. "Though I have no memory of carrying it anywhere."

"Maybe one of the workmen moved it."

Minnie looked out through the porthole; there was nothing on the jetty or the quayside.

"It could be in the house," Natalie said at last. "It's very valuable, an antique. Someone might have taken it up there for safekeeping."

"Who?" asked Minnie blankly.

"Please, Minnie. It must be up there somewhere."

"Okay. I'll go and look, but it'll be no easy task fighting my way through the crowds."

"Minnie," said Natalie, lovingly and with the sweetest smile. "Would I demean you with an easy task?"

Minnie laughed happily.

Minnie ran from room to room, dodging through the crowds, opening and closing cupboards, staring under people's feet to see what was the object that they sat upon. She pushed against a human tide which swirled and eddied where it listed. As Beryl had observed, Minnie scurried up and down staircase after staircase, moving ever faster like a spinning top whipped by an unseen child. There was a pain forming in her chest and she breathed in gasps. She imagined the coffin, the size and shape and weight of it; she imagined dragging it back onto the yacht and laughing with Natalie at her speed, her haste, her fright. Finally it occurred to her to try Renée Vivien's office. There was no reason for the coffin to be in there but she was weary, near hysterical, from searching again and again the same empty places. There was a rule that said one finds the thing one is seeking in the last place one looks. As she climbed the vanadium spiral, Minnie knew what she would find but there was no triumph in her step.

"How did she get it up here?" Minnie asked aloud, for Natalie's coffin stood upended in the corner. "And when?"

Then came the heaving, panting, muscle-aching stumble down the stairs, and out through the empty corner where the 1900 Room had stood. Minnie scrabbled through the dusk and if any of the partygoers saw her, they mistook her for a gardener and her burden for dead leaves. By the time she reached the parapet and could put the coffin down and slide it along the grass, let gravity draw it to the water, she knew it was too late. It was always too late, it had been too late before it started. She knew that if she looked, the yacht would no longer be there. That Natalie had sailed as soon as Minnie was out of sight.

"Hey, Natalie," she shouted into empty air, "I found your coffin. I've brought your coffin back."

She shouted but did not look up. Instead she dropped her bur-

den over the parapet where the cliff was steepest, and she watched
as it fell and broke and splintered. Not a moment too soon, it was,
or she would have carried her lover's coffin all her life. For it is not
a torch one carries longest, that flame burns out. Far below, the
crimson padding was ripped and scattered like clots of blood upon
the ground. The wreck of wood slipped into the river and was
washed along for some drowning mariner to cling to, maybe, in
some other time.

Or was it her own great failure of imagination which dissolved
the yacht just as she was about to sail away upon it? A fatal hesitation, lack of faith? Was this last-minute salvation or pusillanim-
ity—the worst, the only unpardonable crime of the lover?

"How could she do this to me?" Minnie demanded of the silence.
"How could she plant her own coffin up there where I would not
find it for long enough to launch the yacht. What cold-blooded,
practiced artifice. Why did she buy me roses, why did she call me
darling if she planned to leave me so?"

Minnie's voice was replaced with wracking sobs. "Was it all mere
blandishment? Did she never love me, though she said she did, she
said she did. She whispered in my ear; she took my whole ear in
her mouth and she licked my earlobe. She was a courtesan; she
flattered me; she would praise the rotting litter in the streets if she
thought it could in some way serve her."

And there would be hours, days, months, years in which Minnie
never heard from Natalie again.

"I never should have let her give me those knickers, that bra."
Minnie's rage and shock looked for solid objects to arraign. "It
could only have reminded her of the difference in our ages. Clean
underwear! It is what one wears the day one is run over by the
bus."

And there would be hours, days, months, years in which Minnie
never heard from Natalie again.

"She must have panicked, she must have fled. She was terrified,
a terror that she would lose Renée and could not survive without

her access to the blood banks, was no longer capable of fending for herself among the poor and dispossessed. She sent me away so that I would not watch her collapse, would not have to look after her. Oh, she is dying, she is killing herself out there on the high seas and I cannot reach her."

And there would be hours, days, months, years in which Minnie never heard from Natalie again.

If Natalie had lied to her, with such anticipation and on such a scale, what then was true? Renée, Nea, Natalie: had Minnie invented them, fashioned them out of air and her own pain? Minnie turned from the empty waters of the Swan toward the house behind her, in which every room was lit and full of people. Noise, which she had not heard before, having no ears for anything but the distant splash of a boat which might have signalled Natalie returning, the noise of the party now filled Minnie's ears. For a moment she thought she heard music, the song of the sad countess, *"O mi rendi il mio tesoro, o mi lasci almen morir!"* ("Either bring my darling back to me, or let me lie down and die!") Minnie was struck with the bitter certainty that she could no longer find joy or solace in opera, for Natalie had written all the operas in the world, acted each one out in turn and many times. But the song which was playing was not music at all but a pop melody to which the only words were "Woe woe woe" and "Love love love."

As her mother before her, so Minnie gazed through the uncurtained windows. On the ground floor, alone in the vast kitchens, were Beryl and her John. Beryl asking at last what "NORWICH" meant, and why, and why tattooed on John's left thigh? John, shy, embarrassed, but explaining: "Nickers Off Ready When I Come Home," his search, like Minnie's, for something irrevocable and irrevocably his. Beryl laughing: oh no, not at her John, but with him. On the first floor, Ingrid and the projectionist, which latter had probably proposed by now and suggested that he adopt Lollipop as his daughter. On the staircase, Moira. How long would the tattoo parlour last? How long till she could add "Elysian" to the Scrabble board and score an extra fifty points for a lucky landing? On the second floor Laura opened the window and waved.

I.O.U.

Item: one piece of air (with lightning)	Judy Grahn
Item: one ward of amnesiacs	Olga Broumas
Item: one covered cock with cumin	Alice B. Toklas
Item: the words to every thought (but one)	Emily Dickinson
Item: one tortoise (dead)	Joris-Karl Huysmans
Item: one parrot	Raymond Queneau and Gustave Flaubert
Item: one lobster	Jean-Paul Sartre and Gérard de Nerval
Item: one shark (sight unseen)	Isidore Ducasse, Comte de Lautréamont
Item: one spleen (personal property R. Vivien)	Charles Baudelaire

ABOUT THE AUTHOR

Anna Livia was born in Dublin in 1955 and grew up in Africa (Zambia and Swaziland). Her family lives in Australia; for the last twenty years—bar two—she lived in London. The other two were spent in Paris and Avignon. She is currently living in Berkeley, pursuing a doctorate in French linguistics. It was that or the Foreign Legion. She's had the usual series of jobs bus conducting, theatrical dressing, dispatch riding, and database managing. From 1983 to 1989 she worked as an editor and publisher at Onlywomen Press in London. She is the author of three previous novels: *Relatively Norma, Accommodation Offered,* and *Bulldozer Rising,* as well as two collections of stories, *Incidents Involving Mirth* and *Incidents Involving Warmth. Incidents Involving Mirth* was published by The Eighth Mountain Press in the fall of 1990. Her translation of an anthology of the "Best of Natalie Clifford Barney" entitled *A Perilous Advantage* will be published by New Victoria Publishers in 1992.

ABOUT THE COVER ARTIST

Claudia Cave is a prominent Northwest artist. Her work is known for its feminist sensibility and its unique blend of the zany and the weighty. She lives in Salem, Oregon, and is represented by the Laura Russo Gallery in Portland, Oregon. The cover art is gouache on paper.

ABOUT THE BOOK

The text typography was composed in Berkeley Book; the cover typography was composed in Mistral. The book was printed and bound by McNaughton & Gunn on acid-free paper. Marcia Barrentine, a Portland freelance graphic designer and artist designed the cover for *Minimax*.

THE FLIGHT OF THE MIND
WRITING WORKSHOPS FOR WOMEN

Explore and strengthen your writing skills in a community of women.
Week-long feminist workshops offer formal instruction, time for
work, and the opportunity to exchange ideas with other writers.
They are held at a retreat center on the scenic McKenzie River in
Central Oregon, which also offers hiking trails, swimming, river
rafting, hot springs, lakes, waterfalls and lava beds. Past teachers
have included: Ursula K. Le Guin, Valerie Miner, Barbara Wilson,
Evelyn C. White, Judith Barrington, Gillian Hanscombe, Suniti
Namjoshi, and Elizabeth Woody. College credit is available. To
receive a brochure, send a first class stamp (not an envelope) along
with your name and address to: Flight of the Mind, 622 Southeast
29th Avenue, Portland, OR 97214 or call (503) 236-9862.

THE EIGHTH MOUNTAIN POETRY PRIZE

The Eighth Mountain Poetry Prize was established in 1988 in honor of the poets whose words envision and sustain the feminist movement, and in recognition of the major role played by women poets in creating the literature of their time. Women poets worldwide are invited to participate. One manuscript is selected each year by a poet of national reputation. Publication and an advance of one thousand dollars are funded by a private donor. For entry guidelines, send SASE (29 cents) to The Eighth Mountain Poetry Prize, 624 SE 29th Avenue, Portland, OR 97214.

OTHER BOOKS FROM THE EIGHTH MOUNTAIN PRESS

Incidents Involving Mirth
short stories by Anna Livia

An Intimate Wilderness: Lesbian Writers on Sexuality
edited by Judith Barrington

Dreams of an Insomniac:
Jewish Feminist Essays, Speeches and Diatribes
by Irena Klepfisz
Introduction by Evelyn Torton Beck

A Few Words in the Mother Tongue:
Poems Selected and New (1971-1990)
by Irena Klepfisz
Introduction by Adrienne Rich

Cultivating Excess
by Lori Anderson
Winner of the 1991 Eighth Mountain Poetry Prize

Fear of Subways
by Maureen Seaton
Winner of the 1990 Eighth Mountain Poetry Prize

The Eating Hill
by Karen Mitchell
Winner of the 1989 Eighth Mountain Poetry Prize

History and Geography
poems by Judith Barrington

Trying to Be an Honest Woman
poems by Judith Barrington

Cows and Horses
a novel by Barbara Wilson

The Eighth Mountain Press was formed to publish literary work of exceptional quality written by women. We began in 1982 with the publication of limited edition letterpress poetry broadsides and published our first trade paperback in 1985. For a complete catalog of books in print, send a 52¢ stamp along with your name and address to The Eighth Mountain Press, 624 Southeast 29th Avenue, Portland, Oregon 97214.